THE LAWMAN'S FIERY PUGILIST

The Silk Knuckles Saloon
Book 1

by

Nicki Pascarella

ARE YOU SIGNED UP FOR DRAGONBLADE'S BLOG?

You'll get the latest news and information on exclusive giveaways, exclusive excerpts, coming releases, sales, free books, cover reveals and more.

Check out our complete list of authors, too!

No spam, no junk. That's a promise!

Sign Up Here

www.dragonbladepublishing.com

Dearest Reader;

Thank you for your support of a small press. At Dragonblade Publishing, we strive to bring you the highest quality Historical Romance from some of the best authors in the business. Without your support, there is no 'us', so we sincerely hope you adore these stories and find some new favorite authors along the way.

Happy Reading!

CEO, Dragonblade Publishing

Additional Dragonblade books by Author Nicki Pascarella

The Silk Knuckles Saloon
The Lawman's Fiery Pugilist (Book 1)

The Lyon's Den Series
The Lyon's Pretty Pugilist

PROLOGUE

September 1813

EDWARD ROBINSON STRUTTED through the rookery, whistling a happy tune. Just let one of the loitering reprobates try to ruin his good humor, because he'd plant a facer that would have them seeing double.

A few days ago, Edward had discovered he was a deuce of a pugilist. With a single punch, he had knocked out a thief who had tried to pick his pocket. Edward was of the not-so-humble opinion that when one was blessed with innate talent, they should cultivate said talent, even if they had to traipse down a street that smelled of ripe sewage to reach their goal.

Days earlier, Edward had thought being one of Fielding's Bow Street Runners was his higher calling. He'd dreamed of wielding a brass tipstaff engraved with the message, *City of London*. But things had changed seconds after his fist met flesh, and now he knew his destiny was to be a champion in the purist of all sports.

Rumors circulated that Coach Valentine was one of the best coaches in the city. Some in the boxing circle known as the Fancy claimed he was even better than Gentleman Jackson. Valentine was probably more affordable than Jackson, and since coin, or the lack thereof, was now a concern for Edward, Valentine was the logical choice.

Not to worry, bloke, Edward assured himself because blunt was about to fall from the sky and rain down over his head—so much blunt that he could rent a lovely flat and hire a cook. Not that he gave even half a shite about riches, but he favored the idea of being the best at something. Having a lovely home and a full belly also appealed. His father owned a garment factory in the East Midlands, so he'd been raised in a certain amount of comfort that he aimed to maintain now that he'd moved to the city.

A toothless man in filthy rags barred Edward's path and extended his hand palm up. "Kind sir, can ye spare a coin for a hungry mate?"

Not one to turn his back on a person in need, Edward ensured no one was watching. He couldn't feed every indigent person on this street, after all. Fishing in his pocket, he produced his last coin. " 'Tis all I have today." However, he'd be rolling in winnings soon. He placed the coin on the beggar's palm.

The man wrapped his fingers around it. "Bless ye, mate."

Shoulder back, his gaze focused in front of him, Edward sauntered forward. He could not make eye contact with anyone else if he meant to reach the olive-green building at the end of the street without further interruption.

"Gov, ye too fancy to fight with yer bare fists?" some arse off to his left side called.

If the imbecile was referencing the mufflers hanging over Edward's shoulder, he could sod off.

Evading his daft heckler, Edward almost careened into his next adversary. The blighter poked him in the chest. "Look at the pretty boy. How much ye wanna wager he is on his way to get them perfect teeth knocked out?"

"Won't last in there for more than a minute," another bloke said.

"I don't know." A short round ball of a man with a red nose barred Edward's path. "I wager he makes it at least five minutes."

Edward couldn't help that he was well-made, and he would not be made to feel shame for it. More importantly, there was no way someone could knock him out. Stepping around the portly fool, he continued toward his destination.

Unfortunately, the group of scalawags tagged along behind him, calling jeers about his fancy clothing and pretty face. Although his garments were not fancy, they were clean.

Keeping his temper in check and ignoring his unwanted parade, Edward entered what he hoped was The St Giles Gymnasium.

"Ahh, yes." He inhaled the scent of physical exertion, which was a more palatable odor than the piss and filth on the other side of the door.

Humming with energy, the room was large enough that two roped rings still left plenty of space for a half dozen men to pound on sandbags hanging from the ceiling. Edward smiled. This was where he belonged.

His gaze settled on the closest ring. Two young women, their hair secured in tight plaits, wrapped fists raised, circled each other. Even more shocking than the sight of comely chits in a boxing ring was their state of dress. "Undress" might be the more appropriate description, since their frocks were unbuttoned. Their lowered bodices exposed white chemises, and the dress sleeves knotted around their trim waists held their skirts in place.

Edward should look away, but he was much too fascinated to peel his gaze from the beauties. He'd heard female pugilists existed, but he had never seen one back home in Nottingham. A wave of masculine inclinations shot to his cock.

"May I help you?" someone behind him asked.

If he faced whoever approached he'd have to take his eyes off the pleasing scene in front of him, and it wasn't every day a man got to watch two half-dressed chits engaged in sport. Feeling slightly disappointed, he swallowed his lust and turned.

A red-haired man in his middling years eyed him up and down, snuffing what was left of Edward's arousal. "Here to train?" the man asked.

"Yes," Edward said. "I'm looking for Coach Calder Valentine."

The man grinned. "You found him."

This was easier than Edward expected. "Edward Robinson." His grip firm, he shook the coach's hand. "I just moved to the city last week and heard you are the one to see if I'd like to be a prizefighter."

"You think you got what it takes to be a champion?" Coach Valentine asked.

"Yes, sir," Edward said, his chest confidently thrust forward.

Coach Valentine *tsk*ed. "You need to gain a stone."

Edward stiffened. He wasn't exactly small. Hell, his biceps bulged, and his thighs were practically tree trunks, but arguing with his new coach might not be the best way to start this relationship.

"I plan to hire a cook with my winnings," Edward said.

Coach Valentine sniffed and then wrinkled his nose as if Edward's words stunk. "How are you paying me?"

Wait. Didn't pugilists compensate their coaches when they won? Bloody bollocking hell, he hoped so because he'd used the last of his blunt to pay for two weeks' rent, mufflers, and a meal for some hungry street beggar. On second thought, he'd probably bought the chap a pint of ale. Not that it mattered. The point was, his money was gone.

"I thought I could pay you with my winnings," Edward said. "I can start fighting right away."

"What's your record?" Coach Valentine asked.

Inwardly, Edward suffered a maelstrom of self-doubt. Outwardly, he displayed delusional confidence as he dodged the question. "I used to spar with my brothers, and I knocked a thief out the other day. One punch and he was on his back seeing stars."

From behind Edward, a female scoffed.

Even though he couldn't see them, Edward knew both women glared at his back because the scent of feminine sweat infused with rose-scented soap tickled his nostrils.

He whirled to face them. Hands on hips, the brunette stared

at him as if he was maggot dung. Although quite pretty, she must be daft because he was a damn handsome bloke, and no woman had ever looked at him with such scorn. Obviously, she'd taken too many blows to her brain.

However, the redhead watching him with curiosity stole his breath. Her green eyes assessing, she pinched his bicep, then pursed her lips. "You need to gain a stone."

Coach Valentine chuckled. "That's what I said."

Since ladies didn't pinch men in public, Edward was rather taken aback. He did not appreciate being treated like a hunk of meat.

Actually, that wasn't quite true. He rather enjoyed the spark of heat her touch elicited, but he could do without her wrinkled nose. He definitely did not favor the brunette's sour puss countenance.

"These are my girls. Frances is my daughter, and Josephine Martin is my ward," Coach said. "This is Edward Robinson. He wants to be a prizefighter."

"We heard," the brunette said. "But what's a toff doin' in St Giles?"

"I'm not a toff," Edward said.

The brunette snorted a few times as the redhead continued to rake her gaze over him. If only she found him as attractive as he found her. Then he decided it didn't matter because if she was his new coach's daughter—hopefully, his new coach—then she'd have to be off limits, and his ward would be, too.

"Step into the ring with Franny, and let's see what you got," Coach said.

What the bloody hell? Edward shook his head. "Sir, I am not getting in the ring with a female."

That must have been the wrong thing to say because the redhead bared her teeth like a rabid wolf and hissed. How unfortunate that she was as brain injured as her sparring partner.

"Go on, son," Coach Valentine said. "Let's see what you got. No trading punches for now. Just move around and let me see your footwork."

The brunette, who must have been Josephine, smirked. "Franny'll punch ye after we see yer footwork."

Edward would not allow himself to be baited into this absurdity. "How about I spar with him?" He pointed at a large bloke enthusiastically pounding on one of the sandbags.

"How about you leave my gymnasium," Coach Valentine said.

Nonplused, Edward sifted through the conversations that had transpired since he'd entered the gymnasium. Was he being dismissed because he refused to punch a woman who could not be more than eighteen years old and barely came to his chin? Good God, he was a man of one and twenty and had to be three stones heavier than her.

Coach Valentine could sod off. Edward would be one hell of a prizefighter, and he'd find a coach who believed in him, and if not, he would become a lawman. He'd be damned if he'd apologize or kowtow to this lot after the way they'd treated him, which was a crying shame since the redhead made his blood pump wildly, and he'd like to see what lay beneath her chemise and frock.

Huffing out his exasperation, Edward turned and marched toward the exit.

"Son," Coach called to his back.

Although reluctant to stay in the gymnasium a second more, Edward faced him.

"You have no idea why I am turning you down, do you?"

"Because I won't punch your daughter?" Edward stared into Franny Valentine's eyes. "Who, I dare say, is exceedingly beautiful." Perhaps he was a lecherous rat, but she should know he *had* been interested.

She glared at him.

So be it. He was a man who dealt in truths.

"No," Coach Valentine said. "Because you did not trust me to know what I was doing when I asked you to get in the ring with her. I can't train an athlete who doesn't trust me. I also doubt you have enough patience and self-control to be a champion. You haven't exhibited a lick of either since you barged in here like a cocksure fool."

"Ye are an arrogant horse's arse, ye are," Josephine said.

Edward's cheeks heated. He'd been tested and failed.

"Are you going to get in the ring with me or not, Edward Robinson?" Franny asked.

It seemed they were giving him a second chance.

Since the three of them glared at him expectantly, he nodded. Franny was not wearing mufflers, so he dropped his onto the floor. He removed his tailcoat and waistcoat, untied his cravat, unbuttoned his shirt, and tossed his clothing on top of his mufflers. After a quick stretch, he climbed between the ropes.

He held up the ropes for Franny to join him. As she climbed through them, she accidentally brushed his shoulder. She had the nerve to scowl at him as if he were an uncoordinated clod.

They centered themselves in the ring and stared into each other's eyes.

He drowned in the depths of her bright emerald irises. Meanwhile, she seemed to judge him to his very soul. Unfortunately, her face contorted as if she did not like what she saw. Strange indeed, because most women found him charming.

He moved with her as she weaved around the ring. Although he was aware of the freckles bespeckling her nose, her every breath, and her intoxicating female scent, he did an admirable job of ignoring his libido, which wanted nothing more than to reach out and touch.

Many of the men stopped what they were doing to watch him bob and weave around Franny.

"Good," Coach Valentine called. "Don't let her jam your reach."

The tables turned, and instead of chasing her, he took the defensive as she crowded him.

"No contact yet," Coach Valentine instructed. "But add combinations as if you are sparring with your shadow."

Franny's fist shot out in a flurry of quick jabs that came remarkably close to Edward's face but did not hit him. Heat radiated from her compact little body as she landed a right-left-right hook combination that brushed his bare obliques.

"Fran-ny! Fran-ny!" the spectators chanted.

"Son, let me see your combinations," Coach Valentine called. "But no contact."

Unfortunately, Edward was beset with numerous problems. Firstly, she hadn't even looked at his bare chest. Other women who'd witnessed his muscles had been rendered speechless. Secondly, Franny's endurance was commendable, and her footwork was fast, so he needed a moment to catch his breath. However, his hubris would never allow him to admit this aloud. Thirdly, he had no idea how to throw a punch that didn't make contact with his intended target without looking weak. And finally, he was fascinated by the binding that peeked out from the top of her chemise.

How large were her breasts? Would they bounce if they were unbound? Were her nipples pink like her lips or red like her hair? And speaking of red hair… did scarlet curls cover her quim?

He still hadn't thrown a single punch when Franny backed him up against the ropes, stepped close, and pulled her power from her uppercut.

Her fist lay passively on his gut as she hissed in his ear, "Are you staring at my breasts?"

Of course he was. Any sane man would engage in fantasies while watching her chest as she inhaled and exhaled.

Franny stepped back and glared at him. "You bloody arrogant arse!" Unfortunately, this time when she jabbed, she made contact with his nose. Twice. Make that three times because she nailed him with a powerful cross.

Blinding pain shot from his nose to his brain, and blood spattered as he shielded his face with his forearms.

Her breath heaving from both anger and exertion, Franny

turned her back to him and stomped to the opposite side of the ring.

"Boo," their audience chorused.

It took him a moment to realize he was the object of the audience's ire. Being booed was akin to having monkey shite thrown on him. Neither fate had ever happened to him before, though he was fairly sure he'd prefer the monkey shite to the public disdain.

Edward wiped his forearm across his face and stared at the red smears streaking his arm. "Bloody hell," he mumbled. His damn cock was always getting him in trouble. He should have treated her as if she was a male opponent.

Easier said than done. Men didn't have pretty eyes, dainty wrists, and heaving bosoms. They certainly didn't smell like bed sport and roses when they perspired.

No one said a word to him, and he was too ashamed to make eye contact with anyone as he left the ring, got dressed, and exited the gymnasium.

Ill luck continued to plague him as his blasted hecklers from earlier approached.

"Well, I'll be. Jasper, ye won. The pretty boy made it almost twenty minutes," one of the men said.

"But his nose ain't straight no more," another of the blokes said. "And he's gonna have double shiners. One eye is already turnin'."

"I wager he got beat up by one of them girl fighters." The butterball of a troll burst into chortles.

Edward halted and stared at the bulbous target in the middle of the guffawing face—protruding, bright red, and only inches away. He dumped his mufflers onto the ground, pulled back his hand, and threw out his fist.

Pow!

The man screeched as blood flew from his hairy nostrils.

Ignoring the throbbing in his knuckles, Edward stalked toward the wide eyed men who had nothing better to do than badger him. "Anybody else want to mention that a chit hit me in the face?" he asked with a snarl.

The pathetic excuse of a street gang held up their hands and backed away.

"That's what I thought." Edward retrieved his mufflers from the mud and tossed them over his shoulder. No use leaving them since he might be able to trade them for a few pasties and a mug of cheap ale. For now, he had best get hoofing if he meant to reach Bow Street before it grew dark.

CHAPTER ONE

Five years later, August 1818

NOW THAT SHE'D finished the week's bookkeeping, Frances Valentine took a moment to rest in front of her office door and survey her queendom. Over the past month, she'd stood in this spot more times than she could count, pride coursing through her. A palpable energy zinged from their patrons, infusing the old-factory turned gymnasium with life-affirming vibrations. It mattered not that the scent of sweat tickled her nostrils, or that the crack of knuckles against flesh echoed, because despite her past trauma she loved the sweet science, and here at The Silk Knuckles Saloon, the mind, body, and soul were nurtured. Who would have guessed that the daughter of a boxing coach could create something so perfect? Alongside her father and her best friend, Franny had done just that.

Tonight, London's heavyweight champion Pete the Trojan was studying with Franny's father. His anvil-sized fists flew at her father's straw-filled mitts. Surely, if Pete became a regular patron, other pugilists of great repute would follow.

The reigning female champion, Lady Jabbing Josie, was, in fact, Franny's best friend and business partner, and she currently led a half dozen women in an exercise session involving defense techniques. To Franny and Josie's delight, these female mavericks had forsaken their reputations to frequent the scandalous boxing gymnasium and saloon.

"Shocking, I dare say," the minister next door had said upon meeting his new neighbors. "A club where women drink upstairs and punch each other downstairs."

"Men can also train with us," Franny had explained. "They just aren't permitted upstairs in the women's saloon. There are many clubs in London they can frequent, but women have so few spaces."

The vicar had gasped. "Indecent!" He'd stared at Franny and Josie as if he might be exorcising demons. Good luck with that. Franny rather liked the devil occupying her left shoulder.

"You are encouraging women without chaperones to run around the streets at night." The vicar had brought a hand to his heart.

"Exercise keeps ladies nimble and healthy," Papa had explained. "And we encourage them to walk with other women."

Most of the ladies arrived in carriages but that was none of Vicar Williams' business. Although with the way he spied, he had to know this already.

"*Ironic*, indeed." Now that Josie had married into the aristocracy, she enjoyed showing off her "fancy" vocabulary. She'd even lost her heavy East End accent. "They won't need a chaperone if we teach them to protect themselves. Besides, we can't carry all of our equipment to their homes."

True; they had tried. Aristocratic ladies quite enjoyed hitting and kicking bags of sand, and lifting dumbbells, but the heavy equipment did not make for easy travel.

Unimpressed after their first encounter, Franny exaggerated a friendly wave whenever she saw the vicar wandering around the church gardens. Without fail, he ignored her greeting and scurried in the opposite direction. Deep inside, watching him run away like a cowardly chicken gave her a thrill. Men could be such silly creatures.

Not all men, though. Franny knew two exceptions, her father being the first and most important. He believed in female equality. He'd even risked his reputation to go into business with his "girls."

"If a man chooses not to train with me because I am supporting my girl's dreams, 'tis his loss. I am the best coach in London," Papa often said.

Yes, indeed, she'd been blessed with the best father in the world.

And then there was Harry Simpson, her loyal friend and The Silk Knuckles' caretaker. His admirable work ethic kept the building and grounds immaculate.

If she were honest with herself, maybe she was being a bit prejudiced towards men. Currently, her father's students showed her tremendous respect. Hell, many had even studied with her or Josie. Yet, her father had lost many students when he left the gym in St Giles to move into their new, safer space on Tavistock Street. Franny wasn't naive. Those defectors would never patronize a place co-owned by women.

Josie caught her gaze and curled her finger, motioning for Franny to join the class. "Shall we demonstrate a knee to the bollocks for the ladies?" she yelled across the gymnasium.

"Only if I get to be the knee," Franny called. She didn't care if she played the perpetrator or the victim in a demonstration. However, she enjoyed being the reason the ladies broke from their calisthenics to giggle. Prizefighting might not be fun and games, but these female empowerment classes should be enjoyable if they intended to attract women and turn a profit.

Franny was halfway to the sweaty females when the front door opened and two blokes in threadbare greatcoats strutted in like they owned the place.

Slightly unnerved by their bold entrance, Franny pivoted and charged toward them. "Hello. I'm Frances Valentine, one of the owners. Can I help you gentlemen?"

"Well, damn. If ye ain't prettier than a princess." A stocky bloke who looked like he had taken a hundred too many blows to his face doffed his tweed cap. "I wasn't expectin' that."

Franny glowered at him. "What were you expecting?"

The man thumbed to his swollen-eared companion. "Whale here with girl parts."

Since the man reminded her of the largest mammal on earth, she assumed he was a Whale instead of a Wale and she did not want to in any way be compared to him. Both her jaw and fist clenched.

The man held up his hands in surrender. "Hold on there, miss. I'm here on friendly business. Adam Thorton at your service. But you can call me 'Bear'."

Franny considered the name Adam Thorton. It sounded familiar. "Are you a pugilist?" she asked.

"Retired," Bear said. "Now in the business of hosting and promoting fights, and I have a particular interest in lady pugilists. I find they are the best way to start off a night. Get the wagers rolling in, they do. I find enthusiastic female fighters to be way more interesting than disgruntled blokes pounding the shite out of each other."

"And why are you telling me this?" Franny asked.

"I want you, Fiery Franny, and your mate Jabbing Josie to fight for me."

Franny swallowed. "You must not have heard but I've retired from prizefighting."

He leaned close to whisper, "I heard about your unfortunate fight. But that was over a year ago. It's time to get back on the horse."

Unfortunate was not a strong enough descriptor. Franny had knocked out her opponent, Laughing Lucy. It had taken Lucy so long to recover that she'd been carried away on a litter, as Franny tried not to cry in front of the blood-thirsty spectators. Her opponent had struggled with her memory for months. Franny visited her while she was recovering, and thankfully Lucy eventually returned to her normal self, although she'd never climbed back into the ring.

Neither had Franny. She might live and breathe the pugilistic lifestyle, but her prizefighting days were behind her. For good.

Forever. There was no climbing back on that bucking stallion for her.

"No thank you, Mr. Whale and Mr. Bear," she said. "I appreciate your offer, but I must decline."

Josie approached. "Can I help ye gents?" she asked, her accent appearing as it often did when she was emotional or trying to blend in.

"You must be Jabbing Josie." Bear tipped his cap. "Why, you are also as pretty as can be. A gymnasium full of lovely chits. I wouldn't believe it if I weren't seeing it with my own eyes." His grin showcased emptiness where his front teeth should be. "Whale and Bear at your service."

Just as Franny's had, Josie's fists clenched and unclenched by her side.

"They want us to fight for them," Franny explained.

"What do you get out of it?" Josie asked.

"Fair question. Since I promote both pugilists and the fight in general, Whale and I keep ten percent of the night's purse."

Franny rested her hands on her hips. "In other words, you make out no matter who wins?"

"Absolutely," he said. "Keeps the fights fair. No fixing fights at The Purple Rabbit."

"I'm not currently prizefighting," Josie explained. "I'll return at some point, but for the time being, I'm focused on The Silk Knuckles Saloon and my family." Trying to have a baby to be exact. Although to Franny's knowledge, Josie's womb remained childless.

"Anything we can say to persuade you to change yer mind?" Bear asked.

"Not currently," Josie said.

"Nothing," Franny said. Not unless they could snuff her memories of that tragic fight.

Whale swung his finger toward their female students.

Bear nodded. "Any of those ladies promising fighters?"

Franny regarded their group of aristocrats, some who were in their middling years. "I'm afraid not."

Bear wrinkled his nose as he surveyed the ladies. "Enh. I suppose you're right. But if either of you change your minds, you can find us at The Purple Rabbit in Whitechapel."

"Fighting within the city is illegal," Josie said.

"Only if ye get caught," Bear declared with his toothless grin.

"Whitechapel?" Franny huffed. "Do you run a brothel?"

"We don't tup our fighters," Bear declared, his shoulders thrown back defiantly.

Whatever in the devil that meant.

"Thank you for your offer," Josie said. "But we must return to instructing our class."

"Of course. Have a fine evenin', ladies," Bear said with a flourish of his cap.

Franny's shoulders sagged the second the door closed behind the men. Perhaps she'd been too hasty in her dismissal of their offer. Deep inside her soul, a small part of her ached to compete again. Damn her cowardice to hell, but she couldn't return to the ring where winning at all costs was all that mattered, even if it meant maiming another human. Hell, people died in boxing mills all of the time. *No, thank you.*

Josie seemed to read Franny's mind because she wrapped a comforting arm around her shoulders. "Lucy was not your fault."

But everything about that exceedingly violent fight was entirely her fault. Every decent fighter knew facial bones were hard on their knuckles, so they kept hits to areas with less flesh to the minimum. In her zealous enthusiasm, Franny had aimed at Lucy's face and head multiple times.

"And she recovered, so you need no longer fret," Josie reminded her.

Despite the constant encouragement from her friend, Franny continued to struggle with her fears and worries.

If she were entirely honest with herself, she needed to consider the obvious. Perhaps she was terrified of being at the end of a punishing blow that stole her intellect. It wasn't every day that the daughter of a boxing coach could read and write as well as any scholar and do sums like a clerk. Her late mother's tutelage was a gift she was not willing to trade, not even for glory in the ring.

The front door opened again. Franny and Josie whirled around.

Franny expected the peculiar Whale and Bear to barge back in, but instead their youngest student, Sky Johnston, stumbled to them.

"Fire," Sky panted. "The building is on fire."

Franny froze in place. What was he talking about? The building was just fine. Unless the sudden tang in her nostrils was smoke?

"Hurry, Harry is dying," Sky yelled.

Heart hammering, Franny sprinted to the exit to care for her beloved caretaker.

THANK HEAVENS, TEN Thames watermen had ridden in on their horse-drawn cart and pumped water at the building. They'd saved most of the structure, although part of one wall was now timber and ash.

Apparently, Vicar Williams had been taking his evening constitutional when he'd seen the flames. He'd immediately sent his altar boy to notify the Fire Office. Afterward, the vicar callously confessed he had not saved their building due to heroic kindness. He'd been fearful that the fire would spread to his church. Had the wind been blowing in the opposite direction, the nasty curmudgeon probably would have left the gymnasium burn to the ground with a dozen people inside.

By the time they'd extinguished the fire and called for a doctor to attend to Harry's injuries, it was well after midnight. Luckily, the second floor was untouched by fire. A haze of gray smoke that caught deep in one's lungs still permeated the upper floors. They sat occasionally coughing in Josie's second floor office, all the while discussing what was to be done about their singed dreams.

Exhaling loudly, Franny dropped her head on the table.

"The Davenports will take care of Harry," Josie's husband, Nicolas Wentworth, the future Earl of Shiredale, said. "They will allow him to stay with them until he is healthy. He will be so well fed and entertained that he will never want to leave."

"That is true. I loved my stay with the Davenports." Josie patted Franny's back. "I could have stayed there forever. Harry is in good hands."

Franny knew with every fiber of her being that Nicolas's dear friends, Viscount Davenport and his mother, the Dowager Viscountess Davenport, were kind and generous and would make sure Harry had the best doctors. Over the past few months, they'd welcomed her and Papa into their home and treated them as if they were equals. She was also reasonably certain that Lady Davenport romantically fancied Papa. However, Papa was much too set in his ways to allow himself to be seduced by a woman— especially one not of his class, even if she was as lovely and generous as Agatha Davenport.

Although Franny feared that nothing would ease the pain from Harry's burns, there was no time for despair, so she pulled herself together and sat tall. "Why would someone hit Harry from behind? Everyone adores him. And who would want to destroy our business?"

Josie harrumphed. "That nasty vicar next door."

"That makes no sense." Papa's soot-covered brow furrowed. "Why would he risk his church burning?"

"Because the arse didn't realize the wind would carry the flames toward his building," Josie said.

Franny wholeheartedly agreed.

Nicolas sighed. "Unfortunately, you can't rule out that there are many men who do not believe women should have a business or teach female empowerment classes."

"What are you saying?" Franny asked. "Do we have numerous enemies? Could one of them tried to burn down our building?"

"Unfortunately, that is precisely what I am saying," Nicolas said.

"Bloody infernal hell," Josie said.

Franny's sentiments exactly.

"Whoever they are, they picked the wrong people to wage a war against," Papa said.

Oh, had they ever.

CHAPTER TWO

FOLLOWING A SERIES of triple raps on his door, Edward Robinson was struck with a sudden urge to leap out the window of his office at Number 4 Bow Street. To break a leg or listen to Samuel Baker, the blowhard, blabber on and on?

After weighing his options, Edward decided he'd ignore the knocks and continue perusing *The People's Hue and Cry,* the weekly publication that provided lawmen with reports on stolen goods and criminals. Unfortunately, the door flew open, and the overbearing arse barged in without an invitation.

"Hell, Robinson, I wish I could concentrate like you," Baker bellowed in an outside voice. "Didn't you hear me? I knocked three times."

Edward peered over his newspaper. "Nine times."

"Nine?" Either oblivious to or unfazed by Edwards's irritation, Baker plopped onto the chair in front of his desk and pointed at the paper. "Any valuable information in there?"

There was almost always valuable information in the newspaper, but Baker had made a habit of not doing his own research, and Edward would not hand feed or enable the lazy arse.

"I'm actually quite busy working on the case of Lady Celeste Milton's missing jewelry," Edward said. "Do you need something?"

Baker smirked. "You lucky arse. They say bedding the young

widow is a rite of passage for every bloke in the *ton*." The shite waggled his brow. "Does she also tup us working chaps?"

Edward would never, not in a million years, tell a piece of shite like Baker that the widow had invited him to spend the night in her bed. And damn, Edward had been tempted. It had taken every bit of discipline to pretend he wasn't interested and walk away, especially when women were his Achilles heel. He was no saint, but he took his job seriously, and he did not bed the women he was assigned to help.

"Fine. Don't answer. Keep her all to yourself, you selfish shite." Baker leaned back in the chair and plunked his mud-covered boots on Edward's desk. "Anything in there about the fire at The Silk Knuckles Saloon?"

Edward glared at the fool. "Bloody hell, Baker. Remove your feet from my desk." Since he had no desire to engage in conversation with the swine, he swallowed his curiosity and did not ask what The Silk Knuckles Saloon was or what had happened there.

As usual, Baker nattered on, his foul-smelling footwear stinking up Edward's desk. "The Duke of Griffendale brought the case to the magistrate's attention and is paying my fee. Someone tried to burn the building to the ground." Baker chuckled, needling Edward's last nerve. How the soulless arse kept his job was anyone's guess. Lawmen should be upstanding and honorable.

"What in blazes do you find so humorous about arson?" Edward asked as he finally shoved Baker's feet from his work area.

Baker teetered in the chair, righted himself, and kept on blabbing. "Well, they got what they deserved. Those damnable women thought they could open a scandalous business in a respectable part of town. They should have stayed in St Giles, where they belong."

As Edward had learned many years ago, no woman should set foot in St Giles. Unless, that is, she was as fearless as Franny Valentine. Five years later, Edward still remembered everything about the alluring hell-on-carriage-wheels pugilist. He still compared every woman he met to her and found them lacking in spirit and passion. Too bad the chit had taken an instant dislike to him because he'd been frustratingly attracted to her. Perhaps he should detest her for ruining his perfect profile, but time had a way of making a man mature and see the error of his ways, and Edward *had* been an arrogant, insufferable arse. Besides, his crooked nose gave him a rugged look that women favored, maybe even more so than his once "pretty" face.

Edward sighed. "I hope you plan to investigate this with integrity. And, keep in mind, bedding prostitutes in the line of duty is not ethical."

"Bugger off, Robinson. I'll bed whoever in the hell I want." Baker's chuckle sent another prickle of annoyance up Edward's spine. "Although I don't think these chits bed men. I suspect they are—" Robinson leaned close to conspiratorially whisper— "Sapphists. But they aren't prostitutes, to my knowledge."

Sapphist or not—not that Edward begrudged anyone their lifestyle choice—no woman should have to deal with the weakest investigator on the force.

"If they don't own a house of ill repute, what type of scandalous business do they own?" Edward asked. And what was the duke's interest?

Baker stared at him as if he was a dolt, which was ironic indeed since the man had the intellect of a worm.

"The Silk Knuckles Saloon is a gymnasium that teaches women to defend themselves. Ridiculous, I say. Women are not strong enough to defend themselves. Men must protect the weaker sex. Well, when they need protection, that is. Sometimes, though, they need a firm hand."

Again, memories of the feisty redhead who'd broken his nose bombarded Edward's memory. Those images were pushed aside by a fantasy about Samuel Baker being castrated by a bevy of angry women in a dark alley. Edward chortled.

"Would you believe that Pete the Trojan was there the night their building caught on fire?" Baker said. "Apparently, he was training with that coach who supports women's pugilism. That aristocratic fool who writes *Meanderings of a Gentleman* may be trying to shove female sports down everyone's throat, but I, for one, ain't fallin' for it. Seems like The Duke of Griffendale and Viscount Davenport are also supporting these absurd women. I wager it's because they are there looking for cunny." Baker chortled. "Women are only good for two things. Milking cows and tupping."

Swallowing his fury, Edward sorted through Baker's nonsense. Could Franny Valentine and Josephine Martin be the owners of The Silk Knuckles Saloon? Holy bollocks, was Lady Jabbing Josie, the new champion of the prestigious Duke's and Damsel's Mill and the future Earl of Shiredale's wife, actually Josephine Martin?

"Are you talking about Coach Calder Valentine?" Edward asked.

"*Pfft*! That daft fool could be one of the greatest coaches of all time, but he lets his daughter and that partner of hers run amuck. No idea why The Trojan would want to be associated with that man and his pair of hoydens."

Baker was an unholy arse.

"Wait a minute," Edward said. "Are you telling me that the Valentines opened a gymnasium called The Silk Knuckles Saloon, and a few days ago, someone tried to burn it to the ground?"

Baker rolled his eyes. "Where have you been, mate?" He chortled. "Got your head stuck in that damnable *Hue and Cry* so often you are missing the real news."

"I've been busy doing my job," Edward said, his temper barely contained. "Was anyone injured in the fire?"

"Yes. The gymnasium's caretaker," Baker said. "Severe burns but alive."

"And the magistrate assigned *you* to the case?" Edward asked, his indignation evident in his high-pitched lilt.

"Yes," Baker said. "I know. Bloody preposterous, isn't it? But I have no intention of wasting much time on it. Like I said, they got what they deserved."

Edward's blood pumped so forcefully that he feared his eyeballs might explode from their sockets. So much for Fielding's intention to have the most intelligent, skilled, and well-trained force protecting their country. Their beloved patriarch would roll over in his grave if he knew an unscrupulous, indolent ignoramus like Samuel Baker was one of his beloved Runners.

Growling, Edward leaped from his seat, grabbed Baker by his collar, and pulled him onto his feet. Edward hissed, and his saliva spattered Baker's face.

"If I find out that you do anything to jeopardize a thorough arson investigation, I will take it out of your hide." Unable to control his temper, Edward shoved Baker so hard, the ignoramus lost his balance, crashing against the chair.

Baker harrumphed indignantly, but Edward was much too busy gathering his pistol and tip staff to pay attention to the pouting fool.

CHAPTER THREE

ONCE THEIR VOLUNTEERS departed, Franny stood back and admired the repaired wall. Many of their members had worked around the clock these past few days, so now The Silk Knuckles Saloon was almost ready to reopen. Unfortunately, if Franny inhaled deeply, she still caught a whiff of smoke. But, if they kept the windows open the fresh air, if one could call the London air fresh, filtered into the gymnasium.

The hard work over the past few days seemed to invigorate Josie. The woman was a machine that never quit, and her resolve did not falter. Meanwhile, Franny had wallowed in an ugly rage. How could someone hurt Harry? And who would want to destroy their dream? Whoever had done it could have killed everyone inside the building. What kind of person did such a thing? Surprisingly, it was Josie, the belligerent orphan Papa had brought home thirteen years ago, who had remained optimistic while Franny stomped about grumbling blasphemies.

Franny recalled the first time she met Josie in vivid detail. Smiling and with an upturned palm, Papa had presented a scrawny child dressed in rags as if he were offering Franny a puppy.

"Franny, this is Josephine Martin. I found her in an alley, beating the hell out of a bully twice her size. She doesn't have a family, food, or a place to live, so I thought she could live with us.

What do you think?"

"I think that is a boy." Franny had wrinkled her nose in disgust. "And he stinks."

Josie had growled, bent low, and charged Franny, knocking her on her arse. The second Franny regained her wind, she'd jabbed the filthy urchin in the nose. Then the two of them had rolled around on the floor, wrestling, punching, and calling each other unseemly names children shouldn't know.

After taking a few elbows to his breadbasket, Papa managed to pull Franny off Josie. Thereupon, he'd sent his own flesh and blood to her room without dinner. Later that night, a pretty girl who smelled like Franny's soap and wore one of her old night dresses snuck into her room and held out a biscuit.

"I saved this for ye," the girl said.

Since Franny's belly gurgled, she took the offered food and shoved it in her mouth.

"I favor your Papa, I do," Josie said. "I'd like to live with him and have biscuits every night. I ain't had noffin to eat in forever. And yer house is so pretty and fancy."

No wonder their visitor was gaunt. Although their house was far from fancy, it was cozy and almost clean, and it probably did appear pretty to a girl who'd spent her life sleeping next to rubbish bins.

"You haven't eaten in forever, and you are giving me your biscuit?" Franny asked. She wasn't sure she'd give someone one of her biscuits, especially if she were hungry.

Josie had plopped onto the floor, sat cross-legged, and rested her chin on her knuckles. "Ye are lucky. I don't have parents."

A lump had formed in Franny's throat as she dropped to sit beside Josie. "I don't have a mother. She died last year. She used to be a governess before she married Papa. She taught me to read and write, and she had pretty red hair."

"Ye have pretty red hair, too." Josie frowned. "I guess ye loved your mum. If she was as nice as yer da, no wonder yer sad."

Franny's tears flowed as Josie, a girl who had no home, wore dirty boy's clothing, and had no one to love, patted her back and soothed her heartbreak.

From that second forward, they had been like inseparable sisters, reading, writing, dancing around the kitchen, boxing, terrorizing Papa's male students, and generally being pains in the arse.

Last year, when Franny had injured Lucy and retired from prize fighting, it was Josie who had comforted her. It was also Josie who had supported her when Franny announced that she wanted to open a new gymnasium in a safer part of the city so that women could exercise and learn to defend themselves. Franny's dream had become Josie's dream, and together with Papa, they'd made it come true. Even when Josie won the ultimate female prizefighting championship and married a handsome aristocrat, she remained Franny's loyal friend.

Josie wrapped her arm around Franny's waist, bringing her back to the here and now. "Franny, since our building is whole again, why don't you get some sleep before tonight's meeting? And Coach…" Josie grasped his hand. "You need rest, too."

"Jojo you are probably correct," Papa said. "I am exhausted. I think I'll lie down in my office for a bit." Thank goodness he acquiesced since dark half-moons underlined his eyes.

"I am going to hire a hackney to take me to the newspaper office," Josie said. "I'd like to visit with Nicolas. That is, if the two of you don't mind?"

Franny had never found it in her heart to dislike Nicolas Wentworth. Not even when he took Josie from her. The man was the heir to an earldom, and still, he had taken a humble job as a journalist for *The Daily Dispatch of London*. He even wrote informative articles about women's sports. And his very best quality was that somehow, he had managed to turn Josie into a proper lady, without snuffing the passion or spirit that made her larger than life, all while making her happy.

"Enjoy your afternoon, Jojo," Papa said. "And, Franny, you get some rest too."

"I'll be back in time for our meeting," Josie called as she scurried to the exit.

Papa kissed Franny on the cheek, then left her alone. As exhausted as she was, she craved a blood-pumping, mind-clearing training session. Although she loved having the gymnasium full of people, sometimes it was nice to have the space to herself.

She tugged the bodice of her gown down, then tied the sleeves around her waist. She started her session with Papa's prescribed calisthenic routine, which included one hundred deep knee bends, fifty lunges, and fifty squats. Dropping onto her belly, she performed fifty push-ups. Since nervous energy still coursed through her, she performed another twenty-five before leaping to her feet, hopping about, and shaking out her arms and fingers.

She skipped to the far wall to retrieve one of the long ropes. Once upon a time, she'd jumped over it one hundred fifty-seven times without making a mistake. Today was the perfect day to try to beat her record. She'd aim for one-hundred seventy-five.

She sifted through the ropes, looking for the one with the orange dot on the end because it was the perfect length. "Ah, ha, there you are," she said as she tugged it from the hook.

"Hello," someone said.

She startled, then faced the main entrance as the rope slithered to the ground. A man who carried the staff of a lawman had entered while her back was turned. A different Bow Street Runner, with lecherous eyes and a dismissive attitude, had visited yesterday. He'd asked a few questions about the fire but hadn't bothered to listen to the answers. Papa, Josie, and Franny agreed; they'd been assigned a useless investigator.

Franny experienced a moment of déjà vu as a five-year-old memory of a handsome, arrogant man barging into their old gymnasium hit with a thud. She froze in place as her visitor swaggered toward her.

This couldn't be him. Could it? That man had been as pretty as a prince and lean-muscled. This man was formed from warrior sinew and had a rugged, masculine jawline. His crooked nose looked as if someone had punched him. Hard. But he had the same dark hair, and just like the man in her memory, his eyebrows and lashes were thick and dark.

"Frances Valentine," he said.

Heavens above. He also had that same cocky grin that had addled her those many years ago. It was as if he was about to say something outrageously witty that only he could understand. Franny did not like feeling confused. Not one single bit. And this man befuddled her.

Her heart skittered, flipped, and then flopped. "If it isn't bloody Edward Robinson," she said with a horrified snort. "What in the bloomin' hell are you doing here? Didn't I punch you hard enough the first time?"

CHAPTER FOUR

Assuming that Baker had done a half-arsed job, Edward had spent twenty minutes combing the outside of the building, searching for clues. A fishy smell permeated the area, indicating that whale oil had been used as an accelerant. The wall of the building that butted up against a narrow alley had recently been rebuilt. He'd kicked at the stones, uncovering black ash and a few chunks of charred timber.

When his toe brushed up against something that glittered amongst the black, brown, and gray, he had crouched down to unearth it from its hiding place and then lifted it to hold a plain gold button in the lone ray of sunlight poking into the alley. Since it might be evidence, Edward had dropped the button into his pocket beside his ever-present notebook, and made his way to the front of the building.

Thereupon he had entered the gymnasium where a woman with a well-formed backside and a long red braid talked to the wall. Her chemise was visible because her blue dress was knotted around her waist.

And then Francis Valentine swung around to face him, and Edward questioned his judgement in coming.

Since he was older, more mature, and better able to control his randy beast, he knew better than to look at the nipples poking through Frances Valentine's sweat-dampened chemise. He would not think about her prodigious, bouncing, unbound bosom. No sir. Not this time. He averted his gaze to stare into her emerald eyes.

Beautiful eyes.

Make that beautiful but furious eyes.

Shite! This woman looked at him as if he were Satan come to Earth. It seemed she hated him so much that she'd even remembered his name. Not that he would ever forget hers. It wasn't every day a man got his nose rearranged by a woman half his size.

Left floundering at her acerbic question, and wanting to protect his nose, he cleared his throat, trying to come up with a witty retort that would show her how charming he was. Luckily, he was a quick thinker.

"As you can see…" He held up his lawman's staff. "I never did become a prizefighter." He chuckled.

She scowled.

So much for charming her with his self-deprecation. He shook off his frustration. "I heard that you had an unfortunate accident a few nights ago, and I wanted to offer—"

"Unfortunate *accident?*" She lunged into his space and lifted her chin, which only made it more difficult for him to avoid looking down her chemise. "It was no accident. Someone tried to burn down our building, with us inside it." She jammed her finger into his chest and poked him half a dozen times. "My dear friend Harry was seriously injured. Someone hit him over the head, left him for dead, and his skin is covered with burns."

"I'm sorry about your friend," he said in all sincerity. "But could you stop stabbing me?"

She stared at her index finger pressing into his chest. Although her aggressive posture relaxed, she did not move her hand.

"Maybe we should start over," Edward said.

Seeming to come to her senses, she dropped her hand and stepped back.

"As I was saying—" before she'd rudely poked him to death—

"I heard what happened to your gymnasium and wanted to come in person to offer my assistance."

She stared at him as if he'd said men could fly to the moon.

"Why don't you tell me exactly what happened," he said.

One strawberry-gold eyebrow rose as she tilted her head to regard him. "If your pudding-headed partner had listened to us, I wouldn't have to repeat myself now."

Baker was such an arse. When Edward returned to the office, he would throttle the man. Hell, he'd do more than that. He would lodge a complaint with the magistrate.

"Baker is *not* my partner," Edward said.

She squinted at him as if confused.

"Baker came into my office earlier today to tell me what happened and explain he'd been assigned to the case," Edward said. "He mentioned that two women and a well-known coach owned the building and that arson was involved. I made the connection, and after I confirmed that it was your building, I wanted to do what I could to help you." Best not to mention that Baker was an incompetent, misogynistic blowhard.

Now that Edward had said it out loud, he realized how impulsive his response had been. He had no authority to interject himself in this investigation, and it wasn't as if he had a friendship with Franny or her business partners. His concern seemed quite irrational. Damn his honesty to hell when it made him divulge information he had no desire to share—such as a five-year fascination with a woman who detested him so much that she had broken his nose.

He was pathetic. No wonder she disliked him. He should turn around, walk away, and mind his own business. And he was about to do just that when he heard the door behind him open.

Franny's gaze slid to whoever had entered, and her face lit up. Thunderation, her smile was pretty, genuine, and downright sweet. He'd be thrilled if she ever turned that delighted expression on him.

"If you will excuse me," she said. "I believe I have new students who are here to learn about my gymnasium."

She stepped around him and approached the three women. The oldest of the group, as well as a short brunette, tutted. A pretty little blonde shifted her weight back and forth uncomfortably. Edward would wager his hard-earned blunt they were not there to learn about the sweet science, since the gray-haired woman held what looked like a Bible to her bosom.

Unfortunately, he had to pass by the women to reach the exit. *'Tis none of your business, you fool*, he berated himself as he stuck to the outskirts of the room. Still, he eavesdropped because Franny's downcast eyes and red cheeks broke his heart.

"Good heavens. Dressed like that! And in the company of a man," one of the women said. "The vicar is correct. This is a den of wickedness."

Franny crossed her arms over her chemise as if she were embarrassed by being caught in the middle of a workout in her own gymnasium.

No way in hell would he allow these women to shame her. He turned on his heel. Dodging exercise equipment, he charged across the room.

CHAPTER FIVE

NEVER HAD FRANNY felt as exposed and humiliated as she did at this moment. She'd approached these women, expecting them to say they'd heard about the admirable work The Silk Knuckles Saloon did to empower women. She'd honestly thought they were new students. But instead, her cheeks heated as they looked down their noses at her.

Meanwhile, her chemise was showing, and an arrogant man who messed with her common sense watched as these women chastised her. If only she had bound her breasts earlier, she might not be currently crossing her arms over her chest, preserving her modesty. Upon further introspection, Franny concluded she was also trying to protect her heart from their ugly words.

"The vicar is correct," the tall gray-haired woman with high cheekbones who seemed to be in charge said. "This is a den of wickedness."

Never at a loss for words, Franny's tongue refused to work. *Say something. Defend yourself, you daft fool!*

"I was training," she finally said, her normally bold voice sounding meek. "You see…Well, I cannot move freely and punch in stays and a tight bodice. And then Runner Robinson came in."

"We hear a group of rebel rousers also meet here," the woman declared. "The rumor is they plan to overtake Parliament."

"We don't plan to overtake Parliament," Franny said. However, they did want to send a petition to Parliament.

"I shall pray for your lost soul." The woman opened her Bible and read: "Proverbs 7:10-12. *Passing through the street near her corner; and he went the way to her house, In the twilight, in the evening, in the black and dark night: And behold, there met him a woman with the attire of an harlot, and subtle of heart. She is loud and stubborn; her feet abide not in her house: Now is she without, now in the streets, and lieth in wait at every corner.*

"Amen," the short, dark-haired woman said.

How dare these judgmental biddies compare her to a prostitute. The arrogance it took to barge into her place of business with the damnable proverb marked and ready was both startling and unsettling.

Franny's temper snapped. "You bloody sanctimonious—"

"Ladies," Edward Robinson said as he infiltrated their group. "May I be of assistance?"

At Edward's approach, the petite blonde who had not said anything winced and looked at her feet. When she lifted her chin, Franny noticed the bruise on her cheek.

"Have you ever heard such language?" asked the eldest woman, her tone imperious. "Are you here to serve her a writ for breaking the law?"

Franny planted her hands on her hips. "Ladies, we teach women how to protect themselves, we exercise, and we train prizefighters. We are not a bloody brothel."

"Oh!" the short brunette cried. "Oh, Mrs. Brown, I feel faint. I believe I need to sit."

What a dramatic ninny. Franny rolled her eyes. "Feel free to sit on the floor."

Ensconcing them in his smoldering gaze, Edward smiled at the women. "I'm here to investigate the fire."

Franny looked right into his eyes and scoffed twice. Only a fool would misinterpret her disgust.

Fool that he was, he also grinned at Franny.

Edward Robinson's lashes might be long and thick, his brown

eyes might be filled with passion, and he might have a sculpted physique, but his flirtatious personality would not work on Franny or these holier-than-thou women.

"Probably God himself set the fire because he is cleansing our city of Satan's immorality," the biddiest of the biddies, who seemed to be married to the unfortunate Mr. Brown, said.

Franny fought her urge to grab the woman's Bible, throw it on the floor, and stomp on it. "My dear friend was burned in the fire. He is the kindest, most moral man I know. If you continue to be disrespectful, I must ask you to leave my gymnasium." Franny swung her arm, index finger pointing toward the door.

"I've never encountered such rudeness," Mrs. Brown, the bald-faced liar, said. Franny would wager with a personality so bereft of charm the nasty woman had encountered far worse insults than she'd just dished out. "Treated like this when we are here in the Good Lord's name to pray for your souls," Mrs. Brown added.

Franny was of the opinion that the Good Lord wanted women to be strong and independent. However, he probably did *not* want her to punch this sour puss. She unclenched her fist.

"Ladies," Edward Robinson said, gazing at the timid little blonde. "Why don't I walk you outside where you can fill me in on all of your concerns." He smiled at each of the unwelcome visitors. "I am a lawman, after all."

The second he grinned at these mean-spirited humans as if he were their savior, Franny's unease around him grew tenfold.

Mrs. Brown raised her chin and then sharply dropped it in prideful acquiescence. "Yes. Thank you. A man of reason, just like my sons. They are both good men who have welcomed God into their hearts. Are lady pugilists not illegal?"

"Ladies learning to defend themselves is not illegal," Edward said. "And as far as I know, no mills are taking place here." He flashed Franny a look that said, *at least there better not be.*

Edward Robinson could sod off!

Strolling alongside these horrible women as if he were their ally, Edward escorted them across the room. They were almost to the door when the blonde peered over her shoulder and sent Franny a look that reminded her of a child who had lost her only toy.

"You ladies seem quite observant," Edward said. "Have you seen anyone suspicious lately? Or anyone that you don't trust?"

"Besides these pugilists?" Mrs. Brown asked.

The door closed, muffling Edward's response.

The last few days had been sheer hell. Three women she'd never met barging into her gymnasium accusing her of being a prostitute in league with the Devil did not improve her mood. And then there was Edward Robinson showing up after five years, claiming he wanted to help her. Why in the dickens did a man she found attractive frustrate her so?

Franny untied her sleeves and slid her bodice into place. Most of the time, she did not give a whit what she looked like, but since she admired Lady Davenport and Lady Siddons she had no desire to smell like perspiration at their upcoming meeting. She wrote Papa a quick note letting him know she was walking home to bathe and change clothing and slid it under his office door.

Franny was halfway home when she stopped short and thunked her palm against her forehead. Someone, probably an angry man, had used his fist on the timid little blonde. Franny had been so self-centered and too absorbed in her indignation to look out for another woman's wellbeing.

Trepidation skittered up her spine, putting her on high alert. Too many unusual things had happened over the last few days. She needed to pull her head out of her arse and focus.

CHAPTER SIX

AT THE END of his long day, Edward trudged from Bow Street to his lodging house on Henrietta Street. As usual, the dutiful Mrs. Benson lit the lamps and set out Edward's brandy, ensuring his comfortable welcome home. He hung his coat on its hook, poured a drink, sank into his favorite chair and contemplated his day. As stressful as the last twelve hours had been, Edward's life was quite fulfilling. He favored his job, his home, his landlady, and his cat.

He did not require excessive wealth, but he did enjoy a certain amount of comfort and Runners barely made enough to feed themselves. Along with a few other lawmen, he'd honorably earned additional blunt by pounding the streets twice a week, trying to rid Drury Lane of pickpockets. He gave the money to Mrs. Benson who, in turn, took excellent care of him. His long workdays on his feet had the additional benefit of maintaining the muscular physique with which he'd been blessed. Additionally, twice a week, he visited a men's gymnasium where he skipped rope and hefted dumbbells.

Loudly meowing, Zigzag leaped onto his lap and nudged his hand.

"Damn tough one," he told her as he caressed her soft cheek. "Would you like to hear about it?"

The ball of orange and white striped fur meowed, her golden

eyes flashing.

"There is this infuriating female pugilist, the same one who broke my nose years ago."

Zigzag swatted at his hand, reminding him that he needed to keep the pats coming if she was expected to listen.

"Yes. I know. I am a fool to find her attractive but that is not the point. Someone tried to burn down her business."

"Meow."

"Exactly. I went to her gymnasium today, and let me tell you, she was none too happy to see me. Three angry women probably saved me from having my nose broken again." He paused, recollecting. "Who were these women, you ask?" Edward let out a lip vibrating huff. "Angry, self-righteous sheep who don't believe a woman should learn to protect herself or work outside the home. And God forbid a woman wear less than five layers of clothing and sweat."

Edward raised his voice to imitate the imperious Mrs. Brown. "'Indecent, I say. Did you see her state of undress'?"

Oh, Edward had seen it alright. Except Frances Valentine was not trying to tempt a man or call forth Satan. She was simply exercising alone in her own building.

Zigzag stretched and yawned, almost knocking Edward's drink from his hand.

"Am I boring you?" he asked.

She blinked as if to say, *Continue if you must, but be quick about it so I can sleep.*

Allowing his bossy pet to dragoon him, Edward increased the pace of his storytelling and the length of his caresses. "These women and their vicar want The Silk Knuckles closed down. They believe it is akin to a brothel. The real concern should be that someone hit one of the women on her cheek. I know what a bruise from a punch looks like, and her injury was caused by one hell of an angry fist. I tried to question her about it, but Mrs. Brown wouldn't let the poor woman speak for herself. Tried to tell me her daughter in law ran into a door. Ironic, don't you think? I'd wager the young Jane Brown needs to learn to protect herself from her husband." Edward exhaled a huff of disgust.

"Stupid arse that I can be, I returned to work and barged into the magistrate's office telling him that Samuel Baker was not the best person to investigate The Silk Knuckles fire. You can imagine how well that went."

"Meow. Meow?"

"Then, I asked why the Duke of Griffendale hired us to look into the fire. Would you like to know what I discovered? Good, because I'm about to tell you. He sponsored Jabbing Josie, one of the instructors, to be his champion at the mill he co-hosts with the Duke of Paulsgrove. Now, do you want to know the most interesting part? The magistrate demanded I keep my nose out of it because Maxwell Whitehill, this lord with clout in Parliament, is demanding The Silk Knuckles be permanently closed. It seems two influential aristocrats are interested in the saloon for different reasons. One is trying to protect it. The other is trying to destroy it."

Aghast with the absurdity of it all, Zigzag sprang onto all fours and dug her claws into Edward's thighs.

"Ouch. Easy, please!" He lifted her slightly. When she'd sheathed her claws and settled down again, he continued, "I know. Suspicious as hell, isn't it? Why would Whitehill give half a shite about a pugilism school? And then I had to go to Celeste Milton's townhouse and explain that I had no leads on her stolen jewelry. And do you know what she said?"

Zigzag plopped down and nudged his hand so hard his glass tipped, and brandy spilled onto his lap. At least his soggy crotch kept his cock from reacting to the memory of the dowager thrusting out her prodigious bosom as she said, "Edward, darling. Why don't you stay the night?"

His common sense may have been screaming, *Don't do it,* but his damnable prick had been ready to sink deep inside her. Reason had prevailed, however, and he'd left the lady looking as if she might cry at his rejection.

" 'Twas a shite day all around," Edward told his purring companion.

Mrs. Benson stepped into the parlor, and placed her hands on her ample, aproned hips. "You are quite late. Your dinner is getting cold."

"I was just telling Zigzag about my day," Edward said.

As she often did when Edward was in one of his thoughtful moods, Mrs. Benson sat in the wing backed chair across from his. "Tell me all about it."

Edward rested his head on the back of the chair and closed his eyes. "Stuck my nose in a case that wasn't mine."

"I see," she said. "And the magistrate told you to stay out of it. Again."

"Yes."

"Would you like my opinion on the matter?" Mrs. Benson asked.

There was no point in saying *no* because she had a habit of offering unsolicited advice.

"Was the man who makes a muddle of his cases assigned to it?" she asked.

"Yes."

"And you think that a real injustice has been done and if you don't step in someone could get hurt?"

Mrs. Benson was more than just a meddling landlady, cook, and maid. She was also a wise woman and a dear friend. He opened his eyes and tilted his chin to see her better. "Yes."

"You always do the right thing when it comes to finding the truth, holding criminals accountable, and protecting others. You are one of the good ones, Edward."

He was no saint, but he appreciated her vote of confidence. "So you think I should continue investigating a case I've been told to stay out of if I think someone may be in danger?"

"I do. Just be sure you are working on your other cases. If need be, do it as a citizen, not a lawman. Of course, I don't need to tell you that. You are the hardest working, most honorable person of my acquaintance." She tapped her forehead. "And for a man, you are quite intelligent."

Edward chuckled.

"Is there a beautiful woman involved in this case you are not supposed to be investigating?"

"What would make you ask that?" he asked with entirely too much indignation.

Mrs. Benson grinned, and her apple-like cheeks rounded even more.

"How did you know?" he asked.

"You have that haunted look of an infatuated man."

He moaned.

With a hiss, Zigzag leaped from his lap, then sprinted beneath his desk. Her tail slapped the carpet as she angrily swished it, giving away her hiding place.

"Oh dear. Zigzag didn't like that." Mrs. Benson stood. "Your dinner is on the table and your breakfast is in the larder. I'll stop up tomorrow afternoon." Before departing, Mrs. Benson sent him a compassionate smile. "Get some sleep. You won't be good to anyone if you fret all night. I'll wash those wet trousers tomorrow morning. You have a clean pair in your wardrobe."

"Thank you," he called to her back, then he closed his eyes and exhaled.

Bloody hell, if Mrs. Benson sensed his attraction to Franny he must beyond hope.

"I'm in deep shite," he told Zigzag as she peeked out around his desk.

"Meeooow," she scolded.

CHAPTER SEVEN

A COOL BATH and a brisk stroll to The Silk Knuckles invigorated Franny so much that she now eagerly anticipated tonight's meeting of The Ladies' Autonomy League. Pride overflowing, she stood beside Josie surveying their inviting parlor.

Thankfully, they had followed Lady Davenport's decorating advice because the light purple wall coverings juxtaposed against the dark purple upholstery and draperies made what could have been a very ordinary room exceedingly elegant. Colorful landscape paintings adorned the walls, and a gilded clock ticked from the fireplace mantle. The large table in the center of the room held pastries, sweetmeats, and the hand-painted teacups that Lady Davenport had gifted them.

Franny stepped up to the polished rosewood side table that held a variety of libations. She poured two glasses of brandy, handing one to Josie. After settling into the plush wingbacks, they sipped as Franny relayed the details of their uninvited afternoon visitors.

The old Josephine Martin would have thrown a tantrum at being invaded and insulted. The new in-love Josie attentively listened, and then calmly said, "We will survive the unfortunate circumstances of the last few days, so I believe we should put on brave faces for the other ladies this evening."

"I agree," Franny said. "However, I think we should be honest about having an adversary." She feared they might have multiple enemies. However, she kept this disconcerting notion to herself.

Although Josie nodded her acquiescence, her brow furrowed. "Franny, has it occurred to you that Edward Robinson heard about the fire and remembered you from long ago because he was, and still is, attracted to you? Mayhap his offer to help is sincere."

"Have you forgotten how arrogant he was?" Franny asked.

"That was years ago. Could he have changed?"

Franny snorted. She adored Josie, but ever since falling in love, Josie had become much too trusting of the male species. Not that they were all hideous. There were Papa and Harry and a few of their students. But Edward Robinson did not fit into this category. It was obvious that the Bow Street Runner thought himself the most handsome man in the world. He just might be, but still, he did not have to strut around like a cocksure fool acting like she was insane if she didn't bow at his feet. And the way he'd flirted with and charmed Mrs. Brown and her entourage soured Franny's stomach.

"Nicolas heard from Viscount Davenport this morning," Josie said. "Harry slept well last night. The doctor said he is ready for visitors."

It never ceased to amaze Franny that Josie, an incorrigible foundling, called aristocrats by their given names. Not that Franny minded or begrudged her for it. In fact, she very much appreciated that she benefitted from Josie's new status. The Davenports even graciously shared their exquisite Mayfair townhouse and fabulous cook with her and Papa. If only their next visit was under more favorable circumstances. Poor Harry lying in bed with painful burns was far from a joyous occasion.

"I passed Papa on the way upstairs," Franny said. "He is going to The Spotted Octopus for a drink while we are meeting. I'm worried though. He looks so very tired."

"He does," Josie said. "But do not fret over much. Your father is resilient. What other man would give up his own career to support his daughter and ward? A man who is as strong and heroic as a titan, that is who."

True. Papa was Franny's hero.

"Are you speaking about Calder?" The Dowager Viscountess Davenport swept to them, her green skirts swishing against her ankles. A pearl dangled from each ear and a delicate strand adorned her neck. Her gray hair was piled high in an intricate updo. The woman looked as if she was attending a ball instead of a weekly female-only meeting. It was not lost on Franny that the lady overdressed for her Papa, or that every time he entered the room, the dowager's eyes and smile brightened even more.

"Good evening, Agatha. You are the first to arrive." Josie stood and kissed the viscountess on her cheek. "Yes, we were discussing Coach. He looks quite tired, but I suppose we all are. We worked hard to fix the damage so that we can reopen."

Agatha Davenport wrinkled her nose. "I can still smell the smoke. But the building looks much improved. Where is Calder? I did not see him downstairs, and he is not in his office."

"At The Spotted Octopus," Franny said.

The normally smiling Lady Davenport frowned. "Fiddlesticks. I had hoped to say hello." She sighed. "Oh, well. You will visit Harry tomorrow, will you not? I believe he is enjoying our maids' attentions. Still, I am quite sure that he would be pleased if the two of you visited. He has been asking after you." She winked at Franny.

The viscountess needed to stop turning everything into a romance. Franny and Harry were simply friends. They may have kissed years ago, but that had been curiosity, not love.

"I will come around tomorrow early afternoon," Franny promised.

"As will I," Josie said.

"I do hope Calder will join you," Lady Davenport said, a faraway expression in her eyes.

"I am sure he will," Franny assured her.

Lady Davenport smiled, her green eyes twinkling. "I shall have one of his favorite trifles prepared."

"Trifle? I do hope I am invited?" Bridget Wentworth, Josie's sister-in-law and feisty aristocrat extraordinaire entered, bringing with her a palpable energy and a few young bluestockings.

Lady Helena Siddons and the pinch-faced, skeptical Lady Lucille Hillcaster arrived within moments of the debutantes. Following enthusiastic greetings, the ladies chose drinks and arranged themselves around the room.

"Are we ready to begin?" Lady Siddons asked.

The ladies chorused their *yeses*.

"Let the Merry Maidens of Mayhem commence their battle plan," called the never serious Bridget Wentworth.

Franny chortled so hard she choked on her brandy.

Lady Davenport tried to stifle her chuckle with a palm over her mouth, but it did not hide the sparkle in her eyes.

With a smug grin, Bridget opened the leather-bound meeting notes.

Lady Siddons waited for the ladies to stop sniggering and then projected her voice. "I call this meeting of The Ladies' Autonomy League to order." She shot Bridget a look that screamed *'tis time to be serious.*

The irreverent Bridget was so busy attending to her notetaking she did not seem to take notice.

"As I am sure you have all heard," Lady Siddons said. "Someone tried to burn down The Silk Knuckles Saloon a few days ago, and Harry was injured."

Moans and groans of disgust echoed.

"My nephew, the Duke of Griffendale, hired our brave Bow Street Runners to look into the fire," Lady Siddons declared.

Franny had mixed feelings about Tristan Keats. According to rumors, he was an arrogant rake of the worst sort who bedded women in alarming numbers and seemed to take pleasure in breaking their hearts. Conversely, he had made Josie his champion in the Duke's and Dame's Mill where she won a large purse. He also supported Nicolas's marriage to Josie even though she was not of his class. Additionally, Lady Siddons, who Franny respected, loved him like a son. Furthermore, he cared enough about Josie to go to the magistrate on her behalf. Come to think of it, someone should tell the duke that Samuel Baker was an incompetent arse since it was his coin the man was wasting.

"The Duke is not our only ally," Lady Siddons continued. "Josephine's husband, Nicolas Wentworth, the future Earl of Shiredale, has taken up our cause in *The Daily Dispatch of London*. And Viscount Davenport, Agatha's son, is prepared to lend additional resources to uncover who might wish to harm The Silk Knuckles Saloon."

"Hear, hear," chanted all of the ladies except Lady Hillcaster. Why the dreary woman came to these meetings was anyone's guess.

"On to our next topic," Lady Siddons said. "Has everyone started reading *A Vindication of the Rights of Woman?*"

Franny had only read about thirty pages since she'd been busy rebuilding the gymnasium wall.

"I have been reading from it every night," Bridget said. "I find Mary Wollstonecraft to be quite forward thinking. She states that women are only inferior to men because they lack education."

"She also believes in social order founded on reason," Isabelle Stewart, a rather intelligent young woman Franny favored, said.

Lady Hillcaster let out a long, dramatic sigh. "But women are not equal, and Wollstonecraft never claims that they are."

"*Psh*, Lucille." Lady Davenport flicked her wrist. "'Tis obvious that she believes the sexes would be equal if women had better educational opportunities."

"I agree, Agatha," Lady Siddons said. "We shall tackle equal education, and changes to coverture laws so that women have economic rights."

Franny wholeheartedly agreed. One of the reasons she'd never marry was because she refused to be some man's property.

No man would ever become custodian of her share of The Silk Knuckles. No man would ever own her existence.

Luckily these high-born ladies always welcomed Franny's opinions. "Both married and unmarried women must be able to own property," she declared emphatically.

Lady Siddons raised her fist. "First women's property rights. Then educational rights. Someday we will even have a place in Parliament."

Everyone in the room, except for Lady Hillcaster, cheered as they raised a fist in solidarity.

"My nephew has agreed to discuss our concerns with his fellow lords," Lady Siddons said. "If he garners enough support, he will petition our ideas at the next session of Parliament."

Franny had dared to hope as much, and now it seemed as if her dreams might come true. She would definitely give the duke another chance since he had some redeeming qualities. Edward Robinson, not so much.

Augh! She needed to push the insufferable lawman from her thoughts and concentrate on the meeting.

" 'Tis so very exciting," Bridget said.

"Can you imagine?" Lady Davenport sighed. "Maybe there will come a time when women take their own concerns to Parliament. But for now, I am grateful for His Grace's assistance."

A giddiness bubbled through Franny. If the Duke of Griffendale, the future earl of Shiredale, and Viscount Davenport took up their cause, it would be easier to encourage other men to support them and eventually change the status quo.

"Ladies, excuse me," Edward Robinson called, his deep voice slicing a chunk out of Franny's elation. "Does anyone have a carriage?"

The bloody man needed to leave her alone. Franny swung toward the door, preparing to lambaste him publicly.

Instead, she gasped in horror because he supported her severely beaten, bloody-faced father's body weight.

"He needs a physician," Edward said.

Franny dropped her glass as she rushed to the men.

CHAPTER EIGHT

EDWARD STOOD IN the doorway of a guestroom at the Davenport's home observing as he tried to blend into the background. The heartbreak in the room was palpable. Franny knelt by her father's bed holding his hand, and tears glistened in Lady Davenport's eyes. Nicolas Wentworth wrapped his arm around his wife as if helping to hold the champion pugilist upright. Meanwhile, Viscount Jonathan Davenport paced the room, blasphemies flying from his mouth every few minutes.

"Please do not fret over me," Coach Valentine said, his voice weak. "I will be fine. The doctor said 'tis just a few bruised ribs, a dislocated shoulder, and a broken nose."

Edward suspected that Coach Valentine had more injuries than he'd confessed since his pupils were unfocused.

"Papa, your entire body is bruised," Franny said. "I swear to God, when I find out who is behind this, I shall kill every single one of them."

Undoubtedly, she would, because Frances Valentine was akin to a one-woman army.

"You shall stay here until you are back on your feet, Calder," Lady Davenport said. "Both you and Harry are welcome here until you are fully healed."

Edward fought the urge to proclaim that if the injuries continued, Greenpark House might run out of guest rooms.

The viscount stopped pacing. "I wager Whitehill is behind this."

"Whitehill?" Edward asked, breaking his silence. So much for no one taking notice of him since everyone turned to stare.

"You don't look surprised," the viscount said. "Why is that?"

Edward couldn't betray that the magistrate had mentioned the peer's name. However, he could collect information. "Tell me why you think Whitehill is involved."

Franny glared at him. Bloody bollocking hell! Using only his fists, he'd sent the two men attacking her father running for their lives. And still, she appeared to hate him.

"Runner Robinson, how is that you have no idea who attacked my father?" Franny asked, with an accusatory and wholly predictable lilt to her voice.

He would not allow the disgust she laced into her insulting address needle him. But how could she think he was somehow to blame? He'd simply decided to patrol the streets around her gymnasium in order to protect her and her business when he'd stumbled upon the scene in a side alley.

"Frances Valentine," her father scolded. "The men wore masks and may have beaten me to death if Mr. Robinson had not happened along."

"Oh, dear," Lady Davenport gasped. "Thank you, Mr. Robinson. What a miracle that you were there." She sank onto the end of the bed by Coach's legs but then seemed to realize how inappropriate that was and popped back onto her feet as if on a spring.

The others didn't appear to notice her actions. Instead, they hummed agreement with her declaration. Franny, however, still looked at him as if he were rat dung.

"Back to Whitehill," Viscount Davenport said. "He has loudly condemned Griffendale, Wentworth, and me for our involvement with an establishment that supports women. He is afraid that we have so much sway over the House of Lords that we will persuade Parliament to reconsider views on women's property rights. Especially since Wentworth had legal papers drawn up stating that he does not own The Silk Knuckles Saloon."

"Interesting," Edward murmured. "Let me be sure I understand. My lord, although your wife owns a share of The Silk Knuckles Saloon, you do not own any part of it?"

"I do not," Nicolas Wentworth said. "I've thumbed my nose at coverture laws and Whitehill is not happy. 'Tis none of his bloody business. Although I care very much about female autonomy, my decision was made because my family has had financial difficulty, and I won't have my wife bear any of my forefathers' mistakes. Ironically, the angrier Whitehill gets, the more he bellows contradictions, thus solidifying my and other's opinions that women need control over their own destinies."

Lord Davenport grinned. "And I find women are willing to grant me even more special favors if *I* support female autonomy."

Josephine backhanded the viscount.

"Ouch," he said as he rubbed his shoulder. "I was teasing." He smirked. "Although 'tis a nice bonus."

"Do hush, Jonathan." Lady Davenport glared at her son before focusing her gaze on Edward. "We were in the middle of penning concerns for His Grace when Calder was injured."

Franny growled. "What if Lady Hillcaster is telling her arse-kissing sycophant sons about our meetings and they are telling Whitehill? I have no idea why Lady Siddons brings her to our meetings."

"I agree with Franny," Josephine said.

"Ladies," Lady Davenport said. "Lucille may appear stodgy, but she is quite trustworthy."

Josephine harrumphed and Franny snorted.

"Something else is concerning me," Josephine said. "Right before our gymnasium was set on fire, a couple of men showed up asking Franny and I to fight for them."

Why didn't Edward know about this?

"The men who interrupted the women's exercise and defense class?" Coach asked.

"Yes," Josephine said. "We explained that neither of us is currently competing."

"Why is that?" Edward asked.

Josephine grinned at her husband, and he beamed back at her. "We are trying to start a family."

"Why aren't you competing?" Edward asked Franny.

An uncomfortable silence settled over the room. Apparently, Edward had hit a nerve.

"I also don't trust the vicar," Franny said.

The woman was a master of deflection. Luckily, Edward was a master at solving puzzles and he would discover the truth of this matter.

"Williams is always lurking about," Franny said. "I'm certain he sent those self-righteous biddies to harass us."

"What self-righteous biddies?" Coach Valentine asked.

Franny filled her father in on the visitors, ending her tirade with, "Of course, Runner Robinson treated them as if they were not barging into my place of business. He had the nerve to try to charm them as he escorted them out."

As attractive as Franny Valentine was, Edward was tired of her accusations. "I was gathering information, Miss Valentine. That is what I do."

"I'm happy that you have been assigned to our case, Mr. Robinson," Josephine said. "Mr. Baker does not seem very thorough or intelligent."

Edward clamped his lips together, stifling the declaration of agreement he itched to voice.

"Runner Robinson has not been assigned to our case," Franny said. "He's simply sticking his nose in my business."

Edward was over the termagant. He would continue to investigate because it was the right thing to do but Frances Valentine could bugger off.

Nicolas Wentworth's brow furrowed as his gaze traveled back and forth between Franny and Edward. "I dare say, I believe we would be better served to have you, Robinson. Baker has a reputation for being the worst investigator in London."

Franny stopped glaring at Edward just long enough to glower at Wentworth.

"We shall take this up with Griffendale," the viscount said.

"Please don't." Hesitating, Edward rubbed his chin and searched for honest words that did not divulge too much, settling on, "I am investigating on my own time."

"Hah! I told you all." Franny pointed an accusatory finger at Edward.

"Frances!" Coach Valentine grabbed his daughter's hand and stared into her eyes. "He saved my life. Let him help us."

Franny's expression softened for the first time in hours, almost endearing the woman to Edward. *Almost,* because fortunately, he caught himself in time to remember he was over his infatuation. Or whatever the nonsense he felt was.

"Robinson, my good man," the viscount said. "I shall pay you to look into this for us."

Edward shook his head. "I do not require payment. I'm seeking the truth because 'tis the right thing to do."

Franny cleared her throat. "I shall stop by Harry's room and check on him before I leave." She kissed her father on the cheek. "Sleep well."

"Frances, stay the night," Lady Davenport said. "I had a guest room prepared."

Franny dismissed the offer with a flick of her wrist. "I would like to return… Well, return home, of course."

"Stay here," Josephine pleaded.

Shaking her head vehemently, Franny stood.

"Harry is in the last room before the stairs," the viscount said. "But he may be asleep."

"In that case, I shall just peek in." Franny blew her father a kiss. "I love you, Papa. See you tomorrow."

Against his better judgement, and sensing Franny was up to something, Edward stepped to the side to let her pass.

Nicolas Wentworth scratched his head. "I dare say, someone

should stop her. Did you see the look in her eyes? She is going to get herself into a muddle she can't get out of."

"Good luck to whoever tries," Josephine said.

"Mr. Robinson," Coach Valentine croaked out. "Will you keep an eye on my daughter until I am back on my feet? It should only be about twenty-four hours."

Edward wagered it would be at least a week. And unfortunately, even though he no longer favored the sour woman, he couldn't let her run amuck looking for her father's attacker while the poor man tried to regain his health. She would get herself killed and he did not want that on his conscience.

"Of course." Edward bowed slightly, exited the room, and then tracked Franny's delectable rose scent.

CHAPTER NINE

FRANNY TAPPED ON the door closest to the stairwell. When no one answered, she cracked it open and peered into the darkness.

"Harry," she whispered.

A soft snore rippled.

Although she desperately desired to see him, she didn't have the heart to wake a healing friend. If only she had a candle, she could illuminate the room and watch him sleep. A few moments with Harry and a soft flame were all she needed to calm her fretting. Afterward, she would check on her gymnasium. Hopefully it hadn't burned to the ground while they'd been gone. She'd rest on the sofa in her office, and if she awoke every few hours, she could patrol the perimeter of the building to ensure no one was skulking about the grounds.

Franny backed out of the room, her bum smacking into something or someone. "Shite," she murmured as she whirled to face Edward Robinson. "What the bloody hell?" she grumbled.

His fingers clutched her waist as if steadying her, and for some strange reason, a spark of warm tingles shot to her belly.

"I didn't mean to startle you," he said.

"You did *not* startle me," she lied. Her reaction to his touch had been a moment of surprise and nothing else. "Why are you following me?"

His arms dropped to his sides as he stepped back. "Miss Valentine, your father asked me to…" He cleared his throat. "Asked me to help you discover who is behind these violent acts."

The light from the hallway sconces danced over Edward's long lashes and dappled over the planes of his strong jawline. The man was so exceedingly handsome that she ached when simply looking at him. If it were not for his waistcoat and cravat, he might be mistaken for a long-ago Greek God come to life. After she'd told him he needed to gain a stone, he must have spent the next five years lifting heavy objects.

"Miss Valentine, I am a skilled investigator and whoever targeted The Silk Knuckles Saloon is willing to kill to close your business down." His voice was so gentle, it was as if he were afraid that she would skitter away like a terrified kitten if he spoke at a normal volume. "Forgive me for saying so, but you are quite stubborn. I can see your intentions reflected in your eyes. You have the look of a woman ready to track down her enemy on her own."

She winced. She hated that her emotions were always transparent.

"I know you can discover who the perpetrators are without me," he said. "Hell, I think you could single-handedly stop an army. But why not take advantage of my talents and allow me to assist you?"

Was he trying to soften her with flattery or was he sincere? She hoped the latter because she could use some help. The truth was, she was somewhat lost without Papa, not that she would admit this to the officer. However, even through her confusion, heartbreak, and exhaustion, she was aware that her family and business were more important than her hubris. The truth was, not a day went by when she didn't fight with her warring inner voice screaming, *A woman must never be timid. She must be bold. She must not hesitate. She must never let a man get the upper hand.* Unfortunately, these thoughts often led to rash decisions, and this dashed impulsivity would be the death of her if she didn't rein it in.

Franny exhaled, then compromised. "I accept your offer. But on one condition."

His features twisted into a skeptical glare. "What is that?"

"I am in charge. 'Tis my business after all."

"Of course," he said with a slight bow. "I shall see you home tonight."

She gnawed on her lip.

"You aren't going home, are you?" he asked. "You did not tell your family and friends the truth because you didn't want them to fret. You intend to patrol The Silk Knuckles tonight?"

It was eerie how precisely he read her mind. She should not be unnerved or flattered since he probably read minds in general. Intuition made one a valuable investigator, after all.

She expected him to argue and tell her that spending the night at The Silk Knuckles was foolish. Interestingly, there would be a silver lining if he immediately broke their pact, because once he went back on his word, she could tell him to sod off and be rid of the befuddling man once and for all. That is what she wanted. Wasn't it?

At least it was what she had wanted until Edward had saved Papa. She'd still treated him with disdain in front of everyone, but perhaps she'd been protecting herself from the perplexing feelings the man evoked. Whatever the case, deep in her heart she knew if Edward Robinson hadn't stuck his nose in her business, Papa might be… she gasped.

"Are you well?" Edward asked.

"I was just thinking that if you had not come upon my father, he might be…" She couldn't say the words out loud.

"The Davenports have a carriage waiting for us," he said.

Being alone in a carriage with Edward after his warm, steadying hands had awoken a feminine longing deep inside her seemed like a very bad idea. She shivered.

He regarded her with compassionate eyes. "I shall ask the driver to take us to The Silk Knuckles."

Since she was too exhausted to walk, a carriage sounded heavenly, and having someone help her guard the studio while Papa and Harry convalesced held appeal. Still, she hesitated.

"I promise not to behave like a cad," he declared. "I am aware that the way I acted the first time we met was reprehensible."

"Yes," she agreed with one sharp chin bob. "If you ever look at me the way you did that day, I will knock your teeth out." Which would be a shame since he had such lovely teeth. "I'd like to check on Harry before we leave," she said.

"Of course. I will wait here for you."

She stared at the closest candle. At her height, she would struggle to reach it, but Edward was tall enough to pluck it from the sconce. All she had to do was swallow her pride and ask.

He followed her gaze and removed it without her having to say a word. He handed it to her. "Then it is settled. Investigation partners."

She might regret her decision in the morning, but for now it seemed like a good idea. "Partners, Robinson. But do not make me regret my decision."

Because the second he acted like a reprobate, she would knock out those perfect teeth, or perhaps, God forgive her, run her fingertip over his lush lashes.

CHAPTER TEN

HARRY SIMPSON HAD to be more than The Silk Knuckles' caretaker if Franny had kissed his forehead while he slept, then left his room with tears in her eyes. Not that Edward was jealous. There were way too many women in the world to ever harbor that useless emotion. Besides, he no longer felt infatuated with Frances Valentine. The only emotion he harbored was protectiveness. But that was mostly because her father requested he look out for her. Furthermore, the lust making his cock twitch was entirely because they were alone in a carriage.

As important as the truth was to Edward, he forgave himself for telling Franny one harmless untruth—*Miss Valentine, your father asked me to help you discover who is behind these violent acts.* Twisting the facts was in her best interest since she would never allow him to protect her. The minor falsity had probably also saved his teeth and bollocks from her wrath. In truth, it was a genius plan because now they could work together instead of butting heads like tetchy rams.

It would be difficult to protect her while doing his actual job. *But where there's a will, there's a way,* he assured himself. After some sleep and a cup of strong coffee, he'd solve his dilemma.

Edward forced himself to concentrate on something other than the woman beside him.

Calder Valentine was a safe subject. Imagine a father so devoted that he'd sacrifice his career to support his daughter's dreams. Edward's admiration for Coach grew every time he was around the man. Since his innovative club supported women while attracting champions like The Trojan, an aristocratic journalist, a popular viscount, and a fashionable duke, it would undoubtedly thrive if it survived attacks from its enemies.

If? What was Edward thinking? Of course it would survive. He would make sure of it.

They pulled up to the gymnasium, exited the carriage, and thanked the driver. Edward's senses were on high alert as he and Franny cautiously approached the building. Like a beacon of hope for all women, a beam of moonlight illuminated the Silk Knuckles sign.

Franny removed a key from her skirt pocket and opened the door. Although she faced him, she didn't meet his gaze. "Thank you for seeing me here safely. Good night—"

"I am staying," he declared. If she threw a fit and told him their partnership was over, he would have to toss her over his shoulder, carry her into the building, bind her hands and arms with the skipping ropes, and tie her to the boxing ring. She'd probably scratch out his eyes but at least he'd keep his promise to her father.

Thunderation, the thought of Franny tied and helpless sent a jolt of lust to his pelvis.

God almighty, he needed sleep. Or a tup. But what he did not need was a sexual entanglement with the feral Frances Valentine.

She blinked, and if he was not mistaken, her cheeks turned the same color as her hair. "I forgot to ask the ladies who locked up to close the windows."

Bloody hell, someone could be in the building at this very minute waiting for Josephine and Franny to return.

To his surprise, she stepped to the side and allowed him to enter. At least he wouldn't have to carry her into her establishment like he was a prehistoric cave dweller and she his petulant woman. He'd have to satisfy that fantasy another time.

For fuck's sake, he was never going to carry this aggravating woman anywhere. He needed to concentrate and check the building for intruders.

Since Edward didn't know his way around in the dark, he stuck so close to Franny that he almost bumped into her every time she slowed down. Eventually she halted. There was the click of flint against steel, and then she blew until a flame sparked in the dark.

Once the lamp glowed, she faced him. "Do you have a pistol?" she whispered.

Edward shook his head. "No." Since he'd taken to the streets tonight as a civilian, his weapons were locked in his desk.

"What good is a lawman without a pistol?" she asked.

Dare he remind her that he'd fought off her father's attackers using his fists?

Lantern in tow, she marched past him. He followed her to the far corner. Leftover supplies from the repairs were neatly stacked. Franny placed the lantern on the floor and rummaged through the pile. The chit must be searching for weapons, and if so, he quite admired her ingenuity.

A piece of wood about the same length and width of his tip staff rolled from the stack to rest beside his foot. Edward scooped it up and tested its weight.

Perfect! Just let someone try to overtake them.

Franny huffed her disgust. "What are you going to do, give an invader a splinter?"

Since Franny was again rooting through the wood, she missed his eye roll.

"Ah, ha," she exclaimed, hefting a beam as long and thick as his arm from the supplies.

Edward chuckled. If she could swing the heavy hunk fast enough, she would take off someone's head. Hopefully, not his.

She picked up the lantern and held it close to his face. "What are you laughing at?"

He blinked a few times. "I'm not laughing." At least he wasn't now that she was trying to blind him.

"Let's go," she whispered, turning her back to him.

"Let me go first," he said as he stepped around her.

"But my weapon is bigger," she hissed into his ear.

This woman would be the bloody death of him.

SEEING AS HOW they were both so headstrong that they normally clashed, it was a miracle that they combed the building and latched the windows like they'd been working together forever.

Once they scoured every nook and cranny, Edward sighed in relief. " 'Tis safe."

Franny tilted her head and regarded him as if he were a fool. Disappointing indeed since they seemed to make one hell of a security team.

"I'm going to look around outside," she said. "I need to ensure no one is hiding in the bushes intending to harm The Silk Knuckles."

"Why don't you stay inside and I will check the grounds?" Edward asked.

She huffed as she shot past him and out the front door, her hunk of wood poised to maim anyone who got in her way.

Grumbling under his breath, Edward grabbed the lantern and followed, locking the door behind them.

Franny moved quickly, exploring every inch of her property. "If anyone is out here, show yourself, you bloody cowards," she shouted into the dark alley.

Edward clutched his makeshift staff, ready to defend Franny if the need arose.

With a bittersweet sigh, Franny halted and stared at the repairs. "I can't believe we were able to fix everything so quickly."

"I dare say, the three of you can accomplish anything you set your minds to," Edward said as he came alongside her.

Her shoulders softened as the wind blew her long, unbound hair every which way. "We had assistance. We could not have done it this quickly, otherwise."

"You have loyal friends," he said.

Her lips curved upward, almost forming a smile. "I suppose we do."

"When do you plan to reopen the gymnasium?" he asked.

"As soon as the odor is gone," she said. "It was difficult to have our meeting of the Ladies' Autonomy League with the lingering scent. It simply won't do to have people exercising with smoke in their lungs. But now that the windows are closed…" Franny sighed. "How can we keep them open if we are constantly worried about an attack?"

Edward considered recommending they wait at least a week before opening, but what was the point? She was too stubborn to take his advice.

He tapped the dirt with his foot. "Yesterday, I found a button right here. 'Tis on my desk."

She squatted and traced the trail his boot had drawn. "A clue?"

He shrugged. "Mayhap. Anyone could have lost it walking down the alley. Or perchance it was from one of your patrons."

Franny stared up at him, her eyes sad and the wind wreaking havoc with her red locks. "Why does someone hate us so vehemently?"

Because they were powerful women in a man's world but now was not the time to tell her this. He should say something to comfort her so she could sleep peacefully.

"We should go inside," he said. "I think both you and the building are safe for the night."

"I suppose 'tis not safe for us to open until we know who is targeting us," she said.

Thank God, she'd figured it out on her own. "That would be wise," he said.

She stood, then side by side they retraced their path. Once

they were safely locked in the building, she entered her office, calling over her shoulder, "You can sleep in the ladies'-only parlor."

"I will try not to get my maleness all over everything." He chuckled.

She peered over her shoulder. "Please try not to smell up our lovely room."

For a second he was taken aback. God Almighty, did he stink? But then her lips quirked upward. At least she was now taunting him instead of glaring at him as if he were the devil.

"Do you have an extra key?" he asked.

"I have another in my office." Without looking at him, she plucked the key from her skirts and extended her palm.

He approached, and grasped the key, doing his best not to brush her skin. "Thank you," he said, his damned voice coming out in a deep flirtatious rumble he had not intended.

Her back stiffened, and she closed her office door without another word.

Lamp in hand and the key in his pocket, he climbed the stairs and found his way to the parlor. Unfortunately, the ladies had cleared away the food from earlier, so there would be no sating his growling stomach. He tested out the dainty furniture, which was much too small for his large body. He settled into the largest, but still lady-sized chair, and stretched his legs long. Being uncomfortable was probably for the best since he didn't want to sleep the entire night. He set his mental alarm to wake him in one hour so he could patrol the grounds.

Resting his head on the back of the chair, Edward closed his eyes. Since he was no longer attracted to Frances Valentine, he would not think about how her hair blew in the breeze as if she were a forest nymph. Or how brave she was, hefting about her ridiculous hunk of wood. No indeed. And he definitely would not dream about her naked and breathless in the center of the boxing ring because only an unholy ape with an incorrigible libido could conjure such a lascivious image.

Hell, who was he kidding? He could devote his life to protecting others, but deep down inside he was as randy as they came, and he fervently desired the one woman who wanted nothing to do with him.

CHAPTER ELEVEN

Berating herself under her breath, Franny rolled onto her side and shielded her eyes from the morning sun blasting through the window. She had every intention of waking every few hours to patrol the grounds but instead had lazily slept through the night as if poor Papa and Harry weren't injured and her life-long dreams weren't in jeopardy.

Yawning, she stretched her stiff body, reveling in the exquisite release of tension as her muscles elongated. Today, she required an extra-long calisthenics session. But first, she needed food, coffee, and enough energy to get out of bed. She stretched again, perhaps too enthusiastically, because she tumbled off the sofa, crashing onto the unforgiving floor. Her head barely missed hitting the edge of her desk, and her torso twisted. One foot remained on the sofa, exposing her private area to the air.

"Ouch! Bloody bollocks," she grumbled.

Her office door flew open, and Edward Robinson's massive body filled the doorway. His eyes widened, and then he chortled.

Her cheeks burning, she dropped her leg, sat up, rearranged her chemise, and crossed her arms over her chest. Even though he had seen the bodice of her chemise before, she wanted to die from embarrassment. Boxing in a chemise was hardly indecent. But a man seeing you in your undergarments because you were sleeping half naked was humiliating, especially when said undergarments were not covering your body parts. What if he had seen her cunny while she'd been lying there, arms and legs akimbo?

If only she could disappear right this second, so she never had to face Edward Robinson again.

"I slept on the floor," she lied.

Edward smirked. "I can see that."

Obviously, he'd heard the damnable crash and was being facetious. What a smug arse! "What do you want, Runner Robinson?"

"Call me Edward. Get dressed. We have a busy day of investigating ahead of us." Grinning as if he'd just won a major award, he closed the door.

Blinking, Franny tried to clear the morning fog from her brain. The reality of her situation hit her with an exhilarating thud. She was about to investigate with an honest-to-God Bow Street Runner.

On second thought, who cared that he might have seen her girl bits? She had a job to do. As if a strike of lightning animated her, she bolted to standing and threw her dress over her head.

MR. ROBINSON BARELY spoke to Franny as he hailed them a hackney. Even now, sitting across from her, staring out the window, he was oddly quiet. If he was humiliated because he had seen too much of her, he needed to get over it. It was her body, and she was completely at peace with what had happened.

Well, almost at peace with it.

But no one, not even Josie, had ever seen her down there. Her cheeks heated and she gasped as if someone had punched her in the stomach.

Nope, not at all over it. Not if she lived to be one hundred. If they were going to work together, they needed to establish rules, which included no barging into her office without knocking, and this was a good time to make her boundaries known.

As she mentally organized her thoughts, she stared at his profile. His lashes occasionally fluttered. The dark stubble overtaking his chin and jaw was quite masculine and so distracting that his presence muddled her thinking. Perhaps this particular conversation could wait.

"Where are we going?" she asked. Dare she tell him she was starving?

"We are here." He slapped the roof with his palm.

"Where is *here*?" she asked.

"My residence. As you pointed out last night, a lawman requires a pistol."

Since sarcasm laced his tone, she didn't believe for a second they were there solely to retrieve his pistol. However, her overwhelming hunger and lingering embarrassment kept her from badgering him further. She exited the carriage and followed him to the front door of a lodging house, sandwiched between charming storefronts.

They climbed a flight of narrow stairs to the third-floor landing. Edward unlocked a door and held it wide, inviting Franny to enter in front of him.

She hadn't expected the arrogant man to have a cozy home, but it was exceedingly warm and inviting. On one side of the entranceway, an archway led to a room that appeared to be both a study and a parlor. Cream-colored flowers and swirling emerald vines adorned the rich brown wallpaper. Plushily upholstered furniture was arranged in front of a brick hearth. The fire was almost extinguished, but the embers still emitted a glow. Dozens of leather-bound books filled the shelves and the stacks of papers on his desk were neat.

Edward sauntered down a hallway, leaving her standing beneath the archway. Once she lost sight of him, she uncomfortably shifted her weight from foot to foot. She'd never been alone with a man in his home, and she had no idea if she should follow him, stay where he'd left her, or make herself comfortable in one of the big chairs.

Edward's deep voice carried down the hall. "Good morning, pretty girl. Did you miss me?"

What the hell! Who was he speaking to? Did Edward Robinson have a mistress? How dare he strut about like an unbridled stallion.

Her original instincts about him had been correct. The man was an arrogant arse.

Obscene kissing noises coming from the end of the hallway made Franny gag. A man oozing potent masculinity should be a sensual kisser. Instead, he smacked his lips as if he was a clown making love to a brick wall.

"Come meet Miss Frances Valentine," Edward said.

How in the devil was she to face his lover after feeling warm and mushy in his presence? And worse, he'd seen her naked! Still...oh, confound her feminine curiosity to hell. She was no coward, but this entire morning had been too much. This might be one of those moments when being wise was better than being brave.

She headed for the door, but Edward cut her off, a ball of orange and cream fluff in his arms.

"Zigzag, meet Miss Valentine. Miss Valentine, meet Zigzag."

The cat looked at Franny, batted her arm, and let out a vociferous meow.

Some feeling she dared not identify spread over her and Franny found herself giggling at the imperious animal. "Meow to you too, Zigzag." She clasped one little paw between her thumb and forefinger and shook.

"Are you hungry?" Edward asked.

"Famished." Franny rubbed her stomach.

"I was talking to Zigzag," Edward said, his expression quite earnest.

Franny would not fall for his taunting. "Never mess with a hungry redhead, Mr. Robinson."

"Call me Edward." He chuckled. "Follow me, milady," he said as he performed an exaggerated bow while hugging the well-fed cat to his chest.

THANK HEAVENS FRANNY no longer subsisted on a training diet of bone broth and eggs. She licked the sweet honey from her fingers. "Your landlady is a superior baker."

"Yes, indeed." Edward pushed his chair back and stretched his legs long. He had eaten half of the six honey cakes his landlady had set out. Franny had enthusiastically devoured the other three.

Now she poured herself a third cup of coffee. "How many people live in this building?" For some inexplicable reason, she wanted to know everything about the man sitting across from her in his tidy kitchen.

"Mrs. Benson, myself, Zigzag, and Mr. Glasgow, a young tutor, who lives on the second floor."

How pleasant it must be to live in a lovely building with Mrs. Benson cooking and cleaning. Franny and Papa's first-floor flat was slightly bigger than Edward's but not nearly as well-furnished, and Franny couldn't bake bread, biscuits, or cakes to save her life.

Edward waved his hand in front of her face, interrupting her wool gathering. "Tell me about these men who showed up at the gymnasium and asked you and Josephine to fight for them."

"Do you think they could be behind our misfortunes?" she asked.

Edward shrugged. "Since they showed up right before the fire, I'd like to question them."

Franny quite agreed. "Their names are Bear and Whale. Whale didn't speak at all. I suspect he might be hired muscle. Bear said I can find him at The Purple Rabbit. If my memory serves me, Bear was a decent pugilist about a decade ago."

"The Purple Rabbit is a gambling den in Whitechapel," Edward said.

"I thought it was a brothel." Her cheeks heated as if she were a bluenose saying an indecent word instead of Fiery Franny, an intrepid pugilist. She simply wasn't as confident as she'd once been, thanks to her confounding cowardice. A pang of regret squeezed her chest.

Edward steepled his fingers under his chin. Franny hadn't noticed before, but purple bruises marbled his knuckles.

"After we call on this Bear and Whale, I want to speak to your neighbor," he said.

"I wager Vicar Williams is behind all of this," Franny hissed.

"I'm not convinced it was him, although I never rule anyone out until I thoroughly question them." He scraped his fingers through his chin stubble. "The truth is, I want to speak to one of his parishioners."

"Mrs. Brown is a sanctimonious fool." Franny pursed her lips and looked down her nose. *"Have you ever heard such language?"*

Edward frowned as if he hadn't found her impression the least bit humorous. "I wasn't speaking of her. I can't stop thinking about her daughter-in-law, Jane. Someone is beating her."

Franny had forgotten about the poor woman while Edward had been consumed with worry. Perhaps she was heartless and Edward was heroic? Since she admired lionhearted individuals, she wanted to reach across the table and gently run her finger over his bruises.

"I'm assuming you would like to look in on your father and your *friend* today?" He drew out the word friend as he stared into Franny's eyes. How odd. Did he think she didn't care about Harry, or did he assume she and Harry were more than friends?

Taking her new role as investigator seriously, Franny nonchalantly sipped coffee while trying to read Edward's mind.

Unfortunately, his gaze was so intense that she suspected he was simultaneously trying to glean her thoughts. She tried not to think about how handsome he was. Or how much she liked his thick lashes and brows. Or how strong and masculine his hands were. She settled on pondering his fresh bruises.

He opened and closed his fists. "You should see the dunderheads."

Egad! She was correct. He could read her mind. Her cheeks heated at the downright humiliating things she'd been thinking.

"They will think before coming after one of your loved ones again. Their faces look much worse than my hands."

As she suspected, he'd sustained the injuries protecting Papa.

He grinned, and her heart swooped low and then glided high. "I tried to see if either of them was missing a button, but it was much too dark, and I was more concerned about protecting your father."

Of the latter, she was glad.

"First things first. I need to stop by my office."

Franny squealed as if she were a child receiving a new toy. "I've never seen a real courthouse. Is it exciting? Is it dangerous? Are the criminals shackled?"

"Most of the trials take place at the Marlborough Street Magistrate's Court," he said. "Besides, I'm afraid you must wait outside for me. I shan't be long."

Before she could ask him why she wasn't permitted to enter the Bow Street office, he stood. "Make yourself at home in my parlor. I'm going to wash up and change shirts."

How unfair that he could clean himself up while Franny remained unkempt. At least she'd taken time to fix her hair. Not that it mattered because, as usual, the heavy strands were tumbling from her twist. She brushed the long curl tickling her cheek behind her ear.

Edward closed his eyes for a moment and sighed as if exasperated. Without another word, he turned on his heel and stomped from the kitchen.

What in the hell had she done wrong? She'd been disappointed when he said she couldn't enter his office, but she hadn't complained. She hadn't even pulled a face. It was also unfair that

Edward could read her mind when she had no idea what he was thinking.

"He's a bloody pain in the arse," Franny mumbled under her breath as she returned to the cozy parlor, Zigzag at her heels. She plucked a copy of *The Mysteries of Ferney Castle* from the shelf and sank into one of the chairs. The second her arse hit the soft cushion, her frustration dissipated. Good God, she was snuggling into a chair that smelled like Edward's masculine cedary scent.

Zigzag curled into a ball at her feet and immediately fell asleep.

Franny opened the book and tried to concentrate, but it was pointless. She read the first page three times as she fretted about Papa and Harry.

At last, Edward ambled into the room, his scruff shaved clean, his white shirt crisp, and his scent fresh and delicious. Turning his back to her, he gathered some items from his desk. Once he was finished, he removed his blue greatcoat from the hook and slid into it. She swallowed saliva as she shamelessly admired the line of his well-sculpted backside.

It seemed the arrogant, heroic Edward Robinson had tunneled his way beneath her skin, and she simply could not allow this to happen. No man, no matter how attractive he was, would distract Franny from her goals.

CHAPTER TWELVE

WHILE SITTING ACROSS from Franny in the carriage, Edward showed her the button. Unfortunately, she didn't recognize his only clue. Thereupon they sat in silence, staring out the windows. He wanted to strike up a conversation, but his mind was on other things—Franny's safety. Lady Celeste Milton's stolen jewelry. The red curls covering Franny's quim…

Just the memory of Franny's naked cunny made him salivate. After hearing a crash, he'd found her lying on the floor. He'd only had a quick glimpse of red hair against creamy skin, but it was enough to whet his appetite. As the morning wore on, his desire for her grew. God Almighty, even something as innocent as the way she brushed a strand of hair from her eye had his cock twitching. At least she didn't know what he had seen, for if she did, she'd cut off his bollocks.

His palms instinctively and momentarily shielded his crotch from her imagined wrath. He had to pull himself together quickly because if he meant to accomplish all of his goals today, he had to push inappropriate thoughts of Franny to the side.

They pulled up in front of Number 4 Bow Street, climbed out of the vehicle, and he paid the driver.

Hands on her hips, Franny glared at him. The woman's death stare could stoke fear in Atilla the Hun. He knew damned well she wanted to go into the building with him.

"Stay here, Miss Valentine. Please," he pleaded. "If you are seen with me, I could be reprimanded, and then I won't be able to help you."

She sighed. Loudly. "Fine. I'll wait here. But hurry."

An industrious woman like Franny might wither away from boredom if she had to stay in one place for too long. At least she would be safe because no harm would befall her on a busy street in daylight. However, since Francine Valentine did not take orders, there was a good chance she would storm into the building boldly announcing her presence, and then their partnership might be over before it had truly begun.

"Please wait here," he said again. And then, against his better judgment, Edward left her standing a couple of buildings away from his place of work.

Edward's conscience warred as he hurried into the building, up the stairs, and down the hallway to his office.

Yes, he was ignoring directives, and if all lawmen did this, London would be synonymous with corruption and chaos, but he'd given his word to an injured man and his promise meant something. Beyond these conundrums, there was one far more pressing. Men of privilege and in positions of authority must stand against the inequitable treatment females experienced daily, and someone was terrorizing these revolutionary women who dared to defy societal expectations. This all begged the question, what was a man to do when his duty and his morals clashed?

Edward reached his office and breathed a sigh of relief. Whistling as if he was innocent of any wrongdoing, he slipped inside and locked his door.

One of the clerks had placed Edward's mail beside *The Hue and Cry*. A sealed note lay on top of the pile. Hoping it was the news he sought, Edward opened, then read the short, unsigned missive.

Someone came in with the items you described. TW

This was the break Edward needed in his stolen jewelry case.

It meant one more stop in his already busy day, so he needed to keep moving. He slid the note into the same pocket that held the button and then retraced his path, this time calling amicable greetings to everyone he passed.

Franny's disregard for a bonnet meant her wildly blowing hair was visible the second he exited the building. She'd tried to secure it in a twist, but much like the lady, her thick locks were incorrigible and refused to be restrained. Every time another strand escaped its confines, Edward was overcome by the desire to tuck it behind her ear. Wanting to be by her side, he quickened his pace.

As if appearing out of nowhere, Baker approached Franny.

Panic squeezed Edward's lungs. He lengthened his stride, reaching them in time to hear Baker ask, "What are you doing here, Miss Valentine?" Before she had a chance to respond, Baker whirled on Edward. "She better not be with you, Robinson, because you were told to keep your nose out of my case."

Perhaps this was a very bad idea, but it was the only solution Edward could manufacture with his brain erratically screaming *think!* "Miss Frances and I have quite the past together, so when I heard her name again, it brought back memories. I desired to revisit certain parts of our relationship." He wrapped his arm around Franny's waist and pulled her against him. "I don't have my nose in your case, Baker. I have my…" God Almighty, was he actually going to say this? He cleared his throat and lecherously winked at Baker. Thunderation, this felt wrong. Edward might be indiscriminate when it came to bedding women; however, he never tupped and told. "I'm sure I don't need to tell you what part of me I'm about to put in the lady." Acting as if he was a buffoon in a bawdy play, Edward pinched Franny's arse.

Baker guffawed.

Franny startled and then elbowed Edward in the gut.

Edward chortled through the pain as he pulled her closer. "Darling, watch your love taps. You do not want to render me useless." As reprehensible as Baker was, he would understand the innuendo. Hopefully, it flew over Franny's head.

Unfortunately, she stiffened, and her almost imperceptible growl resonated in Edward's chest. Once they were alone, she would probably render him permanently "useless." His bollocks stung at the mere thought.

Baker stepped into Edward's space to whisper, "I'm impressed. How did you convince one of the sapphists to tup you?"

Franny was too close not to have heard the fool. Edward squeezed her, willing her not to react. Meanwhile, his disbelief overshadowed his rage. Baker must not know that one of his so-called *sapphists* was married to and in love with one of the most influential men in the *ton*. How could he not realize he was making a muddle of an investigation in which the Duke of Griffendale had a particular interest?

Beyond that, Edward did not like the sneer Baker made every time he referenced women who loved other women. In Edward's opinion, no one was less than because of who they chose to love. He had no doubts that any female who had a choice between Baker and another woman would be much better served to choose their same sex.

He bit back the insults he wished to hurl at the odious man, turning them into a lecherous wink that Baker would undoubtedly interpret as *I'm about to stick my prick in the lady.*

"I'm growing impatient for time alone, darling," Edward cooed into the top of Franny's head, all the while praying she didn't thrust that deadly elbow into his pelvis.

"Don't let me stop you," Baker said through his unseemly chortles.

Edward spun Franny and forcefully nudged her away from Baker. "Do not say a word," he whispered.

"You are lucky I don't break your nose again with everyone on Bow Street watching," she growled from between clenched teeth.

"Shh," he murmured, knowing his close murmurs would seem like whispers between lovers to Baker as he guided her down a side street.

To his surprise, her muscles relaxed, and she stopped fighting him. "Keep going," he whispered. He turned down an alley and dragged her to the end of it. Wrapping her in his arms, he pulled her torso to his.

She gasped, her breath blowing across his cheek. The hair on the back of his neck rose.

"In case he followed us," Edward said again, nuzzling her extremely soft cheek. Her rosewater scent swirled around him. He couldn't help but inhale. This farce was doing nothing to temper his desire.

Her body, pressed against his, was warm and feminine, but her angry words brushed his ear. "I had it under control. I was going to pretend to be out for a constitutional. If you had used your brain instead of your bloody male hubris, you would have stayed away until he left."

Because he was still pretending to be in a scandalous assignation—and most certainly not because he had wanted to touch her hair all morning—he tucked a silky strand behind her ear imagining how soft her long waves would be, blanketing his lap as her lips enveloped him…

What in the devil was he thinking? She'd bite off his prick, and he would deserve it.

"Franny, a man like Baker is single-minded," he said, his raspy voice betraying his desire. "He would be skeptical that you 'just happened' to be in front of his building. But he *will* believe I am bedding you."

"And why would he believe that, Robinson? *Hmm?*" Accusations laced her question as her eyes flashed with fury.

He was no saint, so how was he to answer?

"If you ever pinch my arse again, I *will* render you useless," Franny said.

Of that, he had no doubt.

"Now, remove your hands," she said.

Edward dropped his arms and backed away.

"My name is Miss Valentine to you," she said as she stomped around him and headed back the way they'd come. "And from now on, knock before entering my office!"

EDWARD TOLD FRANNY as much as was appropriate about his current investigation as they perambulated to Wagner and Son Jewelers. As they walked and talked, she relaxed until she no longer reminded him of a leopard about to eviscerate its prey. She even smiled at every child and animal they passed. If only she would cast some of that joy in his direction.

"Can I go into the jewelry store with you?" she asked.

Assuming she would enjoy looking at all of the baubles, Edward said, "Yes." And then, since Franny was listening attentively and the theft was public knowledge, he rambled on. "A few days ago, I visited the store and described the items I am searching for. I asked Mr. Wagner to let me know if someone tried to sell him the pieces."

"Do you think the thief is dangerous?" Franny asked, an excited breathiness in her question.

"I would not put it past them. I think we are looking for a ring of thieves. Whoever they are, they knew that the countess would be at the Thorton's ball, and they knew about her fine jewelry."

"Don't all aristocratic ladies have diamonds, emeralds, and rubies lying about their chambers?" Franny asked.

"Yes. But most aristocratic ladies don't have masked men knocking out their butler, tying up their lady's maid, and running amok in their townhouse," Edward said.

"This is why we must teach ladies to defend themselves." Franny clasped her hands together as if she'd just solved all of the world's problems. "Mayhap we should train butlers, too. Can you imagine? An army of punching, kicking butlers could rid London of all crime."

Frances Valentine was innovative.

Having arrived at their destination, he held the door wide.

Franny glided past him, stopped short, and gasped. " 'Tis so lovely."

Impressive displays of jewelry and watches glittered and sparkled.

"Good day, Mr. Wagner," Edward called to the gray-haired man behind the counter who was speaking with a well-dressed gentleman. And then he whispered in Franny's ear, "Please just go along with this."

Franny peered up at him through her golden lashes and nodded. If this confounding, unpredictable woman had a fascination with investigating crimes, Edward would finally have a bargaining chip beyond Mrs. Benson's honey cakes.

"Look at these, darling," he said as he wrapped his arm around her waist and guided her to a case of brooches.

"Of course, my dear," she said, playing along. Her gaze drifted over a half dozen exquisite pins glittering beneath the glass. "They are so pretty," she breathed, in a way that let him know she meant what she was saying.

So much for squelching his attraction to her because Edward adored this Franny, the woman in awe of something beautiful. Hell, to be honest, he also rather enjoyed the Franny who punched reprobates in the nose.

He placed his lips near her ear. "Which is your favorite?" His original intent was to remain inconspicuous until Mr. Wagner's patron departed, but now that he'd asked, he truly wanted to know.

"This one." She pointed at a profile of a silver kitten with an emerald eye.

Simple and lovely. He rather liked it, too. Too bad lawmen couldn't afford expensive gifts for ladies they favored.

"Enjoy your afternoon, my lord," Mr. Wagner said as he handed his patron a box. "I hope her ladyship adores the necklace."

Edward waited for the aristocrat to leave before descending on the shopkeeper, Franny glued to his side. "I received your missive," he said.

Mr. Wagner leaned across the counter and spoke so softly Edward had to tilt his ear to make out his words. "A man was here yesterday trying to sell me a rose necklace and earrings encrusted with diamonds and rubies, a sapphire ring, and a necklace dripping with diamonds."

A lead at last, because this was exactly what Edward had been searching for. "Did he give you a name or address?"

Mr. Wagner frowned. "No."

"What did he look like?" Edward asked. Meanwhile, Franny was so close that her breath tickled his cheek. Damn distracting, this chit.

"Tall, scar above his right eye. He said the pieces belonged to his late mother. He was dressed like a gentleman. Also spoke like a gentleman, but I was skeptical. He has been in before with other pieces and each time I explain that our policy requires verification before purchase and that it will take me at least twenty-four hours to complete the process, he leaves. That is our policy, though. We don't want to buy paste."

"People try to sell you fake jewelry?" Franny asked.

"Only once," Mr. Wagner said. "But now we know to be cautious."

Franny's head bobbed enthusiastically as if it were the most fascinating thing she'd ever heard.

"He showed up again this morning with a black eye," Mr. Wagner said. "The same eye as the scar. He asked me to reconsider purchasing the jewelry at a slightly discounted price. He still refused to leave it for me to appraise, so I said 'no' and sent a missive to your office."

"I bet he couldn't sell them to anyone else," Franny said.

Thunderation, the woman was intelligent. "He is getting desperate," Edward said.

"The jewelry is fine indeed," Mr. Wagner said. "I am certain they are genuine. But no legitimate jeweler would take a chance buying costly sets that might be stolen."

Franny *tsk*ed. "He must be very bacon-headed to try to sell very expensive jewelry that someone is surely looking for in the same city he stole it."

Edward wholeheartedly agreed. He mentally sorted through what he knew. He was looking for a tall man, who might or might not be a gentleman, had a scar above his black eye, and had the intelligence of a pudding.

He had to wonder why and how the pudding-head had a black eye. Was it the result of his trying to sell the jewelry to the wrong person, or in a different scuffle? Or was it just something he'd acquired through life as a thief?

"Would you compile a list of all of the pieces he has ever tried to sell you?" Edward asked.

"Of course," Mr. Wagner said. "At least the ones I remember. Once I have the list complete, I shall send a message to your office with an errand boy."

Edward held out his hand. "Thank you. Your assistance is invaluable. Lady Milton has offered a generous reward. She indicated that after this is behind her, she will thank you in person."

Mr. Wagner's cheeks turned scarlet. "Oh, my," he murmured.

It seemed the beautiful dowager had a magical hold over every man with a libido, even the ancient married ones.

He and Franny left the store and strolled down the street side by side. Edward was deep in thought when Franny cut him off by leaping in front of him. Her cheeks glowing and her eyes bright, she bounced on her toes. "Where are we going next?"

As usual, Edward's observations were correct. Firstly, Frances Valentine quite enjoyed investigating. And secondly, when she smiled at him, it was as if a golden ray of sunlight shot through his skin and bones to warm his soul.

CHAPTER THIRTEEN

NEVER IN A million years would Franny have guessed she would accompany a lawman as he investigated crimes. But here she was, standing outside Lady Celeste Milton's townhouse, waiting for someone to answer the door. Later, she'd examine why Edward was dragging her around London. For now, she would ignore her erratic emotions and enjoy the adventure.

Of course, her task would be easier if the man weren't so confounding. One second, she was angry at him for pinching her arse. The next, she was admiring a kitten-shaped brooch as his breath tickled her neck, and goose pimples skittered up and down her back.

The door opened. "Good day, Mr. Robinson. Her ladyship will join you soon." The butler motioned for them to follow.

Franny had never seen the inside of a castle, but she suspected Lady Milton's marble and gilded foyer rivaled anything the royal family might own. Her thoughts whirled. If she extended an invitation to Lady Milton, might the wealthy lady become a patron? Although Lady Davenport and Lady Siddons occasionally joined classes, they were quite spirited and not your average dowagers. Physical exertion might be too much for the elderly Lady Milton. But perhaps she might enjoy a drink in the upstairs parlor of The Silk Knuckles.

The butler escorted Franny and Edward to an exquisite drawing room decorated with rose and emerald damask. Seating fit for the king himself was arranged beneath a chandelier dripping with crystals. Since Franny didn't want to seem like an unsophisticated fishwife, she tried to hide her awe.

Edward relaxed and leaned back in his chair as if he visited houses this fine all the time. Maybe he did. The man seemed to lead an exciting life.

Unfortunately, he caught Franny watching him. Her desire to talk to him overrode her embarrassment. Before she could tell him she quite enjoyed investigating, a beautiful brunette glided into the room, bringing with her the scent of a million roses.

Edward stood.

"Edward, how delightful to see you again so soon," the lady drawled in a sensual voice.

Franny sneezed.

The lady stopped short. Her gaze traveled back and forth between Edward and Franny, and she blinked a half dozen times, her dark lashes fluttering wildly. Then her brow rose.

"Good day, my lady," Edward said. "This is Frances Valentine. She is assisting me today. Miss Valentine, meet Lady Celeste Milton."

But Lady Milton was supposed to be an elderly matron with gray hair and sagging breasts. This woman's decolletage was prodigious and spilled over the bodice of her tight red gown. She looked like she'd dressed for a late morning assignation, and she smelled like seduction. And, as if the lady's appearance wasn't shocking enough, she had addressed Edward by his given name.

Feeling as if she'd interrupted a private moment between Edward and the woman, Franny stood and awkwardly imitated the curtsy Josie had taught her. "Pleased to meet you, my lady," she murmured.

Up and down, the lady's gaze traveled as she took Franny in.

Franny had never cared about her appearance. She suspected she was comely since men regarded her with appreciation, but she simply hadn't given her aesthetics much thought. Physical attractiveness played little part in her old life as an athlete or her new life as a businesswoman. Still, for the second time this morning, Franny was aware that she'd slept in her chemise, and that she hadn't yet used tooth polish. She made a mental note to purchase some for her office since she'd be sleeping there until she knew the building was safe. Wishing she were as stunning as the exotic-looking woman before her, Franny self-consciously pushed a wayward strand of hair behind her ear.

"I did not know there were female lawmen," the lady said.

Should Franny point out that if there were, they would be called lawwomen?

Edward's lips twisted. "I have information on your stolen jewelry."

"How wonderful." Lady Milton glissaded across the room and gracefully sat on the chair closest to Edward. Once she had arranged herself to look like a goddess perched on a throne, she indicated that both he and Franny should be seated.

Franny sat, sneezed, and then pardoned herself.

Edward glared at her as if she'd purposely made the obscene sound. Well, he could sod off. It wasn't her fault Lady Milton smelled like a brothel. Or at least what Franny suspected a brothel smelled like.

Stubborn donkey that she was, Franny refused to relax her glower. Edward eventually sighed and focused his attention on his client—and probable lover—explaining what they had learned from their visit to the jewelry shop.

"Do you know a man who fits the description Mr. Wagner provided?" he asked.

Lady Milton stared into the corner of the room as she tapped her long, feminine fingers on the arm of her chair. Franny regarded her own short fingers and rough-skinned knuckles. Wincing, she tucked them into the folds of her skirt as an odd sensation twisted around Franny's heart.

Celeste Milton was too beautiful, Edward Robinson was entirely too handsome, and Franny did not favor the lightning zinging about the room.

Lady Milton met Edward's gaze. "I do not recall ever meeting a tall man with a scar above his eye."

Wearing a lazy grin, Edward crossed a foot over his opposite thigh. Watching him with a soft-lidded gaze, Lady Milton licked her plump red lip. If the cocksure fool was trying to drive the woman wild with desire, it seemed to be working.

Who cared if the lawman was tupping the curvaceous beauty? Franny certainly didn't give even the tiniest of shites. She was not jealous. She was simply suffering from brain confusion due to perfume poisoning.

"As we discussed," Edward said, "I told Mr. Wagner that you would visit to thank him for his assistance."

"Indeed," the lady said.

Edward clapped a hand on his thigh and stood. "Please excuse us. We have a busy afternoon ahead of us."

Thank the Good Lord above because Franny wanted to be far away from this woman who oozed so much feminine charm that she made her feel like an unattractive, freckle-faced child.

The lady crooked a finger, motioning for Edward to come to her. Biting his lip, he swaggered a few steps to stand over her. She motioned for him to lean down, and the mesmerized fool obeyed.

Holding her breath, Franny watched as the lady whispered something in Edward's ear. His Adam's apple slid with his swallow.

He stepped back and bowed. "I am honored, my lady, but I cannot. I will be working quite late this evening."

Lady Milton waved her hand dismissively as if she was not fazed by his answer, however, the quiver in her lips said otherwise. "Another time."

"You will hear from me as soon as I have more information," he said. "We shall see ourselves out."

Even extending her stride did not help Franny to keep up with Edward as he hurried out of the room, down the hall, and through the foyer. The second the door closed behind them, he bent forward and sneezed until his eyes watered.

As much as she didn't want to admit it, Franny was immensely pleased. "God bless you," she told him. "Let's go."

CHAPTER FOURTEEN

T HE FRANTIC PACE of the morning could not be helped if Edward meant to do his job, protect Franny, and discover who meant to damage The Silk Knuckles Saloon. While Franny visited her father and Harry's sickbeds, Edward joined the Davenports and the Wentworths for a midday meal.

"Calder is being quite stubborn," the Dowager Viscountess Davenport said. "He insists on returning home tonight."

"He is worried about Frances," Viscount Davenport said from the head of the table. "Although you can't blame him. The woman has no regard for her own safety." He tipped his glass to the lovely brunette sitting to his right. "Reminds me of another chit I know."

Catching her bent middle finger on her thumb, Josephine flicked, sending the viscount a lewd hand gesture.

Edward almost choked on his roast beef.

Grinning, Jonathan Davenport winked at his friend's wife. As unseemly as his host's behavior was, it didn't surprise Edward. The viscount was known for being an irreverent rakehell with an endless list of female conquests. And as for Josephine's behavior, he'd expect nothing less from the plucky champion of the Duke's and Dame's Mill.

"Jonathan, please behave in front of the company." Lady Davenport's voice was firm, but her eyes impishly twinkled. "You don't want Mr. Robinson to think we are churlish beasts."

"But we are quite loutish at mealtime." Josephine cast a charming smile at Edward. "Mr. Robinson, you don't strike me as the type of man who stands on false pretenses."

"Please call me *Edward*. And, you are correct, my lady. I do not," he said. However, his mother would have taken away their dessert, and his father would have boxed their ears if he and his siblings had misbehaved at the table.

"See, 'tis settled," Josephine said. "Edward is one of us now."

One of them? The statement warmed Edward's heart. The camaraderie these individuals shared was infectious, so it would make sense that he might want to be included. Maybe it was the delicious meal they'd shared with him, although Mrs. Benson was a fabulous cook, so that hardly seemed a likely reason to wish to be included as "one of them".

Thunderation, he should be honest with himself. His silly sentiment was probably—no, completely—related to the spirited redhead who had turned his world upside down.

"Edward," Nicolas Wentworth said. "I think you should know that last night my wife snuck out for a late-night constitutional, and someone followed her."

"Good Heavens." Lady Davenport brought a hand to her heart. "Josephine, we discussed this. You are not to go out alone until we understand who and what we are up against."

"I did not sneak out," Josephine said. "I simply needed some fresh air, and Nicolas was busy scribbling in his journal."

"Do you know what Josie did?" her husband asked, shooting her a disgruntled look.

The viscount grinned. "I wager she turned the tables, chased the bloke until she tired him out, and then beat the shite out of him."

Josephine grinned, then huffed. "I was minding my own business, enjoying the cool breeze. I was halfway down the street when I realized I was being followed. So, I turned around and yelled, 'Ye better run for yer life because if I catch ye, ye are a dead man.' And I started running toward him. The coward took off. I almost caught him, but he got away because a gig was waiting for him at the end of the street."

Lady Davenport waggled a finger at Josephine. "And what if he had pulled out a pistol and shot you?"

"Exactly." The future earl folded his hands across his chest and glared at his wife. "If she had only asked, I would have gone with her."

"If he had shot me, you would find him and skin him alive," Josephine said. "And besides, if he could have shot me, he could have shot you, too, and that's something I would never allow."

Her husband nodded. "True."

"Without a doubt," the viscount agreed.

Good God, no wonder Jabbing Josie and Fiery Franny were best friends. They were so much alike. Poor Coach Valentine. How had he managed the pair?

"Can you tell me anything about the man who followed you?" Edward asked.

"He was fast," Josephine said. "Otherwise, I'd have caught him, and he'd have a couple of broken ribs."

A couple of broken ribs, a broken nose, and his bollocks jammed up his arse, Edward wagered. Lucky fellow to have escaped.

"Was there anyone else in the gig other than the driver?" Edward asked.

"I don't think so, "Josephine said. "I only saw the driver."

"What did these men look like?" Edward asked, and reached for the notebook and pencil in his pocket. He paused then. This wasn't his case. Should he take notes? Yes, he decided. But still… "If anyone asks, I'm not the runner assigned to this case, and any notes you see me take is the market list for my landlady." He lifted a meaningful brow and opened the notebook to a fresh page. Everyone nodded.

Josephine grunted. "The man who was following me wore a dark hooded cape and a black mask that covered half his face. The other man was too far away for me to see any details."

Edward tucked the notebook away before he spoke, bracing himself for the pugilist's wrath, expecting verbal ire or a feminine fist, and perhaps both. "My lady, your husband is correct."

Instead of punching him, she regarded him with a raised brow, so he continued. " 'Tis probably best that you don't go out alone for now. I suspect those men meant to capture you and put you in their conveyance, but when you yelled—and came at them, something they probably never anticipated—they feared others were alerted." Edward cast his gaze on each individual at the table so they understood his seriousness. "Coach Valentine and Harry should remain here under the Davenport's care and protection, and I will continue to stay with Miss Valentine."

Franny would be the death of him, but it was for the best and for once, his brain and cock agreed.

Speaking of Franny, she'd been attending to Harry for a long time. Was there something between them? His thoughts provided an image of her kissing the man, and his heart clenched. But fortunately, Edward's musings were interrupted when a massive man entered the room at the butler's heels.

"His Grace," was all the butler got out before the red-bearded man rushed past him.

"Tristan." Lady Davenport rose and kissed the newcomer on the cheek.

Assuming this must be the Duke of Griffendale, Edward stood. "Your Grace."

The duke motioned for Edward to be seated. "I just heard that Coach Valentine was injured. Is he here?"

"He was attacked on his way to The Spotted Octopus," the viscount said. "Luckily, Mr. Robinson...I mean, Edward—" he gestured toward him—"came along and was able to stop the attack. The doctor saw to Coach, and he is upstairs resting."

"Unfortunately," Edward said, "the men got away."

The duke regarded Edward, nodding in what seemed to be appreciation. "Ah, the investigator the magistrate assigned to find our arsonists."

"Actually, I am not your investigator," Edward said.

"Hold on." The duke pulled a chair between the viscount and Josephine and sat, then stared at Edward with furrowed brows. "You're not?"

"We got some dolt named Baker," Josephine said. "But Edward is helping us anyway. If you see him taking what appear to be notes, he's actually writing a market list." She grinned like a devilish child who'd just gotten away with a prank. "He is an old *friend* of Franny's."

He most certainly was not an old friend, and Franny gave every indication that she detested him.

"I see," the duke said. "Let me be sure I understand. The magistrate assigned a dullard to my case when a perfectly decent investigator could be working on it?" He drummed his fingers on the table. It seemed like forever before he spoke. "If I find out Whitehill is behind this, I will meet him at dawn."

"He is an arrogant, unscrupulous, misogynistic fool," Josephine hissed.

"Mr. Robinson," the duke said, his tone deadly serious. "Am I correct that Runners may take on private cases?"

"We can," Edward said.

"I've already tried to hire him," the viscount said. "He refused payment."

"I will continue to investigate," Edward said. "But since the magistrate has reminded me that he did not assign me to the case, I am keeping a low profile."

"Interesting," Griffendale said. "So, you continue to investigate without the magistrate's blessing, and Whitehill has the magistrate's ear."

"Yes, Your Grace," Edward said.

Griffendale snorted. "Something about this stinks like an old chamber pot."

"What are we going to do about it?" the viscount asked, a sinister smile spreading across his face.

"The usual," the duke said.

"Ah, yes," mumbled Lady Davenport.

What was this group of aristocrats up to?

"Mr. Robinson?" Josephine said.

Edward faced the pretty pugilist.

"Nicolas and I will stay at The Silk Knuckles tonight so that you and Franny can get a good night sleep. Somewhere where she will be safe. Mayhap your home?"

He expected someone to point out that this was most indecent, but no one said a word because they were all staring into space, grinning. Wickedly. Not at all suspicious. Edward frowned.

NOW THAT EDWARD had seen to his stolen jewelry investigation, taken Franny to visit her loved ones, and filled his belly, it was time to track down Bear and Whale. He excused himself and left the aristocrats to their scheming. At least, he suspected they were up to something nefarious. As he climbed the stairs and made his way to Harry's chamber, trepidation churned in his stomach.

Nervous about what he might see behind the door, he placed his knuckle on the door and hesitated. What did he care if Franny had spent the afternoon kissing Harry? It's not as if Edward had a relationship with the woman. He, in fact, was not ready to pledge himself to any female. Besides, it wasn't as if Franny had confessed feelings for her groundskeeper beyond friendship. This absurd jealousy was obliterating Edward's common sense. He shook off the useless emotion and gently knocked.

"Come in," someone said.

Edward plastered an impassive expression on his face and entered.

To his delight, Franny was not in the chamber. Harry was propped against his pillows. An ointment was smeared over the angry burns covering the right side of his face.

Edward realized he had been a delusional fool because there was no way this poor man had spent an afternoon engaged in lascivious activities. His jealousy turned into shame.

"Good day. I am Edward Robinson. How are you feeling?" Although polite, it was a preposterous question, since Harry's expression was distorted from pain.

"Good day," Harry said, his voice weak. "Franny told me you are investigating who attacked me and Coach, as well as trying to find the arsonist. Do you think it's the same people?"

"Logic says yes, but I don't want to make assumptions." Edward approached Harry's bed. "Can you tell me anything about the man who attacked you?"

"I didn't see him. I was on my way into the gymnasium when I noticed smoke on the side of the building. I tried to investigate and was hit from behind. When I woke up, Sky Johnston was dragging me away from the flames. The lad deserves a medal."

That made four of them who had been close to these criminals and hadn't seen their faces.

"I will let you rest," Edward said.

"Please protect Coach and the ladies," Harry said. "They are good people. I implore you to find who is behind this for their sake."

"I will." So help him God. With everything he had. Edward left the man's room, closing the door behind him.

Edward's next stop was at Coach's chamber. He gently rapped. When no one answered, he cracked the door and slipped into the quiet. A ray of afternoon sunlight caught the sound-asleep Coach in its beam. Looking like a sweet angel come to Earth, Franny was curled up beside her father.

Edward froze in place, afraid to move or breathe. If he awakened Franny, he could not watch her bosom rise and fall with her gentle breaths. He would also be deprived of watching her eyelashes flutter as she dreamed. The woman was so beautiful, and when she slept, he was safe to enjoy it because she couldn't punch or scowl at him.

He brought a hand to his mouth to stifle his chuckle. The subtle movement must have disturbed her, because she stirred. Her lids lifted, and her pupils slowly focused.

"Edward?" she whispered in a voice so serene it wafted over him like a gentle breeze.

"Yes," he mouthed.

She sat up and rubbed her eyes.

"I didn't mean to wake you, but I want to talk to Vicar Williams," he whispered so as not to wake Coach. "Would you like to stay here, or would you like to join me?"

Franny kissed her slumbering father on the cheek. Grinning as mischievously as the aristocrats in the dining parlor, she slipped from the bed and slid into her slippers.

CHAPTER FIFTEEN

AFTER ENSURING THE enemy hadn't sabotaged The Silk Knuckles Saloon while she'd followed Edward around London, they cut across the lawn, scrambled through the shrubbery, and entered the church. The intimidating building with its stone-faced statues of angels and saints seemed to judge Franny. Fighting to take in a full breath of air, she gasped.

A lad whose chin probably hadn't yet touched a razor, approached with a friendly, "Good day."

"Good day," Edward cheerily called. "We are looking for Vicar Williams."

The lad looked Franny over, and his cheeks turned scarlet. His gaze dropped to his feet. "He is out back in the garden."

What had the abhorrent man of God said about her to make this youth so ashamed in her presence?

"Are you the person who alerted the Thames Waterman?" Edward asked.

The lad slowly lifted his gaze. "I am. I ran as fast as I could."

"Thank you," Franny said. "You saved my gymnasium."

His shoulders relaxed. "Is it true that I also saved Pete the Trojan?"

It seemed the shy lad had an interest in pugilism.

"You did," Edward said.

The boy's eyes lit up and his grin consumed his countenance.

Yes, indeed. He had the look of one obsessed with the sweet science.

"Did you see any suspicious characters around The Silk Knuckles the night of the fire?" Edward asked.

"No." The lad shook his head. "I used to watch the gymnasium a lot. I mean, before the fire." He sighed. "But now I just attend to my duties."

Undoubtedly, the nasty vicar took pleasure in snuffing the boy's vitality and spirit. Franny should do something to protect him. Suddenly, a brilliant idea hit her. "Mayhap you could keep an eye out again and let us know if you see anyone skulking about. In return, I could give you boxing lessons."

The boy's eyes widened.

"Miss Valentine is quite skilled." Edward pointed to his nose. "See this here." He turned his head from side to side, displaying his profile from different angles. "She did this. I used to have a pretty face."

Franny quite liked Edward's more rugged features, especially when he grinned like he was right now. A childish giggle burst from her. Edward snorted, then chuckled.

The boy backed away. "Vicar Williams will be none too happy. He says women who fight have fallen further than Eve."

Edward stiffened. The lethal fury radiating from him was so terrifying that it tempered Franny's anger. They both needed to calm themselves since it wasn't this unfortunate lad's fault that the vicar was a prig.

"You don't have to tell him," Franny said. "It shall be our little secret. What is your name?"

Nibbling on his lip, the boy looked around the nave. There was no need, because the three of them were the only people in the church.

"Charlie," he whispered. "I've always wanted to learn to box."

Edward held a finger to his lips and mouthed, "We won't tell a soul, Charlie."

VICAR WILLIAMS TURNED from the flowers he pruned to frown at Edward and Franny. Undaunted, they approached unapologetically.

"Good day, vicar," Edward said.

Franny couldn't find it in herself to greet the man, so she returned his glower.

"I'm Edward Robinson with the magistrate's court, and I want to ask you a couple of questions about the fire at The Silk Knuckles."

"I already answered Mr. Baker's questions," the vicar said.

"Baker is an arse," Franny said. *And you're a pompous bluenose.*

Frowning, Edward sent her a pleading look. "Sir, I am following up. Please repeat what you told him."

The vicar's pale, thin lips formed a straight line, and just when Franny was about to throttle the words from him, he spoke. "I saw the flames and sent the boy—"

His name is Charlie, Franny thought fiercely.

"—to get the watermen. They arrived and put out the fire."

"Did you see anyone strange lurking around the building?" Edward asked.

"Beyond the usual sinners that frequent that establishment?" The vicar wrinkled his nose as he flicked his wrist in The Silk Knuckles' direction.

Rage so intense it made Franny's eyeballs feel too large for their sockets shot through her. She lunged for the vicar, but Edward grabbed her around the waist and pulled her backward.

"Do you have any idea who started the fire?" Edward asked, a dangerous fury in his question, as his impressive strength held her in place.

"No," the vicar said. "But leave it to the wrath of God, for it is written, 'Vengeance is mine, I will repay, says the Lord'."

Of course, he'd throw a Bible verse at them. Fanny struggled in Edward's grip but he held firm. Too bad. The vicar wasn't the only one who could use the Bible against people; if he were a smaller man with a weaker grip, she'd happily give the vicar a beating of biblical proportions. Sometimes the Lord's vengeance came through the hands of his people and not through divine address, Franny thought with satisfaction. At least in this case.

"Well that may be. And speaking of which, vicar, I will need the younger Mrs. Brown's address," Edward said.

The vicar's eyes widened. "Why?"

"That is my business," Edward said.

"I do not give out my parishioners' information, especially to a godless one like her." Williams pointed a long, spindly finger at Franny.

Edward's jaw clenched until Franny thought his cheekbones might slice through his taut skin. It seemed she wasn't the only one in that garden who posed a threat to the clergyman.

" 'Tis not for her, it's for me. And, since you insist upon knowing, it's for the younger Mrs. Brown's protection," Edward said.

The vicar squared his shoulders and lifted his imperious nose. "She has the Lord and her husband to protect her. What could she possibly need from you?"

Franny would not spend one more second listening to this man's poppycock. "Someone is beating on her," she said. "In fact, it probably *is* her husband."

"Shite." Edward hissed in a breath.

If Edward was upset with her for telling the truth, so be it.

" 'Wives, submit yourselves unto your own husbands as unto the Lord'," the vicar bellowed in a sanctimonious tone. " 'For the husband is the head of the wife, even as Christ is the head of the church: and he is the savior of the body. Therefore as the church is subject unto Christ, so let the wives be to their own husbands in everything.' "

Franny rolled her eyes. The drivel wouldn't work on her since she wasn't one of the vicar's sheep.

"You would look the other way while one of your flock is being beaten?" she asked. "And by a bully who is bigger and stronger than her? How can you claim to be a man of God? How can you look in the mirror at the end of each day?"

"Leave my church immediately," the vicar said. "And stay away from my parishioners. Both of you." His eyes contained hellfire. "If you want a war, demon-possessed woman, I will give you a war." He raised a fist. "And I will win because I have God on my side."

"You bloody arrogant arse!" With every intention of inflicting pain, Franny lunged at the vicar.

Edward captured her fist, locking her arm behind her.

"Let go of me," she spat from between clenched teeth.

The lawman effortlessly tossed her over his shoulder. "Come on, Athena," he said. "You can fight the good fight another day."

If he was comparing her to the goddess of war it was an apt reference, because she was not afraid to inflict bloodshed in this battle. "How dare you!" She pounded on Edward's back as he carried her away from the upside-down, gloating vicar.

CHAPTER SIXTEEN

T OSSING THE SLAPPING, growling Frances Valentine over his shoulder had filled Edward with a twisted thrill. He'd never been one for aggressive, angry bed sport, and bondage had never before held appeal. He preferred slow, sensual lovemaking with appreciative women whose bodies were free to writhe as they screamed his name while coming apart beneath him. But God Almighty, what he wouldn't do to tie this woman to a headboard as she hissed and kicked and called him every blasphemy known to man. Then, he could taunt her with touches, and kisses, and licks, until she begged him for release.

Upon reflection, being that close to Franny had been a mistake. Her little fists pounding on his back, as his palms cradled the curve where her thighs met her arse had heated his blood to the boiling point. And now he needed to get himself under control since waddling into The Purple Rabbit with a cockstand would not do. He put her down but kept his hands on her shoulders just in case he needed to push her away.

Since they might need to make a quick exit, he studied the visible doors and windows of the purple building in front of them as she struggled, then let her go and said in the most authoritative voice he could muster, "Miss Valentine, please control your temper this time. I do not want to drag you out of a gaming hell."

Even as he spoke, his salacious side mocked him, reminding

him of the wanton things he wanted to do to this woman.

Apparently chastened, Franny rested her hands on her hips and lifted her chin. "If you ever do that to me again, I will... Well, I will..."

This was new—Frances Valentine rendered bereft of threats.

"You will what?" he asked, knowing full well he was baiting her. *Go ahead, beautiful. Please misbehave so that I can tie you to my bed and play in those fire-red curls covering your quim.*

Clamping her lips together, she stomped past him and barged into The Purple Rabbit as if she visited gaming hells all of the time. Deciding that her once-frustrating stubbornness had become adorable, he chuckled.

Edward entered the building and fought through the crowd to catch up with Franny. Once again, he found himself heating at her proximity as he leaned close to ask, "Do you see them?"

"No." She shook her head. A soft strand of her hair that had come unbound brushed his cheek.

"I think there is another room in the back." Edward inclined his chin toward the exit at the far end of the room.

Turning her back to him, she snaked through the sea of cheroot-smoking men. God Almighty, they'd be lucky if she didn't catch her hair on fire.

He sighed in relief when Franny and her unsinged locks stepped into a less crowded room where gamblers sat at tables, playing cards. Many of the men looked up to shower Franny with appreciative glances. If Edward weren't an honorable lawman, he'd throttle every one of these fools wearing lascivious grins.

"They aren't here," Franny said.

A bald man whose questioning gaze appeared more curious than lecherous approached. "I'm the proprietor, Mister Bunny. Can I help you?" With his round head and tiny eyes, the man looked more like a racoon than a ball of adorable fluff.

"We are looking for Bear and Whale," Edward said.

Mister Bunny crooked his finger, calling forth a giant of a bloke whose biceps were the size of Edward's thighs. Bunny whispered in the man's ear. His probable henchman nodded and hurried toward a door off to the right side. The ill-named proprietor focused on Edward to ask, "Why are you looking for them?"

Franny, predictably, had no patience with being ignored. "No need to be so protective. I'm Franny. They want to talk to me. Just ask them."

Still more curious than lecherous, the man's gaze raked over Franny.

"I am a... a pugilist," Franny stuttered, as if the admission pained her.

"What an honor." Mister Bunny's cheeks widened in a genuine grin, softening his countenance, making one almost understand how he'd received his moniker. He bowed as if he'd just met the queen. "Fiery Franny! One of the two women responsible for panicking the patriarchy."

Edward assumed Jabbing Josie must be the other.

Franny tilted her head thoughtfully. "What?" she asked.

Didn't she realize just how dangerous The Silk Knuckles was to men of power and influence?

Before he could elaborate, Mister Bunny's large bouncer returned and nodded to his boss.

"Shark will take you to them," Mister Bunny said.

Edward and Franny fell into step behind the intimidating henchman.

"How did you get the name Shark?" Franny asked.

He peered over his shoulder to flash a pair of sharp silver teeth.

"Huzzah!" Franny exclaimed.

Edward shivered.

Franny should contain her excitement since there was only one reason for a man to have knife-shaped teeth. What in bloody bollocking hell were they willingly walking into?

THE OCCASIONAL OIL lamp and dozens of sconces lit up the purple-walled cellar of The Purple Rabbit. An elevated, roped ring sat in the center of the dank room. Two men who resembled gargoyles sparred in the ring. One man was lean and quick on his feet. The other had fists the size of elephant feet and looked as if he had eaten too many pork pasties.

"Bear and Whale," Franny called as she rushed to two men attentively watching the pugilists.

"Fiery Franny," one of the men said with a grin. "Take a break," he called to the pugilists in the ring.

The fighters simultaneously dropped their fists and crawled between the ropes. Edward lost track of them since he was more concerned with the very bruised Bear and Whale. The one he suspected was Whale held ice on the side of his swollen face. The one who had greeted Franny stood, and his legs wobbled. He winced and sat.

Franny wrinkled her adorable, freckled nose. "You two look like you had the shite beaten out of you."

Edward's thoughts exactly.

"Mayhap you should learn to defend yourselves if you are going to spend time with fighters." Franny smirked.

Laurels to the woman for her incessant recruiting and astute business sense.

"Damnable heathens," Bear said. "Think they are better than us because they come from the other end. Got their hands in everything and now they are encroaching on our territory."

That sounded as if an East End gang and a West End gaming hell were fighting over territory. Edward's interest piqued.

"Who is he?" Bear pointed at Edward.

"Edward Robinson," Franny said. "Don't mess with him. He works for the magistrate."

Once they were alone, Edward needed to have a serious

discussion with Miss Frances Valentine about her loose tongue. She couldn't announce he was a lawman five seconds after they'd discovered the location of illegal mills.

Whale dropped his ice and leaped from his seat. Shark was instantly in Edward's space, his massive hand pressing on Edward's shoulder blade.

Franny seemed to grasp the significance of her mistake because she stepped in front of Edward as if she could protect him from these reprobates.

"Mr. Robinson is only here to ask questions because someone tried to burn down The Silk Knuckles Saloon," she said, her expression and voice fierce.

"I heard about your little mishap, Fiery Franny. 'Tis quite unfortunate." Bear's eyes morphed into angry slits. "But are you accusing us of arson?"

Franny met his fury and substantially raised him. "Should we be accusing you?"

"We had nothing to do with the fire. Why would we try to burn down your gymnasium when we want you to fight for us?"

Franny pressed a finger into Bear's chest. Meanwhile, Shark's fingers dug into Edward's shoulder. At least the henchman wasn't using his teeth—yet.

"Mayhap you think that if we don't have our gymnasium, we might be more inclined to come fight for you," Franny said, her chin bobbing with attitude.

Did she seriously think she could bob and weave her way out of this situation? If she did not calm down, she would get them both killed. Inwardly moaning, Edward reviewed his battle plan.

If he pivoted to the side, Shark would probably turn with him. He could grasp Shark's arm, quickly bend forward, and toss the beast over his shoulder. The second Shark crashed to the floor Edward would use the distraction to shove Bear into Whale. If he were lucky, they'd fall like dominoes. If he were unlucky, Shark would remove a chunk of his ankle before he could withdraw and aim his pistol.

So, the question was, did he feel lucky?

He inwardly sighed. Not particularly. But he might not have any choice because he could not allow these questionable men to harm Franny. Inhaling a large breath, he prepared for battle.

CHAPTER SEVENTEEN

F RANNY DID NOT consider herself a dolt. Her mother had taught her to read and by the time she was five years old, she'd devoured every book she got her hands on. She'd also taught herself mathematics, and her skills with numbers rivaled any male clerk's. And yet, once again, she'd allowed her desire to be fierce affect her common sense, announcing to a room full of gamblers that Edward was a lawman not to be messed with. Someone should gag her.

An image of Edward, silencing her with his cravat, his eyelids hanging heavy over pupils filled with desire, infiltrated her thoughts. Something was seriously wrong with her. Their lives were in danger, for heaven's sake. However, in her experience, fear tended to muddle one's thinking. She shivered and then stared at her finger pressing into Bear's chest. Her cheeks heated from embarrassment over both her thoughts and her actions. She dropped her hands to her side.

From beside her, she sensed Edward's muscles contract. Her fighter instincts kicked in; he was about to stage an aggressive coup that would get him killed. She had to stop him.

Whatever she did, she could not trigger any of these men, or all hell would break loose. Intending to send Edward a mental message pleading with him to calm down, she slowly faced him. Before she finished her turn, someone grabbed her. With her arms pinned behind her back, she watched with horror as Shark lifted Edward off his feet as if he were as light as a feather. This was no small feat since Edward weighed at least fourteen stone.

Instead of pulling away from her restraints, Franny flung her bodyweight back and into her captor. Her move would have worked if Whale hadn't been the size of a whale. He wrapped his arms around her and growled in her ear. His grip tightened until she struggled to take in a full breath of air.

"Let her go." Edward slammed the back of his head into Shark's face.

Hopefully, the blood spatter was from Shark's nose or his ridiculous teeth biting off his own tongue. Edward pivoted and dropped into a defensive stance. His agile move would have been impressive if the pugilists who had been in the ring earlier hadn't leaped upon him. One of them punched him in the jaw.

Edward hit the ground with a resounding *thud* that rattled Franny's teeth. His attackers wrestled with him until Edward was flat on his back. Holding him in place, they patted him down, removing a pistol from beneath his red waistcoat. For a defeated man, Edward's expression remained proud and lethal. Franny's heart melted.

Shark growled, and the light from the sconces bounced off his teeth. He bent so far forward that Franny was certain he meant to bite off Edward's cheek.

"Wait!" The hold on her windpipe loosened, so she gasped in a breath. "Bear, stop this nonsense. He is not here to serve you a warrant. He is simply trying to find out who is attacking us. Even my father, who is a superior fighter, was almost beaten to death." Although her voice sounded weak due to the recent pressure on her windpipe and lungs, she had at least articulated her thoughts. But her efforts to halt Shark had the opposite effect. His expression pure evil, he leaned closer to Edward.

The intrepid lawman didn't even flinch.

How had she ever thought this man anything but brave and heroic? She couldn't let them hurt him. If these beastly animals wanted her to fight, she'd tackle her fears and return to the ring to save Edward. Simply put, she had no other choice.

Bile rising up her throat, Franny conceded her only bargaining chip. "You win. I will fight for you. Just please… don't harm Mr. Robinson."

"Shark," Bear said, his voice a gentle reprimand.

The monster halted and backed away from Edward.

Edward sat up. So many emotions played across his face that she had no idea what he was thinking. "You don't have to do it, Franny," he softly said.

But she did have to do *it* if she meant to placate these men and keep them from killing Edward. Ruffians probably took pleasure in torturing a lawman. Although she'd experienced some sentimental moments, it wasn't as if she truly cared about him. She simply didn't want his death on her hands. *This is the only reason for your capitulation to these rapscallions,* she assured herself.

"Please, let him up," she begged. "I've given my word. I will fight for you."

Whale's hold on her loosened and she rushed to Edward. The men holding him down backed away as she knelt beside him. "Are you injured?" she asked.

What a silly question. He had smashed the back of his head into a giant Shark and been attacked by two gargoyles.

Edward snorted.

"You have a deal," Bear said. "A month from now. Here. Ladies fight before the men." He inclined his chin toward the ring. "You against Ruth the Jewel."

Franny moaned. Ruth the Jewel was a charlatan who pandered to lascivious crowds. "But isn't she in prison for indecency?"

"She has been released and has changed her ways," Bear said.

Franny scoffed, and then her soul withered as she realized what a fight in this gambling hell might mean. "Must I take a dive?"

Bear stared at her as if she were insane. "Hell, no. My fighters do *not* cheat. This is a legitimate Irish-stand down fight. I told you. There is no fight fixing at The Purple Rabbit."

Edward's brow raised. "Just illegal fights in general."

Bear glared at him. "Don't make me change my mind, lawman. 'Tis time for Shark's evening feeding and he is quite hungry."

Smiling broadly, Shark showcased his teeth. At some other more appropriate time, Franny would examine his mouth to see what held the silver in place. For now, she fought the urge to sob.

"I hope you don't plan on interfering with our mills, lawman," Bear continued. "It would be pointless since many in Parliament support underground fighting within the city limits."

Edward pushed to his feet. "I have no interest in stopping fights. I want to find out who is targeting Miss Valentine's family and business. My instincts tell me you and your associates are not involved."

Maybe Edward finally agreed that the vicar was the guilty party.

"But I think you know everything that goes on in this city," Edward said. "So, I am asking you, do you have any idea who might be behind this?"

Not only was Edward valiant, but he was also quite good at swallowing his pride to lick a man's boots. Undoubtedly, this quality made him a valuable investigator. However, there was no need for Edward to demean himself. What could Bear possibly know about an unpleasant, pious minister?

"You are no longer needed here." Bear dismissed Shark and the two fighters with a flick of his wrist.

The podgy pugilist handed Bear Edward's pistol before taking his leave.

"I'll be keeping this for the time being. I'll return it the night the lady fights for us. Extra insurance." Tucking the weapon into his waistband, Bear proceeded to rub his jaw for a long time before saying, "I was afraid something like this might happen."

"What do you mean?" Franny and Edward asked simultaneously.

Bear clamped his lips together and shook his head.

Franny's temper snapped. "Mayhap you haven't been listening. Someone knocked out my groundskeeper and then tried to burn down my gymnasium. A few days later, my father was violently attacked. If Mr. Robinson had not come along, those men might have killed him. If you know something, tell us."

When he still didn't respond, she gave him her most pleading puppy dog eyes. "You would not allow someone to harm one of your fighters, would you?"

"And someone tried to kidnap Lady Josephine last night," Edward added.

Franny gasped. "Josie was in danger?"

"She was not injured, and she managed to fight off her attacker," Edward explained. "Your friends enlightened me to the details during my visit with the Davenports today."

Franny grinned. Of course, Josie had protected herself. The men were probably nursing injuries at this very moment, and it served them right.

"Ah, Lord Davenport," Bear said appreciatively. "For an aristocrat, I do enjoy his company."

Probably because there was never a dull moment around the fun-loving viscount who wagered without a care.

Franny was done with the stalling. "What do you know?" she asked, her tone firm and her attitude unyielding. These men had gotten what they wanted from her, and she was too exhausted to negotiate further.

"The West End Knights might be involved," Bear said. "And let me tell you, they don't have a chivalrous bone in any of their bodies."

"Go on," Edward said.

"The hang out at The Round Table in St Giles and they are a new entity. Young and reckless. They have their hands in everything from theft to fixing fights."

"What makes you think they are interested in The Silk Knuckles?" Edward asked.

"They followed us the evening we come to see you," Whale

declared, speaking for the first time since Franny had met him. Interestingly, his childish voice did not match his hulking frame.

"Why were they following you?" Edward asked.

"Because they are rotten, thieving arses," Bear said. "They want to pin their crimes on us. But we don't steal. They fix fights. I told you; our fights are legitimate." He held up his finger, signaling he was about to announce the number one reason the Knights were despicable. "And they want to take over The Purple Rabbit. But we showed them." He chuckled. "Whale here beat the hell out of Lancelot last night. Blackened his eye."

Whale giggled like a happy child. "Now he gots a scar and a black eye. I only gots a hurt cheek. And Bear gave me sweets and tickles 'cause I did good."

"A scar above his eye?" Edward asked.

"Yes, sir," Whale said.

Franny met Edward's wide-eyed gaze. Were they thinking the same thing?

"Have you met Lancelot?" Bear asked.

Franny had learned her lesson about providing too much information, so this time she let Edward respond. "We have not yet been formally introduced," was all he said.

Bear sniffed Then, grinning, he pointed back and forth between Franny and Edward. "You two blowing the blanket hornpipe?"

"No!" they both exclaimed.

"Blanket hornpipe." Whales put his hand over his mouth and giggled.

"Fear not, the night has barely begun," Bear said. "Yes indeed. The night is still young."

As the men hooted and howled, Edward grabbed her hand and dragged her up the stairs.

CHAPTER EIGHTEEN

THE BEAST HAD taken Edward's pistol. What in the hell was he supposed to tell the magistrate?

"We will get your weapon back," Franny said as if reading his mind. She pursed her lips. "I'll wave down a carriage."

She'd get no argument from him. A ride home sounded heavenly.

The second Edward's arse hit the squabs, his battered, exhausted muscles relaxed. Franny sat across from him, gnawing on her lip as she regarded him with concern. In the poor lighting, he couldn't discern whether she was worried about him or fretting over her return to fighting.

"Despite the rough handling, I will be fine," he said. "Just a few bumps and bruises." He rubbed the back of his head.

"Thank heavens," she said. "Because I'm famished."

Thank heavens was right. A hungry chit was a problem Edward could solve.

"Mrs. Benson cooks a hearty potato and beef stew," he said, his mouth watering at the thought. "I wager she baked fresh bread today. We can eat and say hello to Zigzag." He dare not mention Franny was staying with him. She would be furious, and he wasn't in the mood for scowls. He'd tell her later, when she was too tired to argue.

Franny nervously twisted her hands in her skirt. "Bread and

stew sound delicious."

"But?" Edward asked.

She sat forward. "We should go to The Round Table for our evening meal. This time, I promise not to say something bacon-headed that gets you assaulted."

Edward suspected Bear's intel was correct, and if so, even though the Knights might pretend to be a better class of criminals, their establishment of choice was no place for a woman, even one with a set of brass bollocks.

Which begged the question, why had this brazen hoyden's voice become sugary sweet? He blinked and then strained to focus on her face in the shadows. Thunderation, her lashes were fluttering like gossamer hummingbird wings. And to think, he'd thought her above flirtatious manipulation.

"Absolutely not," he said. Not because he was sore and miserable; he simply wasn't going to abandon reason.

"Edward," she pleaded.

Damnations. She'd said his name. He crossed his arms over his chest to steel himself from her feminine wiles. " 'Tis much too dangerous."

"After our harrowing day, wouldn't a pint be delightful?" the cunning minx asked. "I hear their ale is the finest in London."

He was indeed craving libations, but drinking at The Round Table was out of the question. "You've heard no such thing," he snapped. "And we are not going to St Giles." He pursed his lips like an uncompromising father talking to an untruthful child.

"Do you think Lancelot is the same man who tried to sell the stolen jewels to Mr. Wagner?" Franny asked.

That is precisely what he'd been thinking. Well, that mixed with the sentimental mush he'd experienced when Franny had said, *"Just please don't harm Edward."* He would do almost anything to hear her say his given name again. And then there was the thrill he'd felt when Bear suggested he and Franny were tupping. Even now his cock stirred at the thought.

He pictured Baker's ugly face, and just like that, his prick rolled over and played dead.

Edward cleared his throat. "Their physical descriptions are the same." But what were the odds that one of his cases was related to Franny? Maybe after a meal and some sleep, he could make sense of the new information.

"We shall just have a look around, eat something, and drink some ale," Franny declared as if visiting a nefarious establishment a notorious gang frequented was perfectly logical. "The tavern will be busy right now. They won't even know we are there. We shall keep a low profile, and we don't have to interact with them." She nonchalantly shrugged. "Besides, one should always study the enemy in their natural habitat."

There was no way she would blend in. One could see her from a street away. Her fire-colored hair was akin to a glowing arrow, and then there was her stunning beauty. He shook his head emphatically.

She leaped from her seat to sit beside him. "Edward, please," she pleaded as she grasped his hand.

Hot-blooded male that he was, he couldn't steel himself from her physical touch. Sparks shot from his fingers to his infuriating rod.

"Bloody hell, Franny," he grumbled. "You aren't playing fair."

She squeezed his palm. "Oh, thank you, Edward."

"I have not said 'yes'," he fired back.

"But you will, Edward, because you are as anxious to get to the bottom of this as I am." She grinned, and his heart thumped against his ribcage.

Her smile might just be worth another beating. Not to mention, they were finally on a first-name basis. He exhaled his acquiescence.

Franny was correct. The tavern was crowded, no one seemed

to be paying attention to them, and Edward was enjoying the best mug of ale he'd ever drunk. Perhaps it was the stressful day, or that the drink was delightfully bitter, or that his companion was lovely making the evening so pleasurable. Although the stew and bread were not as tasty as Mrs. Benson's, they calmed the gurgling in his stomach and eased his headache. He pushed his empty bowl to the side, leaned back in his chair, and let out a contented sigh.

He hated to bring this up, but he needed Franny to know she had made an error so that she didn't do it again.

He cleared his throat. "Franny, I know you met no harm, but you can't run around accusing men of beating their wives until their victims have protection."

Franny blinked.

"I only know this because I am a lawman, and I deal with the aftermath of such things. When these abhorrent men are outed, their violence toward those they see as weaker than them multiplies."

She swallowed. "I'm sorry. I didn't know. I thought I was standing up for her."

"I know," he gently said. "Most people don't know. It's difficult to comprehend such maleficence."

"Will Mrs. Brown come to more harm because of me?"

He would not lay that burden at Franny's feet. It wasn't her fault some men were beasts. He sent her a reassuring smile. "Do not fret. I will help her."

"I have not a doubt," she said, smiling back.

Her confidence in him, along with her smile, punched him in the chest. Edward hid his own smile with a sip of ale and watched as she scraped the last bite from her bowl and hummed her approval as it slid down her throat. What he wouldn't give to watch a few other things slide down her throat, specifically his body parts.

Pushing his ungentlemanly thoughts to the side, he tipped back his mug and swigged.

Franny leaned across the table to whisper, "I don't see anyone who fits Lancelot's description."

Neither had Edward, and against his better judgement, he'd been scanning the crowd since they'd arrived.

"Shall we split up and ask around?" she asked.

"No!" He finished his ale in one large gulp, and then swiped his wrist across his mouth. Her gaze stayed intently fixed on him the entire time. Troublesome woman. "Do you have a death wish?" he asked.

She huffed. "Then what was the point of coming?" She looked away to lift and down half her beer in an impressive chug. Amazing woman.

"Need I remind you that you promised to behave?" Embracing his Frances Valentine impression, Edward raised his voice a few octaves. *"I promise not to say something bacon-headed that gets you assaulted. We shall just have a look around, eat something, and drink some ale."*

"I do not sound like that," she said.

She was correct. Her voice danced along the vocal scale pleasantly. He sounded like someone was yanking his bollocks from his body.

She glared at him. "Cut the shite. You know exactly why I wanted to come here."

How quickly she'd abandoned her female machinations. Perhaps he should be angry, but how could he be? It was his own bloody fault that he'd succumbed to her charms.

"Yes, and luckily the man we seek doesn't seem to be here. Now, may we check on Zigzag? She doesn't like it when I return home late."

Franny's brow rose. "Do you leave her home alone a lot?"

More than Edward was comfortable with, but why did Franny care? He pondered her reasons for asking. He highly doubted she was curious about his life.

Unable to contemplate her motivation, he moved on to his next conundrum. It was imperative he lure her to safety.

"Can I tempt you with one of Mrs. Benson's honey cakes?" he asked.

Seeming to consider his offer, she tapped her finger on the rim of her mug. *Tap, tap, tap. Tap. Tap...* The insufferable woman beat out an arrhythmic tune that probably confused many an opponent in the ring but was bloody infuriating, since she was stalling.

"Franny, it isn't that I don't intend to investigate these men." He just planned to do it when she was tucked safely beneath her counterpane. "You see, I always take my time and think things through before I act. I honestly don't know what these thieves have to do with your gymnasium, and obviously, we are dealing with dangerous people. I don't want you injured."

"Mayhap you overthink things," she said.

"In my younger days, I didn't think them over enough. I had to learn many a lesson the hard way." There was the time he'd been so excited that he'd barged into a room on the wrong floor, startling an elderly woman who'd suffered an apoplexy on the spot. While he was caring for her, the thief got away. Lesson learned. Now, he double-checked addresses.

Another time, he hadn't studied his environment ahead of time and was cornered by a bloodthirsty hound. He'd eventually made friends with the animal, who quite enjoyed belly rubs, but not before a scalawag of the worst sort fled onto the London streets to commit a half-dozen more dastardly crimes.

Now, he prepared for his investigations as if he were a surgeon saving a life.

Come to think of it, returning without backup was a fool's gambit. "I will come back in the daylight and see what I can learn," he promised.

She continued to tap.

He slid the mug out from beneath her finger, caught her gaze, and held onto it. "I do solve most of my cases," he assured her.

Emotions warred in her beautiful eyes. Softness beat out the heated fury, and she sighed. "I can be most impatient."

"As can I, so I've worked hard to be less so. An impatient lawman has a short life span."

She dropped her gaze to stare at the table. "I suppose I don't want you to die. Yet."

"Yet?" he asked.

When she looked up, her eyes twinkled with mischief. "Well, we must keep you alive until we figure out who is targeting my business and loved ones."

"So, you will turn me over to the enemy after that?" he asked.

Feigning that she was seriously considering his question, she tilted her head from side to side. "Fine, mayhap we should keep you alive because I enjoy your company."

He preened like a cocksure fool.

"Just a teeny tiny bit." She used her thumb and forefinger to measure a pinch. " 'Tis such a miniscule amount that you should not flatter yourself."

He chuckled. "Shall we take our leave?"

Her shoulders slumped. "Fine. But I want at least a dozen honey cakes."

"You have yourself a deal, Franny," he said, testing out her name to see if their rules truly had changed. When she didn't correct him, he celebrated his small triumph with a grin and a trek to the bar, Franny at his heels.

Flashing a coin, Edward caught the tavernkeeper's attention. "Old chap, do you know a man named Lancelot?"

So much for digging his feet in the sand and telling her no, but the truth was he was as anxious to get to the bottom of this as she was. He also seemed to be experiencing some type of euphoria from her attentions that made him akin to a brainless sap. Besides, he wanted her to think highly of him. Yes, indeed, he was a fool, risking her safety so she would think him courageous and intelligent.

The tavernkeeper's eyes widened, reminding Edward of precisely how foolish this inquisition was. But now that he'd started, he should finish. He dropped the coin onto the counter and pushed it toward the tavernkeeper.

The man crooked his finger.

Edward leaned forward and tilted his ear so that he could hear over the crowd. "The Knights are quite dangerous. Heed my warning. You should not take a lady to the third floor."

"The third floor," Franny said, causing an eight-legged arachnoid kind of panic to crawl up Edward's spine. In the second it took him to face her, she was already pushing her way through the inebriated crowd.

CHAPTER NINETEEN

FRANNY HAD NO intention of actually climbing the stairs, she simply wanted to examine the scene like a proper investigator. She was almost to the exit when someone caught her around the waist and tugged her backward. Pressed tight against a solid torso and caged in by the jug-bidden throng, the hair on the back of her neck stood on end. Contracting her tricep, she prepared to elbow her captor in the chin.

"Where do you think you are going, Franny?" Edward asked, his raspy voice vibrating all the way to her core and his warm breath in her ear causing goosebumps to scatter over her skin.

She turned her head until her chin swept along his chiseled jawline. Her heart pirouetted at the intimacy. "Nowhere," she said, her panted whisper betraying her arousal.

"Good," he rumbled in his deep baritone. "Don't break your promise."

What promise? She couldn't think, with her body on fire. If she stopped ramming her arse into his thigh, she might cool down. Except, she couldn't. Not yet, anyway.

"Franny," he growled in her ear.

Hoping to hear that delicious utterance again, she ground her buttocks against him. If she wasn't mistaken, his arousal grew hard and insistent.

"Good God, woman." He groaned.

Groan. Growl. Either one. She didn't care which. She rather liked his beast-like noises. What did he sound like when he spent, deep inside a woman? Deep inside her? Her breath and heartbeat quickened.

Enough is enough. She didn't require a man's touch or attention. The ale had affected her common sense, making her susceptible to masculine sorcery. She steadied her erratic breathing.

"We need to leave right now," Edward said.

So much for trying to pull herself together, because she wasn't ready to let go of this euphoria washing over her. It would take an earthquake to remove her from this man's intoxicating grasp.

Edward loosened his hold and nudged her forward. How dare he awaken her primitive needs, then push her away. The blighter.

His large fingers entwined with hers, dwarfing them. The tingling in her fingertips was a pleasant distraction, filling the void created when their bodies separated. She did not fight his pull as he tugged her out of the tavern and into the sobering breeze.

IF ONLY EDWARD was holding her hand like a lover might. Instead, she suspected his tight grip was to keep her from scaling the side stairwell to the third floor because once the tavern was behind them, he dropped her hand.

Her cheeks heated from humiliation. She had rubbed her body against his like a strumpet. At least he had the decency not to say anything as they strolled side by side. She, for one, couldn't take the uncomfortable silence another moment.

"I'm sorry," she blurted. " 'Twas the ale." Drinking one or two pints had never before made her behave like a cat in heat taunting a tomcat. But she had to blame something, and her pride would not allow her to admit she found Edward alluring, and dare she admit it—wonderful?

"I know you are disappointed that we didn't confront Lancelot," he said. "But I have no idea what we would have encountered if we had climbed those stairs. I shall take another lawman with me when I return."

But she hadn't intended to climb the stairs. At least not tonight. She just wanted to see where the men were staying. Since he thought she was about to break her promise, he could have nagged her about that, or pointed out her dissolute behavior, but instead he'd acted professionally, turning their conversation back to the case. She owed him a sincere apology.

She halted.

Seeming absorbed in his thoughts, he continued a few more steps before returning to her. A ray of moonlight illuminated one side of his face as he regarded her, a straight line to his lips and his expression serious.

"I'm sorry for behaving like a wanton," she murmured, so ashamed she could barely speak. "I don't know what got into me."

He stepped so close that a butterfly would be hard-pressed to flutter between them without its wings brushing their torsos. "Franny, it has been a long, emotional day. Neither of us is thinking clearly. Let us check on Zigzag, then get some sleep. By the by, the Wentworths are staying at the gymnasium tonight. You are staying with me. Your aristocratic friends made the decision."

In his rooms? If they thought she and Edward were saints, they were mistaken. Currently she was feeling the opposite of innocent and virginal. Her lascivious feelings from earlier had returned the second his warm breath blew across her cheek. Years ago, she had not enjoyed Harry's tongue sloppily sucking on hers, but a man like Edward, one who exuded such potent masculinity, must know how to use his tongue to pleasure a woman.

On second thought, she might like to stay at his cozy residence.

What would he do if she rose onto her toes and pressed her lips to his? There was only one way to be certain. But before she succumbed to her feminine desires, she had to know one thing.

"Do you have feelings for Lady Milton?" she asked.

The moonlight shimmered over Edward's ebony lashes as he blinked. "What?"

"She is quite beautiful, even though she smells like a brothel," Franny declared, unable to hide her true feelings.

Edward threw his head back and chortled so hard that his chest quaked with each chuckle.

Franny lifted her chin indignantly. "I'm delighted you find my question so humorous," she said, sarcasm oozing.

Composing himself, he swiped at his teary eyes. "I do not tup the women I am responsible for helping, Franny. And I'm not laughing at your question. It's your observation I find humorous. The lady is lovely, and she does indeed smell like a brothel. But no, I have no carnal interest in her."

Franny glared at him. "Have you frequented a lot of brothels?" Seconds after asking the witless question, she wanted to disappear.

Edward's humor died a quick death, replaced by a tangible anger that radiated from him. "That is none of your concern, and most certainly not a question a well-bred lady should ask."

She should have kissed him when the moment was right. Now she would never know what it felt like to have his lips touch hers. To taste his tongue. To run her hands over his sinewy chest and back.

"I'm sure you have noticed that I am hardly a well-bred lady," she said, her fists balled at her sides. She winced as all of her worse-than-abysmal attempts to flirt with him slammed her memories.

He rubbed his jaw until she feared he might remove a layer of skin. "What about you?" he asked. "Do you have feelings for Harry?"

"Harry?" Franny shook her head. "Our kisses meant nothing."

Edward growled. "I knew there was something between the two of you."

She never should have mentioned the kisses. She was a disaster times ten.

"'Twas long ago, and it was curiosity, nothing more. He is my dear friend, and I care about him, but I have never harbored romantic inclinations toward him." She swallowed both the lump in her throat and her pride. "I've never wanted to kiss a man romantically until…" *Until you, Edward.*

Perhaps he read her mind because he moved swiftly, catching her off guard. Wrapping his arms around her, he pulled her to him. His lips crashed against hers, stealing her breath. Her legs trembled and her knees buckled. She feared she might tumble to the ground, so she clasped his broad shoulders and hung on for dear life.

"Oh, Franny," he murmured into her mouth between his scorching kisses.

She arched into him, pressing her aching breasts against his firm chest.

His tongue teased and taunted her lips with delicate licks and gentle nibbles. Her lips parted on a moan, and his tongue slipped inside her mouth. She cradled his cheeks in her hands. His evening scruff tickled the pads of her fingers. She imitated his swirling tongue that still tasted like ale. Tingles took hold in her lower feminine places, then wound upward to tickle her nipples.

Her heart, soul, and body were being incinerated, and this public display of affection where anyone might come across them was most indecent. Except she didn't give a fig, or a farthing, or a single shite about any of that.

He withdrew his tongue to trail kisses along her jaw and nibble her ear.

Unable to control her desire, she gently touched his silky lashes. "Oh, Edward, they are so soft and pretty."

"Say my name again," he demanded in a wickedly deep voice.

"Edward," she whispered.

"Christ, Franny." He claimed her lips in an aggressive assault that she eagerly succumbed to.

While his hands roamed up and down her back, her fingers tunneled in his hair, gently tugging until he was moaning into her mouth. His hard bulge poked her in the belly.

Panting, he pulled back and rested his forehead against hers.

"*Mmm*," she murmured with a smile.

"I second that," he said. "I believe we have both been jealous fools."

"Yes," she agreed. There was no way she'd admit that she'd been physically attracted to him from the very first time he'd strutted into the gymnasium those many years ago. For now, she'd revel in this glorious encounter. In fact, she wanted more.

She popped onto her tiptoes and reached her lips toward his.

He pulled back. "Shh," he mouthed, one finger to his mouth, the other subtly pointing behind her.

His owlish eyes, combined with her fighter's instincts, chilled Franny to her bones. She slowly peered over her shoulder. At least eight men, their movements predatory, clubs poised, slunk toward them. While she and Edward had been behaving like animals, hunters had cornered them.

"Get them," one of the men yelled.

Edward grabbed her hand. "Run!"

Her heart pumping wildly, a chilly sweat dripping from her forehead, Franny easily kept pace with Edward as footsteps clobbered the cobblestones behind them. All they had to do was stay out in front of their assailants. Franny had the endurance to run all night if need be. She suspected the athletic-looking Edward also had an impressive lung capacity.

Edward's night vision seemed to be superior to hers since he guided her through the winding back alleys and side streets. Thankfully, she wore her rubber-soled slippers that kept her from slipping in the ring. Occasionally, she tripped over something in her path. Sometimes the item felt like a loose cobblestone. A few times, something furry brushed her ankle. Thank heavens she could not see, because she did not favor rats.

Eventually, some of the footsteps fell away. *Huh!* The lazy blighters had shite stamina. If she had to guess, only a few men remained in the chase.

"This way." Edward's labored breathing and his fingers entwined with hers became her anchor in the pitch dark. He dragged her behind a wall of what felt like shipping crates. "Shh," he whispered.

The space was so tight that their torsos melded together. His arms were around her, holding her protectively as they mingled into one being, hell-bent on survival. She pressed her face into his heaving chest to stifle the sound of her breathing.

"I don't see them," someone managed to yell raggedly while gasping for air.

"Bloody hell. They didn't just disappear!"

"Come out, come out, wherever and whoever you are," a third man merrily sang as if playing hide-and-seek with a child.

She should take solace in the fact that these men didn't seem to know who they were, yet tiny fists of fear pummeled her.

Time stood still. Blood whooshed in her ears. She shivered as unpleasant gooseflesh washed over her skin. Beef and ale soured in her stomach.

"When we find you, I am going to bloody kill you," one of the men yelled. "But first, I will make you watch as I teach your lady a lesson. No one asks about Lancelot and survives."

Edward stiffened. With her face burrowed against him in the confined space, she absorbed the quickening *thump thump* of his heart.

Her legs trembled, and a tear trickled down her cheek. If only she hadn't badgered Edward into going to the tavern. Hell's teeth. She'd shamelessly flirted the entire time they were there, hoping he'd do her bidding. And what had it gotten them? She'd become a mass of wanton inclinations, and now these men were about to kill Edward and do unthinkable things to her.

"Do not move," Edward whispered so softly she had to strain to make out his words. "I'm retrieving my pistol." He struggled to fit his hand between them.

But he no longer had a pistol.

"Bloody bollocking hell," Edward whispered.

"There they are," someone shouted.

For a moment, Franny expected to be wrenched from their hiding place and yanked from Edward's arms, but instead a noisy commotion erupted not far from them.

"Stay away from The Purple Rabbit," someone who sounded like Bear said.

Fist and wood pounding skin and bones, as well as blasphemies of every sort, echoed in the alley as warfare broke out.

"Bloody hell," Edward whispered.

Franny's thoughts exactly, although she was too terrified to express anything more than a soft whimper.

"There is an open window above us," Edward whispered. "Can you climb?"

In her youth, she'd climbed trees as skillfully as an energetic lad. Hopefully, a stack of shipping crates wasn't much different.

"Yes," she whispered.

Without further ado, Edward hoisted her onto the crates. She stretched and easily caught the edge of the window. Using her upper body strength, she lifted herself to the pane and tumbled into the building. She landed on a hard floor with a loud *thud* followed by an "Oomph." She bounced onto her feet and hopped into her fighting stance.

As her eyes adjusted, she made out the outline of crates stacked to the ceiling.

Someone soared through the window, startling her.

" 'Tis just me," Edward whispered.

The cacophony from the vicious battle beneath them continued as Edward grabbed her hand and guided her through the maze of crates.

Putting all her trust in him, she followed him along a narrow corridor, then down a flight of stairs. He opened what she suspected was the building's main door and peered into the night.

"Ready?" he asked.

She nodded.

"I will be right behind you," he said. "Head west and run as fast as you can."

So, she did, as if her life depended on it.

CHAPTER TWENTY

PURRING CONTENTEDLY, ZIGZAG rubbed against Edward's leg. He reached down and scratched between her ears as she nuzzled her nose into his calf. At least one of the females in his kitchen was happy.

Unfortunately, Franny sat across from him, staring at the plate of honey cakes, her skin so pale, she looked almost green. Truth be told, their evening had also soured his stomach.

Her teary, red-rimmed eyes were partially his fault. Franny was a bold woman trying to discover who was targeting her. He was a lawman who knew better than to ask about a criminal in a crowded tavern.

"You are safe here," he promised. "The men chasing us didn't seem to know who we were." Which begged the question, *Why?* Was this because these reprobates had nothing to do with the attacks on Franny's gymnasium and loved ones, or because they hadn't seen their faces in the dark? Once they'd finally hailed a hackney, he'd studied their surroundings. He was certain they were no longer being followed.

She swiped at her tears, instantly composing herself. "I'm sorry I behaved like a terrified ninny."

"I thought you were quite courageous," he sincerely said. "You outran those men, and I have no doubt you can outrun me." Not to mention, she'd climbed upon those crates as if she had spider legs and then hurtled herself into an empty building as easily as a squirrel changing tree limbs.

She swished her wrist as if her athletic prowess meant nothing. "I was a fool. I've been fighting you every step of the way." She chewed on that same lip he'd recently kissed. "Women are rarely taken seriously. So it makes me defensive. I can also be combative and impulsive."

With a few honest sentences, he had a glimpse into Franny's soul. If he were a woman, he would feel the same way. Hell, if he didn't consciously fight his impulsivity, he was a combative arse of the first order. "Understandable," he said.

"I made so many blunders today. You see, I didn't know that by speaking against the younger Mrs. Brown's husband that I was putting her in danger. I thought I was standing up to a perpetrator and protecting her. I feel like a daft fool."

"You are not wrong," Edward said. "She requires people to stand up for her. But first, we must get her far away from her husband if he is abusing her, which is easier said than done. There are not many places for an abused woman to go." Edward fought the rush of rage he felt every time he thought about bullies.

However, Franny had suffered enough tonight. She didn't need to witness one of his fits of temper. He called forth his rational lawman. "Men in positions of power must pave the way. We must make it known that abusing those who are vulnerable is unconscionable."

Franny tilted her head, regarding him thoughtfully. "Men like you, Nicolas, and Lord Davenport. Even Lord Griffendale, who is the worst rake in all of rakedom, is outspoken about caring for his fellow humans."

"Yes." Edward didn't have as much power as an aristocrat, but he did possess a certain amount of privilege that he never took for granted.

"And someone like the vicar could preach kindness and female equality in his sermons," Franny said.

"True. He could do a lot. People tend to listen to their religious leaders."

" 'Tis a lot to think about," she said. "When dealing with the underbelly of society, how do you stay positive?"

"I suppose this is my calling. And on the days I question humanity, Zigzag and Mrs. Benson are here for me."

Franny's nose wrinkled. "Does Mrs. Benson look like Lady Milton?"

Was she jealous of his motherly landlady? If so, it was rather flattering, and it might be fun to taunt her after everything she'd put him through.

Maybe another time, he decided. For now, she needed to feel safe. To relax. To sleep. Unfortunately, this meant he could not carry her from his kitchen, toss her onto his bed, and finish what they'd started in the middle of the street.

Thunderation, how was he to spend the night under the same roof with her and not touch her feminine curves? Kiss her full lips? Taunt her nipples? Play in her decadent cunny curls? Taste the sweet cream between her thighs? Suddenly, his trousers were too tight. He shifted in his chair to relieve the pressure.

He needed to think about anything but Franny's kisses and sensual voice whispering his name. Since her last question still hung in the air, his landlady made a perfect conversation topic.

"Mrs. Benson is a delightful woman in her middling years," he said. "She has kind blue eyes and cheeks that remind me of apples when she smiles, which is most of the time. When she cooks, she hums. Even though she wears a mobcap, her curls— they are gray in case you are wondering—hang below it and bounce when she moves." Hopefully, his description had done justice to one of his favorite people. "Oh, and her most delightful quality is that she smells like a bakery, not a brothel."

Franny's snort turned into a chuckle, and her cheeks flamed the same color as her hair. Although he should let her sleep, he didn't want this intimate time with her to end, and he still needed to thank her for saving his life.

"Thank you for agreeing to fight for Bear," he said. "I know it pained you to acquiesce. I could see it in your eyes."

Franny's gaze dropped to the table, and she frowned. "Another of my foolish mistakes today. Telling a group of men with questionable ethics that you are employed by the magistrate's court was unwise. Obviously, I wasn't thinking. I wanted to intimidate them. It was my fault, so I couldn't let them hurt you."

"I know this is not my concern, but seeing as how we seem to be in this muddle together, why don't you compete anymore?"

Using her index finger, Franny drew circles on the table. Her knuckles were roughened and a bit too large for her small hands. Eventually, she looked at him, her expression one of untold grief. "The last time I competed I knocked my opponent out and it took her so long to recover, I feared I had permanently injured her or mayhap even killed her. She did physically recover but I… well, I never fully healed. Mentally, that is. You see, I am fearful of suffering from a brain injury myself. Isn't that cowardly? I can't fight because I'm afraid I will lose my ability to read, write, and think. Those are skills my mother gave to me, and…well."

Brain injuries were not unheard of in boxing. Brutality went hand in hand with the sweet science. It was both understandable and heartbreaking that Franny carried guilt and fear on her shoulders. He wanted to reach for her. Comfort her. But if he touched her, even innocently, his self-control would snap, and he would drag her to his bed.

"I love boxing. 'Tis part of me," she said. "But I think it is the physicality and the lifestyle I enjoy. Actual competition now terrifies me even though a part of me misses it. Josie, on the other hand, loves the glory of being a champion. Once she has a child or two, I suspect she will return to the ring and fight until her old bones insist she retire."

Franny paused for a long while. Assuming she had more to say, Edward forced himself to exhibit patience as he waited for her to continue.

"Occasionally I miss the excitement and the pride I felt winning," she finally said. "But I prefer to train others to fight. I believe my true calling is to empower other women and teach them to protect themselves."

This bold, passionate woman stole his breath. "That is a very noble pursuit, and nothing to be ashamed of."

"It has been so long since I have competed that I am no longer in peak physical shape. I suppose I must start preparing tomorrow because I have grown quite soft."

Did she mean her body? Because it was perfect. All hips and breasts and gentle curves with strong arms and shoulders thrown in for good measure. He'd been too busy gawking at her cunny to notice her legs when she was flat on her back in her study. But any woman who could dash across London like she recently had, had to have shapely thighs.

There went his misbehaving cock, smacking at his trousers like a snake flicking its tongue as it peeked out from its hiding place. He willed his uncooperative cobra to behave, which took every bit of discipline he possessed.

If she meant that her personality was soft, she was wrong on that account, too. She was a raging fire one moment, and a simmering flame the next. He wanted nothing more than for her to share his bed. But…

"You can sleep in my bed, I shall take the sofa," he said.

She shook her head so emphatically that the last strands in her disheveled twist tumbled about her shoulder. "No. I can't."

God above, her hair was glorious and would soon be fanned over his pillow. Too bad he would not be there to witness the sight.

He held up his hand to halt her protest. "You are my guest. I insist, and I will not hear another word about it."

She opened her mouth but then slammed her lips tightly. Her cheeks puffed up with whatever words she wasn't saying.

"I need to run downstairs for a moment," he said. "I shall be right back. Mrs. Benson always warms water for me to wash at night. There will be enough that we can both freshen ourselves before bed."

He pushed his chair away from the table and sauntered from the kitchen.

"Bloody bollocks," she whispered with a groan.

He suspected he wasn't meant to hear her. However, her guttural utterance echoed in his mind, and he wholeheartedly agreed with her sentiment.

EDWARD UNTUCKED HIS shirt and stripped to his small clothes. His sofa, which was quite comfortable to sit on, left much to be desired as a mattress. His feet and ankles hung over the edge, and when he rolled over, his protruding arse exceeded the width of the cushion. He desperately needed a restful night if he was to continue functioning, and there was no way this would happen when he didn't fit on his makeshift bed.

And this wasn't even his most pressing problem since his cock ached for the woman sleeping down the hall. He was a man with needs, after all. And right now, if he couldn't have Franny, he required a mind-numbing, muscle-relaxing release.

Instead of accepting his miserable state, he should take matters into his own hands. He reached into his small clothes, grasped his hard-as-stone rod in both palms, and twisted.

Pleasure pumped into his blood as he imagined Franny's hair spread across his lap, her mouth hollowed around him. His beautiful fantasy sucked him in and licked him on the way out. His toes curled, and his eyes rolled back in his head.

"Edward?"

This might be the best self-pleasure session of his life since he could hear Franny calling to him. The mirage was so life-like that when he inhaled, her freshly washed scent wafted into his nostrils.

"Are you asleep?" she asked.

Life-like his arse. This was no fantasy. Franny was in the room, talking to him. Wincing, he halted mid-stroke and slowly withdrew his hand so as not to bring attention to what he was up to. The sofa creaked as he rolled toward her voice.

Franny stood in the doorway, a candle in one hand. Her soft red waves cascaded over her shoulders, her feet were bare, and the only thing she wore was a calf-length chemise.

"Oh, splendid. You are awake," she said. "Although you look quite uncomfortable. You are much too large for that settee."

No shite! But that hadn't stopped her from relegating him to dainty furniture the night before. "Do you need something?" he asked, his irritation flaring.

Seeming unfazed by his tart response, Franny stepped closer. "I shall share your bed," she announced.

Holy bull bullocks! The wind was literally knocked from his lungs. Was she saying what he thought she was saying?

"It won't be indecent," she said. "We can put blankets between us."

But he wanted to be deplorably indecent. This was an insane idea. There was no way he could sleep beside her without touching her.

"I should stay out here," he said.

"Please." Her voice was a soft caress over his heated skin. "I cannot bear to think of you being uncomfortable on my account."

Was this compassionate woman the same person who had broken his nose and caused him untold grief these past few days, or was he in the middle of a nighttime fantasy?

He sat up and planted his feet solidly on the floor. He wiggled his toes in the soft carpeting. A rush of sensation alerted him that he was indeed awake. How utterly disappointing because if it had been a dream, he would have crawled into bed with her and sunk himself to the hilt. As it was, he would bitterly and begrudgingly do the right thing.

"Franny, I'm staying here. 'Tis for the best."

It was no surprise that the minx ignored him. She grabbed his hand and tugged. "Zigzag misses you."

On cue, Zigzag stuck her head into the parlor and indignantly meowed her *time-to-go-to-bed-human* alarm.

"Bloody hell," he groaned as he succumbed to Franny's tug and Zigzag's meows.

"You are quite grumpy," she said. "Mayhap because you are exhausted."

Exhausted, sore, and randy as hell. And her warm hand clutching his as she guided him down the hallway, the promise of sensual delights almost within his grasp, wasn't helping matters.

Maybe she was playing coy, pretending that this was innocent, when what she wanted was for him to pin her to the bed and make love to her all night long.

Yes. Please. A man could pray and dream.

He held his breath as Franny placed the candle on the nightstand, rolled up his counterpane, and situated it in the middle of the bed. "There." Brushing her hands back and forth, she smiled. "Nothing indecent."

Edward let out his breath with a dramatic scoff. No way in hell would a rolled-up blanket protect her from the things he wanted to do to her body.

Thankfully, she did not punch him. However, she might have rolled her eyes. It was difficult to tell in the shadows with his desire overtaking his intellect.

She lay down on one side of The Great Wall of Counterpane, pulled the covers to her chin, and tapped the nest she'd created for him. "I shall sleep better knowing you are comfortable."

He'd sleep better if he tupped her until he passed out.

Zigzag leapt onto the bed, curled up beside Franny's feet, and meowed at him.

Resigning himself to a night of torment, he stretched out on his side of the mattress.

"See, isn't this cozy?" Franny sat up and snuffed the candle. "Now we shall all sleep better."

No way in hell was he getting any sleep. Not with the sound of this succubus' gentle breath blowing in and out. He folded his arms behind his head, stared at the black ceiling, and planned his seduction.

What would turn Franny back into the woman who'd rubbed her arse against his cock and whispered his name with lust clouding her eyes? Her kisses had been beyond delicious and passionate. Was it the danger? The ale? Jealousy? Coming up behind her and whispering in her ear? *Ah!* The latter might work. All he had to do was roll to his side, rest his head on the counterpane, and whisper her name seductively. Once she was in his arms, the rest would be easy.

He rested his cheek on the counterpane and inhaled her intoxicating scent. "Franny," he said, his voice a sensual rumble.

Her gentle snore rippled.

Well, hell, he couldn't exactly cajole a sleeping woman into bed sport. *You also can't tup someone you are supposed to be protecting, you bloody fool!* He huffed so hard it was a miracle he didn't wake up the two females happily dreaming in his bed while he suffered sheer, hellish agony.

It seemed he was in for the longest night of his life. Wriggling his arse into the mattress, he tried to get comfortable. He instantly found that perfect position, and his muscles relaxed. As a foggy haze swept over him, he closed his eyes.

★

CHAPTER TWENTY-ONE

WITH A CONTENTED sigh, Franny stretched her arms toward the headboard and her legs toward the footboard. If it weren't for her gurgling stomach reacting to the aroma of bacon, she might stay in bed all day. Blast her stringent training diet all the way to hell. Currently, she'd prefer fried pork to training.

Now that her blood was pumping, she reached over the counterpane intending to shake Edward awake. Instead, she found cold, empty sheets. Perhaps this was for the best since she was a dolt in his presence.

Her behavior last night had been atrocious, so from now on, she would not allow her physical desires to dictate her actions. At least she'd behaved after she dragged Edward to bed. Of that, she could be proud. Oh, she'd ached for him to wrap his arms around her and teach her how to make love. After their kisses, she would have been an enthusiastic and eager pupil. But he'd not been himself. He was so exhausted he'd barely been able to keep his eyes open, and he'd been uncharacteristically grumpy. Hopefully, he had gotten a solid night's rest. She had slept like the dead and was better for it. Her resolve was again firm, and in the light of day, and without his presence befuddling her, she knew that a carnal relationship was out of the question.

She crawled from beneath the blankets and regarded Edward's room in the soft morning light. Not only was his bed comfortable, but it was also massive. Someone had taken time to hand-paint a festooning vine of copper and peach flowers on the dark green walls. She'd wager the apple-cheeked, humming Mrs. Benson.

Franny stood on her tiptoes to look at her reflection in the mirror above Edward's dresser. *Ghastly!* She could barely find her face in the disaster of red knots.

She pulled her dress over her head and slid into her slippers. Hopefully, Edward wouldn't mind if she borrowed his comb. After about five minutes of fighting with her rat's nest, she gave up.

Feeling hideously disheveled, she followed the scent of food and coffee to Edward's orderly kitchen.

Edward sat at the table, studying a page in his notebook. An empty plate and a full cup were pushed to the side. He looked up at her and smiled, and for a moment she considered abandoning her plan to behave like the virgin she was. But what was a woman to do when he was masculine perfection, and unlike her, he appeared well-groomed?

"How are you feeling?" she asked since the poor man had taken quite a beating last night.

"Like I was run over by a carriage." He chuckled. "Seriously, I've survived far worse. Mrs. Benson was here earlier. Help yourself." He pointed the pencil in his hand at the food on the counter.

Behaving like a starving guttersnipe who didn't have to get into a boxing ring in a few weeks, Franny piled eggs, bacon, and honey cakes onto her plate. Better to satisfy her appetite for food than her all-consuming ache for carnal knowledge. She poured a large cup of coffee and sat beside Edward.

"How did you sleep?" he asked. Thankfully, he seemed in much better spirits than the previous evening.

"Exceedingly well," she said. "Your mattress is as soft as a cloud." She might like to sleep in his bed every night. Actually, she might like to do other indecent things on that puffy mattress.

Egad! She needed to pull her head out of her arse. She gulped her coffee and burned her tongue.

"Careful, that is hot," Edward said as she schooled her wince. "We have another busy day ahead of us." He pushed the notebook toward her. "Our suspects and errands."

As Franny forked eggs into her mouth, she skimmed Edward's notes. Hopefully, the suspects weren't in order because Vicar Williams was at the bottom of the list.

"Bear, Whale, and the crew at The Purple Rabbit are first," she said. "You have Lancelot and his gang next. Why is that?"

"They are not in any particular order. My instincts tell me Bear is more interested in having you as a fighter than destroying your saloon."

At the mere mention of fighting for Bear, her belly tumbled. She had no choice but to fight her anxiety because, as terrified as she was to compete, she couldn't go back on her word. Instead, she must latch onto the tiny part of her that missed the challenges mills afforded.

"Do you think the Knights are responsible?" she asked.

"I think the Knights have something to do with Lady Milton's stolen jewelry. And I have no doubt, if they had caught us last night, we would not be breathing this morning."

Again, her belly flipped.

"They are exceedingly disreputable," he said.

"But you don't believe either group is responsible for the fire and harming Harry and my father, do you?"

"Bear has an interest in you. But is that motivation enough to cause harm and damage?"

She rubbed at the ball of acid in her throat. "I don't understand why anyone wants to hurt us."

Edward didn't immediately respond because he was pouring himself a cup of coffee. Eventually, full cup in hand, he leaned against the counter, his relaxed pose reigniting Franny's attraction to him.

"Many men are afraid of powerful women," he said. "You are

challenging the status quo."

No matter how many times she heard this, she struggled to grasp how cruel and vindictive people could be.

"I'm going to request the magistrate send a few armed officers to The Round Table with a warrant. If we find what I think we will, we can arrest Lancelot and his men."

She tapped on Lord Whitehill's name. "Lord Griffendale, Lord Davenport, and Nicolas do not favor this man."

Edward leaned over her and peered down at the list. "He is the person who has the most motivation to do you harm. It sounds as if he intends to silence anyone encouraging female equality."

"If there is a Lady Whitehill, she needs a firm talking to," Franny said.

Edward raised a brow and chuckled. "Our first stop this morning will be at Greenpark House to check on Harry and your father. While there, I will ask Lord Davenport to facilitate an introduction to Lord Whitehill. I suspect a friendly *tête-à-tête* will go over better than a lawman forcing his way in and making accusations."

Recalling her image in the mirror, Franny balked. "Mayhap I should stop home and change clothing." While she was at it, she would don stays and a fresh chemise. And tooth polish was a must.

"Of course," Edward said. "We will do that first instead."

"Are we going to confront Vicar Williams again?" she asked.

Edward frowned. "I'm still concerned about the younger Mrs. Brown's safety. So, yes. I will suggest that the Wentworths stay at The Silk Knuckles again. You can stay here."

Of that, she was glad, for she did so like his big, soft bed. Perhaps she should pack a bag. Staring at the honey cakes, she sighed. *Stupid training diet.* However, she could give herself a few hours to adjust to her new regiment.

A faint smile played across his lips as he watched her wrap her cake in a serviette.

"We should be on our way," she said. "We have much to do." Not to mention, she needed to fit in a training session before bedtime. She held up her wrapped cake. "I shall eat this on the way."

"Pack one or two for me, please." Edward squatted to shower the meowing Zigzag with affection.

Franny swallowed. What she wouldn't do to have those strong hands caressing her.

THE MORNING AND early afternoon had been a whirlwind of activity and, unfortunately, mixed news. On the positive side, Papa seemed much improved, and Lady Davenport had miraculously convinced him to continue staying with her. Then there was the negative; Harry's blistered skin broke Franny's heart, and his forced smiles did not hide his pain.

Next, she'd anxiously waited in a carriage as Edward made his request to the magistrate. The second he entered the vehicle, she'd practically leaped upon him, asking questions. He avoided saying anything other than, "Everything is arranged for this evening," and "No, Franny, I'm sorry but you can't go with us. 'Tis official magistrate business." Earlier that morning, she thought she'd be content never to enter The Round Table again, but since she was now denied entry, she wanted nothing more than to barge into the tavern, her fists ready to pound.

She had folded her arms across her chest and glared at Edward. Not that it did her any good. All her temper garnered her were sore muscles from clenching her jaw.

It was late afternoon when she and Edward climbed into Lord Davenport's fancy carriage.

"Where are Nicolas and Lord Griffendale?" Franny asked since she had assumed they would be joining them.

"I decided that Griffendale and Wentworth should stay away

for now," the viscount said. "Whitehill does not favor the two of them. As you know, he and Griffendale are in a heated political war, and he thinks Wentworth 'capitulated to his temperamental wife.' His words, not mine. I'd never say such a horrible thing about Josephine. I'm quite fond of my bollocks." Lord Davenport grinned. "Of course, Whitehill adores me. I dare say, everyone adores me." He winked at Franny.

She chuckled.

Edward's low moan might have been easy to miss if one wasn't paying attention. However, Franny was aware of his every breath. If he was jealous, he need not be. Lord Davenport was an incurable flirt. And yet, Franny had never found it in her heart to dislike him because he had proven time and time again that he was a loyal friend to those he cared about. Despite her favorable sentiment, Franny was not naive. His likability did not negate how unexpectedly dangerous Jonathan Davenport was. She harbored no doubts. The viscount could charm the most stubborn of men into letting him stick a knife in his gut.

"Would you like to hear my plan?" Lord Davenport asked.

"Yes," Franny said with a clap. A renewed enthusiasm replaced last night's trepidation. Thank the Lord above because she did not favor when her fizzled nerves got the better of her courage as they seemed to do ever since her unfortunate fight.

"Go on, Sir." Edward raised a questioning brow.

"I have it on good authority that the Whitehills take tea every Tuesday at The Tea Rose. I shall approach them and say, "How good to see you, Whitehill. Lady Whitehill. Allow me to introduce you to two of my dear friends, Miss Frances Valentine and Bow Street Runner, Edward Robinson. Robinson, you shall take it from there."

Franny had changed into a frock the same shade of green as her eyes, and colorful embroidered flowers embellished the low neckline. She had even tamed and braided her hair, winding the long plait into a coil she tucked beneath her favorite bonnet. However, she knew that her favorite outfit was not fine enough for such an outing.

"Have I told you what a vision you are today, Frances?" Davenport asked as if reading her mind.

"Yes," Edward grumbled. "Three times. But who is counting?"

Edward, for one. Franny, for another.

Instead of reminding Edward of his impertinence and lower station, the viscount smiled. "When a lady is as lovely as Frances, she should hear it at least a dozen times a day."

"Why, thank you, my lord." Franny cast a smug smile in Edward's direction.

"Now that we have become such good friends, I insist you call me Jonathan."

"Very well, Jonathan," Franny said.

Edward folded his arms across his chest and glared out the window.

On her life, she had no idea if she was enjoying Edward's discomfiture because it might be jealousy, or because she was irritated that he wouldn't let her assist with the raid on The Round Table.

"I have given this a lot of thought," Jonathan said. "We shall appeal to Lord Whitehill's sense of importance. He loves it when people bow down to his power. Therefore, we shall beg him to use his influence to help us."

"Beg?" Franny scoffed. Not for a million pounds.

"Trust me," Lord Davenport said. "Flattery will get you everywhere with this man. While we are kissing his arse, he will become overconfident. When men feel invincible, they brag about their wrongdoings."

"They do, indeed," Edward said. "Overconfidence is many a powerful man's downfall."

"I do hope you are both ready," the viscount said. "Because we have arrived."

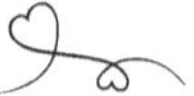

BEFORE THAT DAY, places like The Tea Rose were figments of Franny's girlhood imagination. Now she had evidence they existed, and that families like the Davenports visited them whenever they were struck with a desire to dress up and hobnob.

Pink and red hot-house roses filled the crystal vases in the center of each table, and dozens of small crystal chandeliers hung from the low ceiling. All about the room, three-tiered trays held pretty iced cakes and biscuits; ladies wearing colorful dresses and gentlemen in neatly tied cravats drank from delicate porcelain cups.

"There he is." Jonathan inclined his chin to a couple seated along the far wall. "Follow my lead."

Franny and Edward fell into step behind him.

"How good to see you, Whitehill," Jonathan said as he approached the table. "Laura, you are the first person I noticed when I entered. You are a ray of sunshine."

Lady Whitehill's cheeks flamed so scarlet, they clashed with her yellow dress. "Thank you, Jonathan. 'Tis always a pleasure to see you."

"Allow me to introduce you to two of my dear friends," Jonathan said. "Miss Frances Valentine and Bow Street Officer Edward Robinson."

Franny performed what she hoped wasn't an awkward curtsy.

Lord Whitehill scowled at Edward before turning his unhappy glare on Jonathan.

"*Hmm*," Franny accidentally murmured. It seemed Whitehill did not favor the viscount as much as Jonathan claimed, unless it was the presence of two working-class patrons in a fancy tea house that disturbed him.

"Davenport," Whitehill said. "Lady Whitehill and I were enjoying our quiet afternoon."

Lady Whitehill pursed her lips looking none too happy with her arse of a husband.

Ignoring Lord Whitehill's slight, Jonathan motioned for a waiter to pull three chairs to the table. "Three chocolates and one of those." He pointed at a pedestal holding particularly delicious-looking pastries.

Franny contemplated her dilemmas. Even though she'd devoured her and Edward's cakes while waiting in the carriage, there is no way she would pass up chocolate and these scrumptious-looking delicacies. Secondly, she knew very little about the etiquette of the aristocracy, but she suspected that inviting yourself to join an already seated party might be frowned upon, especially since the server blanched. However, what did she care about these people's etiquette? She sank into the offered chair and anxiously awaited her delights. Looking quite at ease, Edward took the seat across from her.

"Lord Whitehill is a very influential member of Parliament," Jonathan said, situating his tailcoat and sitting beside Franny.

Whitehill stopped scowling to puff up his chest. "I am The Earl of Thingamajig, the Viscount of Whatsthatplace, and Baron of Whogivesashitesshire…" he declared.

Those weren't the precise titles he gave, but Franny couldn't care less about kowtowing to this fool who sneered at her as if she were rat feces.

Edward must have been raised to have more social graces than a female pugilist because he feigned interest in Whitehill's soliloquy of self-importance. As she watched their server move about the room, her mouth watered in anticipation of his return.

The second Whitehill halted to take a breath, Edward commandeered the conversation. "Miss Valentine and I were investigating a fire at The Silk Knuckles Saloon when we ran into Viscount Davenport, and he invited us to tea."

"Are the two of you running around London without a chaperone?" Whitehill asked, his nasally tone needling Franny.

How unfortunate that planting a facer in a room filled with

embroidered linens and velvet drapery was a *faux pas* that might get her removed before she enjoyed her chocolate.

She closed her eyes for a moment, trying to assuage her outrage. This was pointless rubbish. A nice long run would have been a much better use of her time. Edward should have just barged into the man's residence and served him a warrant for being a misogynistic cretin.

"Miss Valentine's father hired me," Edward said.

Lord Whitehill *tsked*. "I suppose pugilists are akin to ladies of ill—"

How in the dickens did he know she was a pugilist? *Suspicious!* Unless he had simply made an assumption because Edward mentioned The Silk Knuckles.

Jonathan cut him off. "We are hoping that since you know everything that goes on in this city, you might have heard who wishes The Silk Knuckles Saloon harm?"

Lord Whitehill swished his wrist dismissively. "Every sane man in this country, which is why women cannot own businesses. Angry men will harm them, and we must protect the fairer sex from violence. Not to mention, women do not have the keen awareness of business that men do. 'Tis been proven time and time again throughout history."

His rebuttal made about as much sense as a foxed man reciting poetry. "Because men wrote the history books," was all Franny managed to refute before Edward's eyes went wide, his gaze tracking someone behind her.

"Thank you for your time, my lord." Edward stood and bowed to Lady Whitehill. "Thank you, my lady, for your hospitality and for sharing a table with us."

Hospitality, Franny's arse.

Edward motioned for Franny and Jonathan to follow him.

"But we are still waiting for our order," Franny called to his retreating backside. "Blast!" She huffed in frustration. The fear of returning to her training diet must be making her crave excessive amounts of food. Besides being hungry, she wasn't finished debating Whitehill's outdated theories.

"Oh, botheration," she mumbled. Excusing herself, she followed Edward as he pressed through the teahouse, dodging servers and fancily clad patrons.

"Edward, wait," she called.

He ignored her, even allowing the door to almost slam into her. Preparing to lambaste him for his rudeness, she exited The Tea Rose. He stood in the middle of the street, looking first one way, then the other.

She caught up to him. "What the devil?" she asked.

"I lost him," Edward said.

"Lost who?"

"A bruised man with a knife-shaped scar above his eye."

"Lancelot?"

"Bloody bollocking hell." Edward scraped his fingers through his hair. "He walked right past us. Exited the tea house and disappeared."

"Was he following us?" Franny asked.

"I don't know. His back was to me. I didn't see his face until he passed our table." Edward kicked at an invisible stone. "Shite." He perused the area. "Where in the devil is Davenport?"

Franny turned in a circle, searching for the viscount. "Mayhap he is paying for our chocolate that we didn't get to drink."

Edward harrumphed and then barged back into The Tea Rose. Franny trotted behind him, almost colliding into his back when he stopped to gawk at something in front of him.

Franny peered over her shoulder to find Jonathan standing beside a potted plant, whispering in Lady Whitehill's ear.

"He is not," Franny mumbled. The woman was older than his mother.

Showering Jonathan with contemptuous glares, Edward stomped past the whispering pair, retracing the path to Lord Whitehill's table. Curiosity getting the better of her, Franny followed. Jonathan and Lady Whitehill joined their parade.

Edward loomed over His Lordship of Holier Than Thou-ness. "There was a man sitting over there." Edward pointed at an empty table. "Who was he?"

Lord Whitehill turned to regard the table. When he faced Edward, his expression had morphed from frustration to anger. "Young man, you seem to be under some mistaken notion that you can speak to me as your equal and interrupt my afternoon with my wife. I suspect you believe I have something to do with that fire at the den of iniquity that Griffendale and Shiredale's disgraced son support."

Undaunted by the blustering aristocrat, Edward stepped closer and stared into Whitehill's eyes. "Did you have something to do with the fire?"

Lady Whitehill's gasp blew across Franny's neck.

The air crackled with danger as Whitehill squared his shoulders and met Edward's intense glare. "The truth is, I am not surprised someone tried to burn that building to the ground. I am not even sorry. But I had nothing to do with it. I have no idea who did it. I will say this; I do not have to lift a finger to discourage female empowerment because others are angry as the dickens. If those pugilists continue to peddle their nonsense to vulnerable ladies, they will remain a target."

Franny clenched her fist and stepped toward Whitehill with every intention of releasing her pent-up anger on his haughty upturned nose. Jonathan grabbed her around her waist and hoisted her backward.

Although Edward's stance remained predatory, the tension in his shoulders eased slightly. Meanwhile, the fire in Franny's soul threatened to explode, and if it did, she might engulf the entirety of The Tea Rose in her flaming orbit.

"And you, Davenport," Whitehill growled. "How dare you?"

"How dare I what?" Jonathan asked with a smart-arse grin.

Did Whitehill know that Jonathan had been flirting with his wife?

"How dare you bring them here?" Whitehill pointed back and forth between Franny and Edward. "You need to keep that out-of-control hellcat on a leash."

Jonathan shrugged. "As far as I know, I can bring anyone I want here, whenever I want. And you might want to temper your insults because if I let go of the hellcat, I am not responsible for what she does to your person."

By now, everyone in the establishment was watching the dramatic scene with wide eyes.

Their server approached. "Is there a problem, sir?" he asked Whitehill, his voice quavering.

"These people are disturbing me." Whitehill waved his hand wildly.

"There was a man sitting over there." Edward pointed at the table in the corner. "He just left. His face is both bruised and scarred. Who is he?"

The server's mouth opened wide, forming an "O".

"Do you mean Lance Gerald Huntington?" Lady Whitehill meekly asked.

"Who is he?" Edward might not be the wealthiest man in that room, but his commanding manner and voice left little doubt that he was the one in control.

"The third son of Lord Michelson," Whitehill said. "Nothing but trouble. Michelson disowned him a few months ago. Why do you ask?"

"He comes in here every Tuesday afternoon and sits at that table," the server added. "Always by himself."

"Lord Whitehill, think," Edward said. "Have you ever talked about Lady Milton's jewelry collection while here?"

Whitehill's brow furrowed, his anger replaced by confusion.

"Yes," Lady Whitehill said. "I told you how much I admired her ruby and diamond set. Do you not remember, Maxwell?"

Whitehill's eyes clouded over. He probably had no idea what his wife was referencing because men like him did not pay women an inkling of attention. Suddenly, Franny hoped Jonathan seduced Laura and brought her a moment or two of pleasure.

"Have you had any recent theft at your home?" Edward asked.

"Yes, my pearls," Lady Whitehill said. "How did you know?"

"My lord, have you discussed your displeasure with The Silk Knuckles Saloon while here?" Edward swung his hand palm up, indicating the tearoom.

" 'Tis none of your concern what I discuss," Whitehill declared.

"Maxwell, was it not you who told Lord Michelson his son was a reprobate?" Lady Whitehill said.

Maybe Jonathan's attentions had emboldened Whitehill's wife to confess truths.

"Bloody fool," Edward grumbled. "I wager you have discussed very personal things sitting in a public teahouse, and Lord Huntington's disgraced son is eavesdropping on your conversations." With that, Edward turned on his heel and stormed from the establishment.

His grip firm, Jonathan escorted Franny outside and did not let go of her elbow until they were in the carriage.

"Lord Whitehill is not behind the arson," Edward said.

"How do you know?" Jonathan asked.

"He is a despicable man, but he told the truth," Edward said. "I could see it in his eyes."

"Is Lance Gerald Huntington Lancelot?" Franny asked.

"Yes. I would not be surprised if he carved his scar to look like Excalibur and took the name Lancelot to get back at his father. He probably sought out an establishment called The Round Table to add even more symbolism to the mystic he is creating, suggesting that this is simply a farce to seek revenge on Lord Huntington."

Suddenly, everything made sense. Franny sat forward. "I've read many versions of Camelot. King Arthur was said to have a strained relationship with his father, Uther Pendragon."

"Yes." Edward nodded.

"But then, why target The Silk Knuckles?" Franny asked.

Edward shook his head. "I don't know. I suppose we will have to ask him after we arrest him." His pointed gaze slid to Jonathan. "Lord Davenport, what were you whispering to Lady

Whitehill?"

"Operation Charm the Wife." The viscount winked at Franny. "Believe me, it never fails. You will see."

⚜

CHAPTER TWENTY-TWO

A SMILING MRS. Benson answered the door, her black dress and apron dusted with flour, and the scent of freshly baked bread wafting about her. "Good evening," she said. "I was just about to deliver your meal." She brushed her finger over Edward's cheek and *tsked*. "The bruise has darkened since this morning. I have a poultice here somewhere that should help you heal."

"The food smells delicious," Edward said. "You are so very good to me, so I hate to be an imposition, but I have a favor to ask."

"Anything for my favorite of Mr. Fielding's People," she said.

"Could you keep an eye on a young woman I am tasked with keeping safe? I must work this evening."

Her eyes lit up and she grinned mischievously. "A young lady, you say?"

" 'Tis not like that," he said with a twinge of guilt. Lying to this dear woman brought him no pleasure.

Edward quickly sorted through the facts. He was responsible for Franny's safety, and although he wanted her on a deep, visceral level, he had not tupped her. Just because they had slept in the same bed, and he had once thrust his tongue into her mouth, it did not mean it was *like that*. This morning, when he'd awoken beside her, he pledged to behave like a perfect gentleman, even if it meant cold baths and taking his arousal into his own hands. He would do the right thing even if he withered away to nothingness from his desire for Franny. *You might be a randy fool, but at least you told Mrs. Benson the truth*, he concluded.

"Does this mean I am finally assisting you in an investigation?" Mrs. Benson asked, her eyes twinkling.

If that was how she wanted to think of it, he would not spoil her fun. "I suppose so. Whatever you do, do not let her out of your sight. If she follows me, her life could be in danger."

Mrs. Benson rested her hands on her hips. "It sounds like your charge might be a handful."

A handful, a pain in the arse, and exceedingly difficult. "Yes, she is," Edward said. "She is an impassioned red-headed pugilist and quite difficult to manage." Not to mention, she sometimes had more attitude than common sense.

"Is this the same woman who broke your nose years ago?" Mrs. Benson asked.

Edward groaned. "You remember that story?"

"Of course. I remember everything you tell me. Despite your denial, I knew there was a woman behind the petrified look in your eyes. Now, help me carry the pork pie. I'll carry the stewed apples and bread upstairs. Just give me a few moments to find the poultice and gather my embroidery. I can work on your new table covering while this wild woman and I get to know one another. We shall have a delightful time while you are out saving the world."

Something told Edward that his two favorite women would have a companionable evening. More importantly, he was leaving Franny with a capable nursemaid.

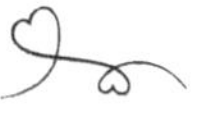

PURPLE AND BLACK clouds striped the sky, and heavy droplets pelted Edward as he waited in an alley for Lancelot and his men to leave The Round Table. Shivering, and soaked to the bones while listening to Baker yammer on about useless drivel while the wind howled, took a toll on Edward's nerves. At least Jenkins and Newton, the other two men assigned to assist them, were respectable blokes.

The downpour had just turned into a lazy drizzle when Newton, the officer stationed near the stairs running up the side of the tavern, held his white glove high.

"Shh," Edward told Baker. "They might walk past us at any moment."

Luckily, Baker stopped talking so that Edward was able to observe in silence as a group of men descended the stairs. They passed Jenkins and then headed in the opposite direction from Edward.

Once Edward was certain the crew of miscreants was too far away to notice them, he swirled his wrist high, alerting the other men that it was time. "Let's go," he said to Baker.

Leaving puddles behind them, the four lawmen entered the tavern. They easily found their way to the bar because the room was not as crowded as it had been last night. Anyone with any sense was at home in front of their hearth. Edward withdrew the warrant from his staff and presented it to the same tavernkeeper he'd encountered the previous evening.

"We are with the Magistrate's Office," Edward said. "Can you point us to the man in charge? We have reason to investigate the party residing on your third floor."

"This is my tavern." His lips pursed, the business owner skimmed the notice. For a moment, Edward thought he might not be able to read, or that he might try to impede the investigation, not that it mattered. They would climb the stairs whether or not they had his permission.

"You were here last night with the pretty redhead," the tavernkeeper said as he handed the warrant back.

From beside him, Baker snorted. "Christ, Robinson."

With his notorious reputation, Baker was not in a position to throw stones. Edward's jaw clenched. along with his fists. Then, upon reflection, he forced himself to relax. He probably shouldn't knock Baker's teeth down his throat while in the middle of an investigation.

The tavernkeeper crooked his finger, inviting Edward to lean close. "The truth is, I've had enough of them. A spoiled lordling playing at being a street criminal to get back at his father is worse than the worst lowlife ruffian."

"I can imagine," Edward said.

"Last night, right after you left, they went out and returned rather worse for wear." The tavernkeeper withdrew a key from his apron pocket and handed it to Edward. "The rumor is that a rival crew got the better of them. I would be grateful if you removed these hellions from my establishment. Just keep me out of it. I don't need trouble." He sighed. "What made them decide to terrorize my business?"

Edward would explain to the owner about how his whimsical choice of a name had become an unfortunate one another time. He took the key and thanked him, adding, "I see no reason to drag you into this."

The tavernkeeper said something, but his voice was so low, Edward had to press his stomach on the bar in order to get close enough to hear him. Obviously, the man did not want to be overheard, which was an understandable caution since the night before someone had heard Edward ask about the Knights, and the consequences had been disastrous.

"Please repeat yourself," Edward whispered.

"The indoor stairway leads to the second-floor rooms," the tavernkeeper said. "The one outside leads to the room the Knights commandeered."

Edward nodded. "May I borrow that?" He inclined his chin toward a candle.

"Yes," the tavernkeeper said.

Edward used his palm to shield their light source from the elements as the three of them climbed the rickety staircase.

Newton, their lookout, stationed himself in a shadow created by the building's eaves.

Holding his finger to his lips, Edward whispered, "Be careful. Someone may have remained behind."

Edward slid the key into the lock and slowly turned. The door creaked open, and they cautiously entered a human-less pigsty that smelled of unwashed bodies and stale ale. Clothing littered the unmade bed and the floor. Dirty dishes and half-eaten food were scattered about.

Edward tried not to breathe in the malodor as he spoke. "We are looking for a stash of jewelry."

The search was slow going with only one candle. Eventually, they found a small lamp and lit it. This allowed Edward to search the drawers as his companion kicked clothing about and checked beneath the mattress.

After about ten minutes, Edward stood in the center of the room, scratching his wet head. The loot *had* to be here, unless Lancelot had sold it. Edward rubbed his temple. *Think, you dullard.* "If you were an angry aristocrat with stolen goods you were struggling to pawn, what would you do with them?" he asked his companions.

"If we find them, I say we each keep a trinket or two," Baker said.

Edward whirled on him.

Baker held up his hands. "No sense of humor, mate."

This had nothing to do with a sense of humor, and if Baker tried to pocket stolen goods in Edward's presence, he would lock him in a cage and melt the key.

"I would hide them until the previous owners stopped looking for them," Jenkins said. "Then I would try to sell them on the continent."

"Brilliant answer," Edward said. Lancelot hadn't had time to travel outside the country between his visits to Mr. Wagner and his sighting at The Tea Rose, which meant Lady Milton's jewelry had to be in this room.

"Check for loose floorboards," Edward said. "The stolen jewels are here. I can feel it in my bones."

While the other men searched, he dragged a piece of round carpeting to the side and dropped to his knees. He placed the candle beside him and pressed on the floorboards. One gave beneath his fingers.

"I think I found something," he called.

He pressed again, and when a corner lifted, he pried the wood loose. In the hollow beneath the board lay a pile of sparkling jewels, including a set of rubies and diamonds, a sapphire ring, a necklace dripping with diamonds, and strands of pearls.

Edward sat back on his heels and grinned. "We have what we need. We will wait for them, and when they return, Lancelot's reign of terror is over."

Baker peered over Edward's shoulder. "Interesting. I've been looking for some of those items."

"What do you mean?" Edward asked.

"Some of the wealthy clients from my private cases are missing jewelry," Baker said.

Who in their right mind would hire Baker? Edward stood, stepped into the man's space, and glared at him. "What the hell? You didn't think to tell me this when you knew I was looking for Lady Milton's missing items? We've had a theft ring right under our noses and have been looking for the same men."

Baker shrugged. "I would have said something, but you wouldn't tell me what was in *The People's Hue and Cry* when I asked, so now we are even."

Edward flexed his fists again. *Do not kill. Do not kill,* his conscience chanted.

"Gentlemen," Jenkins said. "Now is not the time."

Edward rubbed his brow. Jenkins was correct. When Newton's high-pitched tinkling lark's trill sounded the warning, the four of them had no choice but to work together like a well-oiled machine.

CHAPTER TWENTY-THREE

OUTSIDE, THE WIND and rain wreaked havoc on London. Inside, Franny and Zigzag cuddled together on the settee in front of the fire crackling in the hearth. Mrs. Benson sat across from them, her needle and thread dancing in and out of the fabric spread over her lap, and her amusing storytelling helping to pass the time.

Franny laughed until tears dripped down her cheeks as Mrs. Benson related a tale about a goat in a ballerina tutu who once upon a time munched on her slipper. While Franny was bent over holding her ribs in place as she chuckled, Mrs. Benson's story and needle never lost a beat.

Franny had finally contained the chortles rattling her body and was drying her eyes when Mrs. Benson held her project up, turning it for Franny to see.

"What do you think?" she asked.

" 'Tis lovely," Franny said, admiring the winding strands of ivy. "What will it be when it is finished?"

"A table covering for Edward." Mrs. Benson's eyes glimmered with affection. "Then I will make one for Richard Glasgow, the gentleman who lives on the second floor. Mr. Benson, God rest his soul, and I never had children of our own. But now I have been blessed with a lawman and a tutor who are like dear nephews to me. What more could a woman ask for?"

"I have no doubts they feel the same way about you," Franny said. Who wouldn't adore this woman, after all? "I've never had the patience to learn needlecraft."

"I'd be happy to teach you," Mrs. Benson offered.

Franny couldn't help but daydream… Days and early evenings spent at The Silk Knuckles with Papa, Josie, their students, and the women in The Ladies' Autonomy League. Late evenings spent in this drawing room with Zigzag, Mrs. Benson, Edward, a warm fire, and a cup of tea. Franny could learn to embroider and devour Edward's library. Once they crawled into bed, he could shower her with delicious kisses and teach her to make love. How sublime and dreamy. What more could a woman ask for?

Franny exhaled an embarrassingly dramatic sigh.

"Why so sad, my dear?" Mrs. Benson asked. "Embroidery isn't so horrible. Why, I rather enjoy it. It helps me relax so that I sleep better at night."

"Oh, it isn't that," Franny said.

"Then what is troubling you? Is it whatever Edward is investigating tonight?"

Everything about this kind woman suggested trust and compassion, making it easy for Franny to confide in her. "I am a pugilist, and someone tried to burn my gymnasium to the ground. My dear friend was injured in the fire, and days later, someone attacked my father. If Edward hadn't come along, they might have beaten my father to death."

"Oh, my." Mrs. Benson dropped the fabric onto her lap, her sympathetic gaze fully on Franny.

"There are a group of aristocratic ladies who meet at The Silk Knuckles Saloon. They call themselves 'The Ladies' Autonomy League'. Some of them are there to exercise. Some, to gain confidence in their ability to protect themselves. Others are tired of the subservient role women must play to stroke male hubris. One of the women's nephews is a duke, and he is petitioning Parliament with our concerns about coverture laws and female equality. But there are a few lords, one in particular, who will stop at nothing to keep this from happening."

"I see," Mrs. Benson said.

"The minister at the church next door preaches that we are fallen women. He is demanding we be closed down."

"What a rat," Mrs. Benson said.

"A self-righteous rat who does not care if the men in his parish are abusing their wives." And now for the *coup de grâce*. Franny gathered her courage. "Last year, I injured a woman I fought and since then have been afraid to compete."

Mrs. Benson's eyes widened in horror, but her voice remained solicitous. "Bare-knuckle fighting is quite dangerous."

" 'Tis," Franny said. "Yet, it is my life. It is all I know. I love the lifestyle and my gymnasium. But I have been filled with anxiety and unable to compete since that fight. I still train, but not at a competitive level, and I support my friend Josephine, who recently won the Duke's and Dame's Championship. But as for me…" Franny shook her head. There were no words strong enough to capture her nightmarish disgrace.

"I can see the pain in your eyes, my dear. But I don't think you have to compete to empower ladies to exercise, defend themselves, and stand up for female equality."

If only that were true. " 'Tis a long story, but I have no choice. I must fight in a month for a man with questionable associations." Franny huffed. "Which means I must defeat my demons, train hard, and abstain from biscuits, honey cakes, and bread if I don't want to humiliate myself." Franny harrumphed. "Not that the woman I am to fight is skilled. But still."

"Well, that is unfortunate," Mrs. Benson said. "Giving up sweets sounds rather depressing."

"Indeed." Franny did not even try to hide her pout.

"At least you and Edward have found each other," Mrs. Benson declared.

Franny blinked. "But we are not together, Mrs. Benson."

"Why not?" she asked. "You make a lovely couple. You are both unencumbered. He has fancied you for years, and I dare say, you have finally fallen for him."

"But I… I broke his nose the first time we met," Franny stammered. "And he is so…" so very handsome and virile. Meanwhile, she was a wild woman with scandalous hair and more attitude than common sense, some days.

Mrs. Benson chuckled. "Do you not see, Frances? Edward needs a spirited woman to match wits with. He is quite heroic and fights for justice for the common man. Only a woman doing the same by fighting for the common woman could make him happy."

But Franny and Josie had made a long-ago pact to never let a man sway them from their independence. Of course, Josie had met Nicolas. She was happy and in love and had not given up her independence. Could the same happen for Franny?

Egad. Franny was still upholding a pact that no longer existed.

"I can tell you are trying to talk yourself out of a relationship with Edward. But to what purpose, my dear? Stop fighting your feelings and give in to them. You will be much happier. Not to mention, then you can concentrate on the battles truly in front of you instead of this pointless one you invented with Edward."

As if agreeing with Mrs. Benson, Zigzag tempestuously meowed at Franny.

Franny leaned back and closed her eyes. Perhaps she *could* stop fighting her attraction to Edward and let him into her life. It would be much easier than all of these emotional ups and downs. Happiness cannonballed through her.

Yes, she could! And she would tell him she favored him with all of her heart just as soon as he returned.

A CRACK OF thunder awoke Franny. Once her eyes adjusted to the shadows, she perused the room. Mrs. Benson still sewed, the firelight dappling over her profile. The mantle clock indicated it was almost three in the morning.

Panicking, Franny sat up. "Has Edward returned?"

"Not yet, dear. I'm keeping watch. You go back to sleep."

There was no way Franny could sleep with shots of fear being injected into her veins. Now that she'd decided to tell Edward how she felt, something terrible had happened to him. She just knew it. She'd hexed him with the mere thought of a relationship.

Please, oh, please, Lord, let him be safe.

A streak of lightning lit up the room. Thunder boomed, and the large house shook. Zigzag yowled. Her hair spiked as if she were half porcupine, and she leapt from the couch.

Mrs. Benson held a hand to her heart. "My, that strike was close."

"Do you think something happened to Edward?" Franny asked. " 'Tis so late. Shouldn't he have returned?"

"Hush, my dear. Do not fret." Mrs. Benson tilted her head to listen.

Franny followed her lead, discovering a rustling sound coming from the entranceway.

"See, he is home. He is taking off his boots." Mrs. Benson gathered her sewing together and shoved it into her bag.

Holding her breath, Franny swung her feet onto the floor, then perched on the edge of the settee.

With the next clap of thunder, Edward stepped into the room. Lightning illuminated the water dripping from his hair. Wet clothing was glued to his body, and his feet were bare.

"Edward, it's about time. Where in the devil have you been?" Franny's exclamation sounded more like a reprimand than the relief she truly felt.

Mrs. Benson stood. "She was quite worried about you."

" 'Twas just a very long night," he said.

"We shall talk about it tomorrow." As Mrs. Benson passed by Edward, she patted his shoulder. "Would you like some warm water brought up?"

"Thank you, but not tonight," Edward said. "I would like to

dry off, then sleep."

"Good night. May you have sweet dreams." Mrs. Benson peered over her shoulder and sent Franny a knowing look that seemed to say, *remember, the two of you are perfect together.*

As soon as the door closed behind Mrs. Benson, Franny pounced on Edward, wrapping him in her arms. She did not even care that his wet shirt chilled her torso. "I was so worried about you." Hopefully, this was all she needed to confess for him to understand her feelings.

"I'm fine." He ran a soothing palm up and down her back. "We arrested Lance and his crew. They are in the local goal." He pulled back so that they stared into each other's eyes, his expression deadly serious. "Lance confessed to setting fire to your gymnasium and the attack on your father."

"That is splendid," she said. "So, why do you look so concerned?"

He shook his head, water droplets flying from the ends of his hair. "I don't know. Perhaps I'm just tired."

"And soaking wet," Franny said.

He chuckled. "That, too. And I am getting you wet."

She bit her lip and sent him a coquettish smile. "I will share your bed with you again. But only if you take off those wet clothes." Now he should know for sure where her heart stood.

His irises darkened, and he swallowed, his Adam's apple sliding, oh, so seductively. Unfortunately, he dropped his arms and stepped back. "I will sleep on the settee tonight."

The hell he would! She'd made up her mind, and her decisions were final. She would make love to Edward Robinson before the sun rose.

❦

CHAPTER TWENTY-FOUR

EDWARD STRUGGLED TO behave like a gentleman with Franny looking at him from beneath heavy-lidded eyes. As if his self-control wasn't fragile enough, she grabbed his hand and intertwined her warm fingers with his cold, practically numb digits.

"You will catch your death if we do not warm you right away," she said as she tugged him toward the fireplace.

Not only did he require a thaw, but he was much too tired, and truth be told, entirely too curious to fight her pull. Therefore, he simply stood before the flames, waiting and hoping for things he shouldn't want from this confounding woman.

Her fingers quivered as she guided his greatcoat off his shoulders. Hips swaying, she glided across the room and hung the dripping coat on its hook. When she faced him, he barely recognized her. Frances Valentine studied him through eyes clouded over with dark, sensual lust, and her nostrils flared as if she were sniffing out prey. Unless his faculties had stopped functioning due to exhaustion, he was being seduced, and Lord help him, there was no way in hell he was going to put up a fight.

Locking her gaze with his, she swished back to him. Once she was sinfully close, her shaking, albeit nimble, fingers unfastened his waistcoat. She circled behind him, sweeping the fabric heavy with rainwater from his body.

Coming back around to his front, she slowly untied his cravat, her breath tickling his chin the entire time. Her gaze dropped to his torso as she unbuttoned his shirt. Every time her fingers brushed over his skin, he hissed in a breath. The moment he shrugged off the soggy linen, the warmth from the fire became a balm to his chilled skin.

Completely absorbed in her task, she worked his trousers to his ankles. Her gaze raked over his physique as if he were a honey cake and she was starving. She gasped and her eyes widened.

He peered down to see what had shocked her. The outline of his swollen cock was visible beneath his drenched small clothes.

Clenching her bottom lip between her teeth, she gnawed on it as she undid his falls. The last of his clothing dropped to his feet. His unencumbered cock thrummed joyfully, as it strained in Franny's direction.

Moments ago, he'd been freezing. Now, sweat dripped down his forehead and beaded on his chest. Between the blazing fire and her heated gaze raking over his bare cock, he'd become a raging inferno.

She shivered.

"I'm sorry I got your dress wet," he said, his voice raspy. "Did I tell you how lovely you look in it?"

"No." She looked into his eyes and smiled. "And I believe someone recently recommended you tell me at least a dozen times a day."

There was no way he could feel jealousy over a flirtatious viscount, or any man for that matter, not with her worshipping gaze making him feel like a god.

"That dress brings out the green in your eyes. However, I should probably get you out of it because you will catch your death if we do not warm you right away," he said, repeating her taunt.

"We can't have that." She turned her back to him.

He took his time with the tiny buttons and watched with satisfaction as the fabric dropped to the floor. Her chemise and stays followed. As she slowly faced him, he stepped back to take in her perfection.

She was all creamy skin, bespeckled with freckles, feminine curves, and well-defined muscle. Although bountiful, her breasts were high and firm, and her pert, pink nipples pebbled without even being touched. Her waist tapered in and then flared out to luscious, full hips. His gaze lingered at the apex between her thighs where the fire-red curls he'd only recently and briefly admired protected her quim.

He had to swallow a mouthful of saliva to speak his truth. "My God, Franny. You are a work of art."

To lay her down in front of the flickering flames in the hearth or carry her to his bed?

His decision was taken from him because Franny grabbed his hand. Stepping over their clothing, she tugged him toward his bedroom. The perfect crescents of her arse cheeks taunted him all the way to the chamber.

BY THE TIME they reached his bedroom, Edward had used the last of his self-control. He spun Franny around and wrenched her backward, smashing her body tight against his. With their naked torsos pressed together, he slammed his lips over hers.

She tasted as delectable as he remembered, with a touch of apples and cinnamon mixing with her honeyed lips. At first, their tongues waltzed. As they fought for dominance, their graceful dance morphed into a sensual battle. Their lusty war ended with them panting as they clung to each other.

Starting at her cheek, Edward trailed kisses from one freckle to the next, down her neck, to her shoulders. Hell, he could play this game of Kiss a Million Freckles all night long.

"Oh, Edward," she breathlessly murmured.

Her whispered words tickled his ear, raising the hair on the back of his neck. His ache unbearable, he hoisted her off her feet, carried her to the bed, and tossed her onto the middle of the mattress. There would be no counterpane or pillows between them tonight.

Although he was certain she was a virgin, she hardly looked innocent with her wild hair spread out like a crown of fire, just as he'd fantasized, and her body undulating as she reached for him. He must not forget that behind his temptress's sensual show, she was inexperienced. Therefore, he absolutely, positively could not bind her hands, tie her to things, and ravage her, no matter how much he wanted to.

Lowering himself so that he lay beside her, he pulled her into his arms. "Franny, it might hurt your first time."

"I don't care," she said. "I don't mind pain. I am a pugilist, after all."

Bloody hell. She had no idea how tempting her words were, because there was no way she could know that his fantasies involving her were beyond taboo. He needed to tamp his libido, then prepare her by making love to every inch of her perfect body, starting with her mouth.

He brushed his lips over hers. *Gentle. Oh, so very gentle.* He was a feather, and she was stardust that he didn't want to disturb. He administered each kiss and every nibble strategically because her pleasure was all that mattered at the moment. Her lips quirked upward, her subtle smile an arrow lodging in his heart.

He could make a habit of this slow, steady worshipping as long as she was the recipient of his efforts. Nuzzling his nose into the crook of her neck, he inhaled her intoxicating feminine musk. Then, taking his time, he traced her collarbone with his index finger. As goose pimples rose, he warmed and soothed her aroused flesh with his lips.

The further down her body he explored, the more she writhed. Contented little sighs accompanied her wriggling as he stroked along the sides of her breasts. Once he was certain she was drunk with pleasure, his thumb and forefinger circled her nipples in turn, gently spiraling the way inward to her areolas.

Moaning, she arched her bosom toward his face.

"Do you like that, my beautiful Franny?"

"Oh, yes," she said, her voice breathy.

"Do you want more, darling?" he asked, determined to please her.

"Yes," she whispered.

Taking care not to use too much pressure, he pinched her nipple between his thumb and forefinger. She cradled his head and pulled his hair. Taking that as a sign to continue, he plucked her other nipple with a bit more fervor.

She hissed at the same time that a streak of lightning lit up the room.

Hoping to ease any sting she may experience, he leaned forward and blew on one of her pink buds *Lick. Suck. Bite,* her greedy nipples seemed to beg. With a feral growl, he was on top of her, his weight pinning her to the mattress as he suckled one delicious bud. His thumb and index finger drew lazy circles around the other.

"Oh, Edward, more," she said as she pressed on his cheek, to guide his mouth to her other breast.

As the relentless storm beat on the roof and windows, he hungrily devoured her pillowy mounds. Meanwhile, his hands traveled downward, exploring her firm obliques, then the curve of her hips. Shuddering, she emitted sensual sounds that spurred him on. Despite wanting to consume her cunny, he kept his pace leisurely, not moving on until he was certain she was ready.

Once her upper body was pliant, he settled his shoulders between her creamy inner thighs. Parting her wide, he exposed the flower petals of her throbbing womanhood. He blew into the coarse curls before easing a finger inside her.

Her muscles tensed, and she tried to sit up.

He pinned her hips to the mattress. "Franny, relax. Lie back. I am going to make you feel sublime."

She dropped her head onto the pillow, and he started over, gently drawing figure eights on her inner thighs. He wrapped one of her cunny curls around his finger. Then another, salivating as he played in her decadence, the sinful shade of red taunting him mercilessly.

"So beautiful, darling." He slid two fingers into her. This time, her velvety inner walls welcomed him. He circled, then gently pumped his fingers, until they were slick with her desire.

She peeked down at him. He met her gaze and held it as he took his first taste of her musky desire.

Her legs closed around his ears. Growling, he gripped her thighs and held them wide. "I will feast on this delicious cunny if it is the last thing I do, Frances Valentine."

"Bloody hell," she growled back. But his passionate Franny's unseemly utterance held no fight, only surrender. She was finally his.

He lowered his face to bury his nose and tongue in his seductress.

"Oh, Edward. That feels so lovely," she said between her gasps.

"And it tastes like heaven," he managed to confess between his licks and nibbles.

He experimented with his tongue, taking note of what response each swirl and lick produced. When he ran his nose along her slit, she arched her back. When he traced tiny circles around her pearl, she melted. When he nibbled on that nub, she whispered his name. And, when he thrust his tongue deep, she pushed on the back of his head until his face was buried in her secret place, giving him no choice but to violently fuck her pulsing cunny with his tongue.

Thunder crashed, raindrops bombarded the roof, her fingernails dug into his scalp, and her animal-like keening became more frenzied.

He worked his fingers inside her so that he could peel his lips from her pulsing flesh to demand, "Let go. Come for me."

Her hips lifted off the mattress. "Edward. Oh, Edward."

And then she obeyed. Her insides spasmed around his tongue

and fingers, and she screamed his name in the most reverent prayer he'd ever heard, a clap of thunder echoing her joyful cry.

THE STORM OUTSIDE had abated, as had the embodiment of a tempest in his bed, who currently rested her head on his chest.

"Thank you," the formerly feral Franny sweetly said.

Feeling much like Shakespeare's Petruchio, Edward hid his grin in her hair. "No. Thank you."

She playfully slapped his shoulder. "I meant thank you for discovering who hurt Harry and my father."

"How disappointing. I thought you were referencing my skillful bed sport technique." Although he chuckled, something niggled at the edges of his mind.

"Tell me what is bothering you," she said, as if reading his mind.

He'd much rather slide his cock into her cunny, although having her sated and in his arms was delightful, too.

"We delivered Lance and his bootlickers to the gaol without incident. Then we returned the stolen jewelry to Bow Street where we logged it in. I compared what we found to the list with which Mr. Wagner provided us. His memory was quite accurate." How could he articulate what was worrying him when he had no proof, only a hunch?

Franny yawned. "Why did Lancelot, or I should say *Lance*, target The Silk Knuckles Saloon?"

Lance's confession replayed in Edward's memory. *"Yes, I set fire to that Silk Knuckles Gymnasium. Yes, I attacked the old boxing coach. Yes, I did it all, and Merlin and the other Knights helped me. Right, Merlin?"*

Merlin, whose real name was Benjamin Kline, winced. "Yes, sir," he said.

"Why?" Edward asked.

"'Tis fun to catch things on fire," Lance said with a maniacal

chuckle.

"Insanity doesn't always need a reason," the magistrate said.

Perhaps, but Lance behaved more like a spoiled, mischievous hellion who knew exactly what he was doing. Would the courts punish an earl's son? Probably not, since most of the time, men of means got away with their crimes.

Edward needed to stop fretting. A good tup would cure his woes. And what better time than now since his cock was instantly hard? Preparing for seduction, he pushed onto his elbows and looked down at Franny.

Her eye lids were closed and her fire-colored crown looked like a sleeping angel's halo.

Edward flopped onto his back and folded his arms behind his head. "Bloody hell," he mumbled to the ceiling. After accepting his lot, he begrudgingly got out of bed and snuffed the candles.

CHAPTER TWENTY-FIVE

FRANNY HAD SO much to look forward to that she awoke enthusiastic to tackle her day. Now that their enemy was in custody, they could reopen the gymnasium. If she and Josie worked hard and got the word out, maybe they could open tonight. Surely, they would be ready because together, they could accomplish anything they set their minds to.

Giddiness burbled through Franny. Even her outlook on competing had improved, so after she visited Papa and Harry, she'd skip rope, perform calisthenics, and spar. As if all of this wasn't exciting enough, she was falling for a man who made her heart flutter and her toes curl. He also knew how to make her body soar. Waking up beside him was so comforting that she might like to sleep with him every night. Mrs. Benson had been correct. Now that Franny had rid herself of arbitrary relationship restrictions, her heart felt lighter.

She wriggled her arse into the mattress and stretched long. Once her blood vigorously pumped to her extremities, she opened her eyes and rolled toward Edward.

To her surprise, he was wide awake. His thick lashes fluttered, and he grinned. "Good morning."

Her heart lurched. He was so beautiful, even with the bruise marring his face, and messy hair and dark scruff overtaking his chin and cheeks. His muscular shoulders and well-formed biceps peeked out from above the blankets, reminding her again how very male he was. Not that she ever forgot.

Franny scraped her nails through his morning growth. "I favor you, Edward Robinson." She also quite liked the abrasive texture of his facial hair on her fingertips.

His grin widened. "And I am a fool for you, Frances Valentine. I have been since your fist first met my face."

Although he'd tried to make her laugh, she did not find humor in her long-ago indiscretion. She ran her index finger over the disfigured bridge of his nose. "I'm sorry. I truly am."

"I'm not." Grinning, he lifted his chin and angled his head to show off his profile. "I think it makes me look ruggedly dashing." When he faced her, his smirk had been replaced by firm-lipped sincerity. "It is a piece of you I carried with me these many years."

This man was too good to be true. She gently nuzzled his nose before bestowing tiny kisses along its length. She'd intended for her touch to be gentle and loving, but it seemed Edward was easily seduced.

With a feral growl, he pounced and straddled her. His hard cock pressed into her hip as he leaned forward and licked her collarbone.

Tendrils of pleasure twined up her spine.

"You fell asleep before I was finished with you," he rasped in her ear.

It was hardly her fault. She had wanted to spend hours exploring each other's bodies but had fallen asleep because he turned her brain and body into mush.

"I am here and awake right now," she said with a playful eyebrow raise.

His deep growl vibrated her cheek and sent a bolt of awareness to her core.

Tucking his face into the hollow of her shoulder, he caressed a trail over her obliques, leaving heated tingling in its wake. He lifted his hips slightly, running his finger along her vaginal lips.

She melted into the mattress.

He parted her folds, pressing a finger inside of her. She widened her thighs, inviting him deeper. His finger drew heavenly little circles as her cunny cried tears of joy that slicked her passage. She closed her eyes and succumbed to the warm sensation overtaking her.

"Franny," he said.

She opened her eyes.

He looked down at her, his gaze wild with lust. "I've never wanted a woman more than I want you. I'm so overwhelmed with desire for you that it steals my reason."

Her belly twirled about, and she wasn't sure it landed back in its proper place. It seemed too high.

Her core caught fire. She reached to trace the edges of his sensuous mouth with her index finger.

He propped himself on his elbows and hovered above her. "Do you want me?"

Want him? Did he mean his heart? Or was he talking about his cock in her cunny?

"I want everything," she said as she shoved her pelvis against him. To her disappointment, her efforts went unrewarded because her insides still ached, as his rocklike cock poked her belly.

"Everything," he whispered as if the word were a prayer. He moved to line his tip up with her entrance.

She reached between them and, for the first time, touched his steely strength wrapped in soft skin.

He hissed, slid insider her, and then held completely still. The painful pinch quickly morphed into a lightning bolt of pleasure. It was as if her insides were flower petals and he was sunlight as she opened and welcomed him. As they stared into each other's eyes, she ran her hands over the solid contours of his back, a back so strong that, like Atlas, he could carry the heavens upon his shoulders.

"Can you go deeper?" she asked.

He responded with a throaty chuckle as he slid halfway out

and pushed back in. She cried out with rhapsodic pleasure.

"Did I hurt you?" he asked.

"Hell, no," she said.

His pupils grew unfocused as if he were possessed, and a devilish grin spread across his face. He slid halfway out and then thrust, hard.

As deliciously full as she felt, she needed more. "Yes. Please. Deeper," she begged.

Over and over again, he pounded into her, plunging deeper each time. She wrapped her legs around his waist and met his thrusts with equal force.

"So tight and wet," he growled between clenched teeth.

"So hard," she panted back.

To her disappointment, he halted his unrelenting barrage to lower his body weight onto her.

"No!" If he stopped, she'd die from want.

Embedded deep, he rocked his hips, rubbing his pelvis and the lower part of his cock against her clitoris.

"Oh, yes," she roared as her eyeballs rolled back in her head.

"Christ, Franny." Edward slammed into her.

With no distinguishable pattern, back and forth he went. One minute he rocked against her, tickling her pearl in a sweet taunt, the next he was slamming into her, the friction threatening to send her over some intangible ledge.

And then he stopped moving altogether. Sweat coated his chest and dripped from his forehead. She didn't have the patience to wait for whatever sensual trick he had up his sleeve, so she bucked her hips upward, chasing her pleasure.

To her delight, he met her with a thrust that sent the headboard smashing into the wall. Their hip bones repeatedly crashed together, and the pounding against the wall grew louder. He was embedding himself so deeply, it was as if his entire body was inside her. Up, up, up, her pleasure built and whirled.

His jaw tensed, and the veins in his neck protruded. She couldn't help herself; she licked at the purple lines, tasting his salty essence.

"Come with me," he said. He reached between them and pressed on her pearl while at the same time laving a sensitive nipple.

"Oh, Edward," she cried.

"Fuck, Franny!" His cock twitched, his body quaked, and he pulled out. His warm seed splattered on her belly.

She only felt his loss for a second. He slid a finger inside her and circled her pearl. A wave of euphoria washed over her, burning her cheeks. Then, her heart beat in her clitoris. Her spine tingled, her toes curled, and her inner walls spasmed. With one final shudder, she exploded from her body into a sea of pleasure.

She returned to her body feeling as if she were shimmering and shining like a glowworm on a hot summer night. He rolled off of her and pulled her back to his chest.

"My darling, Franny," he whispered into her hair.

If she could have spoken, she'd have told him he was *her darling, Edward*. But since she couldn't yet form words, she remained silently cocooned against him. She steadied her breath as her heart, body, and soul celebrated the dizzying sensation that was Edward Robinson.

CHAPTER TWENTY-SIX

A BOUT THIRTY MINUTES earlier, a gloriously naked Franny had come apart beneath Edward. And now, here she was, sitting at his table, wearing a blue day dress, her eyes sparkling, her hair in a loose plait, and scooping a bite of porridge into her mouth. She swallowed and then smiled at him.

"Even Mrs. Benson's porridge and boiled eggs are delicious," Franny said. "Would you believe that last night she asked me what I eat when I am training, and then she actually prepared it? Even after she was up all night looking out for me." She sighed. "She is so wonderful."

Edward's instincts were always correct. The second he introduced Mrs. Benson and Franny, their mutual affection was apparent, and their budding friendship warmed his heart.

"She has become one of my dearest companions," he said. "I am thankful she took me in when I moved here."

"Where did you move here from?" Franny asked. Her gaze intently on him, she scraped the last of the porridge from her bowl.

For the first time in his six-and-twenty years, Edward wanted to share everything about himself with a woman. He pushed his empty dishes to the center of the table, leaned back in his chair, and settled into storytelling mode. "I was raised outside of Nottingham. My father owned a lace factory."

"A lace factory," Franny said. "How fascinating."

Not particularly, but he wanted her to know even the most mundane things about him. He also desired to know every single minute detail about her.

"I'm the second of four sons," Edward said. "My eldest brother will eventually take over the factory. To my father's disappointment, I never had an interest in the family business. As far back as I can remember, I'd wanted to live in London. I wavered between making my fortune as a prizefighter or living a life of service as a lawman."

"Did I destroy your dreams?" Franny asked.

"Not at all," Edward said. "You helped me discover that my correct path was as a lawman, not a pugilist, and of that I am glad. I have no regrets."

Biting her lip and not looking at all convinced, Franny nodded.

"I had a happy childhood," he continued. "We had a beautiful home, a doting mother, a few servants, and when we weren't helping my father, my brothers and I ran about the countryside. The four of us wrestled and boxed every day. I almost always won, which made me think I was better than I was."

"You were prideful back then," Franny agreed. "But still, I'm ashamed of my behavior."

Edward flicked a dismissive wrist. "You will get no argument from me about my arrogance. I needed to be knocked down a few pegs. Even now, I fight my hubris. In the long run, you made me a better man."

"I suspect you were always a good man beneath that swagger." Her grin was all white teeth and mischief.

Supercilious with a big heart, he supposed. "A few days after moving to London, I was cornered in an alley by a pickpocket. He was taller and broader than me, but I knocked him out with one punch." Edward feigned a jab. Then, pretending to be his unconscious assailant, he tilted his head, closed his eyes, and stuck out his tongue.

His thespian skills must have been atrocious because Franny did not laugh. He opened his eyes and was met with the biggest frown he'd ever had the displeasure of seeing.

"What a terrible welcome to our city. And then you met me, and I behaved abominably," she said.

"And yet I stayed. Truthfully, I love London." Hopefully, his assurance assuaged her guilt.

"Do you ever think about climbing back into the ring?" Franny asked.

"Sometimes. But only to exercise. I have no desire to compete. How about you, Franny? What was your childhood like?"

Her eyes glazed over with a faraway, dreamy look. "Our home was always full of Papa's friends and students. My mother was a governess before she married Papa, and my grandfather disowned her when she married. I don't think she cared because I remember her smiling all of the time. She taught me to read and write. Life was quite jolly until about my ninth birthday. My mother became ill and died soon after." Unshed tears glistened in Franny's eyes. "Papa and I were so sad. Instead of dealing with our heartache, we threw ourselves into boxing. And then one day, Papa brought Josie home. She'd been living on the streets. No parents. No place to live. Nothing to eat. I disliked her at first because I thought she was a smelly boy. But I quickly came to love her like a sister. She brought happiness and laughter to our house again. The three of us worked at the St Giles Gymnasium, and eventually, I begged Papa to open a gymnasium in a safer part of town so that we could attract more female students. Josie fell in love with and married an aristocrat. And here we are today with influential ladies meeting in our upstairs saloon. Josie is a champion. Papa is the best coach in London. And I…" She sighed. "Well, I work hard at bookkeeping and instructing, but I have failed at being a champion. However, I will fight my demons, keep my promise, and climb back into the ring."

Guilt twisted Edward's insides. She was in this predicament because she had saved his life. Of course, his life wouldn't have been in danger if it weren't for her in the first place. Then again, he wouldn't have found his jewelry thief if it wasn't for her dragging him to The Round Table. Hell, who was he fooling? He and Franny were an explosive fervor. Two peas in a pod. Destined to make good trouble together.

"I think you are quite resilient and brave." Edward shrugged. "I, on the other hand, was a cowardly chicken. I had one pint-sized woman punch me in the nose, and I have not boxed since."

Franny brought her hands to her mouth. "Edward, are we both afraid to step into the ring?"

"I don't honestly know."

"How interesting." She stared into the corner.

"What are you thinking, Frances Valentine?"

"Shall we spar together?"

"In the ring?" he asked.

"Of course."

Edward grinned. "I'd prefer to spar between the sheets. But if you insist."

"I insist." She fluttered her lashes. "I shall take it easy on you."

"In the ring or in bed?" he asked. "Because I'd prefer you rough me up between the sheets."

"Easy in the ring. Hard between the sheets." A second after she uttered her scandalous taunt, her cheeks turned scarlet.

Hopefully, the look he sent her was smoldering enough to drench her sweet cunny, because his cock was alive and interested.

"This time, I will not underestimate your ability, and I will take you seriously. Which means I may actually get in a few solid jabs before you knock me out." He was in superior enough physical shape that he suspected he could elude her. And as strong as her punches were, he doubted she could knock a man his size out. But underestimating her five years ago had been a massive miscalculation.

His cock twitched and his balls ached. Hell, he should grab her and drag her back into his bedroom right this very minute.

She feigned a competitive growl as her eyes twinkled. "Challenge accepted. Prepare to lose to a woman." She wriggled in her seat. "I cannot believe it, but I am rather excited to train today."

So much for dragging her back to bed right now because he would not interfere with her goals, but later on, after she'd trained, and when they crawled beneath his blankets, all bets were off.

Unfortunately, having her stay with him no longer seemed to be a safety necessity. He hated to ask, but he needed to know her intentions. "I suppose you will want to go home now that you are safe?" Even as he said this, his intuition troubled him. Lawman did occasionally lock up the wrong men.

Stop being a fool. Lance confessed. You don't want Franny to go home because you want her to warm your bed.

Sighing, she looked at the floor. "I suppose so."

Her voice sounded so meek. Did this mean she didn't want to go? Dare he tell her how much he enjoyed having her stay with him? *No, you fool! What is the point? She can't continue staying with you. You will destroy her reputation.* Not to mention, Coach had entrusted him with his daughter, and he'd taken advantage of that trust. But he could take her to see her father, and he could help her get the gymnasium ready.

"As luck has it, I have the day to myself," he said.

"I cannot imagine you ever taking a day off work to rest."

"I used to work seven days a week, and I even worked evenings, arresting pickpockets on Drury Lane."

"I'm not surprised. You are industrious, and since you aren't working today, you can train with me," she said with an emphatic chin bob. "We can train after we prepare the gym to reopen. Honestly, I don't think we have to do a lot. Just clean up the supplies still on the floor, clear out the smoke, and get the word out. Young Sky and Nicolas can help with that."

And once they had finished with all of her tasks, he could spend the rest of the day between her silky thighs. He cleared his prurient thoughts with a full-body shake.

"I would like to go to Greenpark House first," she said. "I need to visit Papa and Harry. I also want to talk to Josie and Papa about opening the studio back up. They will be thrilled to hear that our enemy is in custody."

"I'd assumed we would start our day at the Davenports," he said.

She bent over and looked under the table. "Goodbye, Zigzag."

"Shall we be on our way?" he asked.

Smiling, she stood. "I'm ready."

Thank heavens, because the sooner they visited Greenpark House, the sooner they could take care of the gymnasium. And the sooner the gymnasium was ready, the sooner they could train. And the sooner they trained, the sooner they could rut like animals. To hell with being entrusted with her reputation. They were way past that. Once he chased her around the ring, or she chased him, both sounded erotic as hell, he would sink himself deep inside this woman who owned his heart, body, and soul.

CHAPTER TWENTY-SEVEN

PERHAPS IT WAS customary to feel wonderful for a long while after making love, because everything about Franny's morning brought her joy.

When she arrived at Greenpark House, Papa was sitting in the drawing room, his cheeks a healthy hue, drinking coffee with the Davenports. Despite Lady Davenport's protests, Papa insisted he was ready to return to his normal activities. A compromise was settled upon; Papa would stay one more night and then go home tomorrow.

Even though Harry had greatly improved over the past twenty-four hours, he had not recovered enough to leave the Davenports. When Franny entered his room, he was smiling at Grace, the chambermaid who sat beside his bed, coquettishly fluttering her lashes. Once he was strong enough to walk, Franny would suggest he invite the infatuated girl to promenade in the park with him.

Just as Franny and Edward prepared to leave, Josie and Nicolas entered the foyer. The perfect timing gave the four of them a chance to talk. Luckily, Josie agreed that it was time to reopen The Silk Knuckles. She and Nicolas had already tidied up and aired out the gymnasium, so there was little for Franny and Edward to do, which meant they could spend the afternoon exercising. Nicolas and Josie agreed to contact young Sky

Johnston to ask him to get the word out to their regulars. Once they left Greenpark House, the newlyweds were going home to ensure that Nicolas's sister, Bridget, hadn't ensconced herself in trouble during their absence. Franny would wager that the bluestocking had not only found trouble but had also instigated it.

In the evening, Josie was to meet Franny at The Silk Knuckles, where hopefully, they would have a gymnasium full of eager students and athletes.

It was almost noon when, feeling positively giddy, Franny pushed the heavy door of her gymnasium open and breathed in the smoke-free air. Edward followed her into the center of the room.

She faced him, looked him over from head to toe, and then panicked. She had no idea how a woman was to act after making love to a man. Could she kiss him anytime she wanted? Should she wait for him to kiss her? What kind of woman wanted to charge across a room, knock a man on his arse, and have her way with him? Apparently, her, for one, hopeless, lustful, sod that she'd become.

Taking in a large breath and exhaling slowly, she centered herself. She absolutely, positively could not make love to Edward in the middle of her gymnasium. Firstly, it was indecent, and anyone might come upon them. Secondly, even though Ruth the Jewel was a charlatan, Franny desperately needed to prepare for their fight.

"Shall we start our training?" Edward asked.

Yes. Right away. Before she did something stupid, like untie his cravat and sniff it.

What in the dickens was wrong with her? Only an insane woman sniffed men's cravats. Although Edward's probably smelled like fresh cedar and tempting man.

"First, we shall do calisthenics," she said, her voice annoyingly squeaky. "One hundred deep knee bends, fifty lunges, fifty squats, and fifty push-ups."

Edward sent her one of his cunny dampening grins. Damn

the man to hell. "Shall we see who finishes first?" he asked.

A contest? How exciting. "Be prepared to lose, Robinson. I will calisthenics your arse off."

Edward chuckled. "Not if I calisthenic your arse off first."

It seemed she found competing with a man to be an aphrodisiac, because her nipples tingled.

Enough is enough, Frances Valentine, she scolded herself. *If you don't concentrate and get yourself mill-ready, Ruth will humiliate you.* Besides, if she didn't pull herself together, Edward would think her wanton and depraved and want nothing to do with her, unless he found depravity an attractive quality in a woman. "Ugh," she mumbled under her breath.

A master contortionist, Franny turned her back to him and undid her buttons. She tied her sleeves around her waist, anchoring her dress in place. By the time she faced Edward, he'd removed his cravat, waistcoat, and boots. With his shirt untucked, he resembled a comely privateer.

Averting her eyes from his tempting form, she hopped up and down, windmilling her arms. From her peripheral, she could tell that Edward imitated her. Every few moves, he edged closer to her.

Once her muscles were loose and pliant, she stepped away from him, claiming her own space. Without meeting his gaze, she asked, "Are you ready?"

"Ready, willing, and able," he said in a deep baritone.

Wait a dashed minute. She was trying to behave, while the bloody fool was trying to drive her wild with desire. Well, she would not take his bait. With a full body shake, she steeled herself against his sensual energy. Once she'd made up her mind, nothing and no one, not even a man as tempting as sin, would veer her off course.

"One hundred deep knee bends, fifty alternating lunges, fifty squats, and fifty push-ups," she repeated.

"I've got it," he said. "Let's go."

She settled her feet hip distance apart and squared her shoulders. "Ready? Begin!"

And they were off, counting in unison.

Franny finished her knee bends and called out, "Fifty, at the same time as Edward. She thrust her left leg forward in a deep lunge. Edward mimicked her movement.

Like a galloping herd of horses, their feet hit the ground, creating a steady beat. "…Five. Six. Seven. Eight…" they counted in perfect synch as they lunged.

Since Franny was going as fast as she could, there was nothing she could do to increase her advantage. But she simply couldn't lose. She was the professional athlete, after all.

"Fifty," they called at the exact same time.

With her strong as oak thighs, squats were Franny's favorite exercise, so now was her time to move out ahead of him. She lowered her body weight into her feet and then drove up through her heels. "One. Two. Three. Four…" she said as she panted. At this point, it took effort to breathe in and out while counting out loud.

How unfair that Edward kept pace with her. She performed this routine at least once, sometimes two or three times a day. She should be winning.

Her breathing became more labored and sweat dripped down her forehead. As soon as she completed her last squat, she dropped onto her belly and balanced on her palms and toes.

Edward landed on the floor at the same time as her. His face inches from hers, his forehead coated in sweat, he smiled.

She growled and lowered her body until her chest almost touched the ground. Keeping her elbows at a forty-five-degree angle, she pushed away from the floor. "One," she called out at the same time as Edward. Thereupon, she made the unfortunate error of meeting Edward's gaze.

The fool lifted a palm high and did a one-armed push-up. "Two." He smirked.

Franny hissed out, "Two."

Once they reached twenty-five, Edward clapped between his

push-ups. Lord help his arrogant arse when they sparred, because she would unleash the fury of a thousand soldiers on him.

"Fifty," they both called as they dropped onto their bellies. The floor cooled Franny's heated cheek.

"Tie!" Edward stood and extended his hand.

Ignoring his offer, she climbed onto her feet, rested her hands on her hips, and glared at the far wall.

"What's next?" he asked.

After she caught her breath, she chuckled. Now that she'd accepted her fate, she found it titillating that he'd kept up with her. Actually, he'd bested her, since he had performed fancy push-ups worthy of a circus routine. "Rope skipping," she said.

"How long are we skipping for?" he asked.

"How about another contest? The first person to make two hundred successful jumps wins." There was no way he would beat her at this. She was the unofficial rope skipping champion of the gymnasium. No one could outskip her. Not even Josie or the male champions Papa coached.

"Prize for the winner?" he asked.

She tapped her finger to her cheek as she pondered what she truly wanted the most in the world. She couldn't ask for him to use his mouth on her cunny again, could she? Her cheeks heated until she thought she might incinerate from a combination of want and embarrassment.

She shrugged. "Glory."

He wrinkled his nose. "Glory?"

"Take it or leave it," she said with a feigned nonchalant shrug.

"Glory." He held out his hand to shake on their deal.

If she touched him, she would melt all over the gymnasium floor, so she bypassed his hand and approached the equipment wall. She easily found her favorite rope.

Edward took his time finding the center of a few ropes, stepping onto them, and measuring where they came to on his body. "Perfect," he said at last.

"Do you see how the end is marked with a blue dot?" Franny

pointed at it. "That is how you know which one is the proper length for you in the future."

"Does that mean I will be invited back?" He winked.

Again, she shrugged. "I suppose that depends on how much you annoy me today." She pushed past him and situated herself in the center of the room. To her surprise, Edward did not follow her.

She faced him to see what had held him up. He stood staring at the rope in his hand, his eyes wide in what looked like horror. He looked up, met her gaze, and even from this distance, she was certain his cheeks turned scarlet.

She didn't take him as a sentimental ninny who'd be hurt by a joke. Still, she apologized. "Of course, you will be invited back. I was teasing."

He blinked half a dozen times.

"What's wrong?" she asked. "Don't you know how to skip rope?

"Oh, I know how to skip rope," he said, his voice so raw and raspy, it landed in her cunny.

"Then, what is the problem? Are you afraid I will beat you?" she taunted.

"That's not what I am afraid of." His throaty voice was both unsettling and arousing. He wrapped the rope around his hands, and then his shoulders slumped forward. His gaze scorching, he stalked toward her. He halted in front of her, looking shockingly predatory.

Her heart beat against her ribcage. Both afraid and aroused, she swallowed.

His lids hung heavy over his eyes. "Are you ready?" he asked.

To be whipped? To be chased down and tied up? To jump over a rope two hundred times?

Surely, he meant the latter. "Yes," she squeaked out, her heart pounding. "May the best skipper win."

CHAPTER TWENTY-EIGHT

S KIPPING WITH A tent in his trousers was no easy task. Blasted miserable, if truth be told. Since his concentration was rubbish, the rope scraped the top of Edward's bare foot. He halted to mumble a string of blasphemies, then picked up where he left off.

"Thirty-one, thirty-two, thirty—" The rope slapped his ankle. This time he sucked up the sting because he deserved any suffering this rope inflicted. Flogging was a fitting punishment for a demented devil who fantasized about tying up women. Well, just one woman. But still…

"Fifty-one, fifty-two…" Franny counted as her rope circled her. Her unbound bosom bounced with each jump.

Hours ago, he'd been devouring her delicious nipples, and now if he meant to display decorum, they were off-limits. Her gymnasium was not a boudoir. More importantly, her determina-tion deserved respect. She must overcome her demons so she could confidently face her opponent in the ring. She needed to concentrate. She did not need some lecherous rat tying her up so that he could ravish her.

He brought the rope around behind him, resumed his count, and watched Franny. Her eyes glimmered like priceless emeralds, and her cheeks glistened with sweat. At least he no longer gawked at her breasts.

"One hundred seventy-five," Franny said as her toe caught on her rope, and she tripped over it. "Bloody bollocks," she grumbled.

She quickly resumed her rhythm, eventually calling, "Two hundred," to Edward's, "One hundred and eighty-four."

"I won. I won," she chanted as she twirled about.

Usually, his competitive nature did not take kindly to losing, and yet, he could not begrudge her a joyful victory. It wasn't her fault he was too randy to control his coordination. *Although you might have won if you weren't so bloody goatish,* he berated himself.

He dropped his rope where he stood. "Congratulations. What's next?" He expected her to say they would hit the sandbags or lift the heavy dumbbells arranged on the corner rack.

"Shall we spar?" she asked.

He couldn't even skip rope without taboo fantasies, so how in the devil was he to be an arms' distance or less from her? "Yes," he said against his better judgment.

Franny popped onto her toes and clapped.

Since he could not extend his arm to punch while wearing a shirt, he undid the buttons and tossed it onto the floor. Arrogant fool that he was, he took advantage of his disrobing and flexed his pectoral muscles.

Showing off had the desired effect; Franny's gaze slid over his torso, and she swallowed. He reached his arms high and stretched, enjoying the way she unconsciously licked her lips. It seemed his newly deflowered virgin was having as much trouble controlling her lust as he was.

Chuckling, he climbed into the ring. She avoided his gaze as she slid between the ropes. Hoping she was now watching, he strutted to the center of the ring and faced her.

"We will pull the power from our punches," she said.

He *should* pull the power from *his* punches. "You can punch me as hard as you want."

She rolled her eyes. "Have you looked in the mirror today?"

"Fine," he said. "We will both pull the power from our

punches."

She dropped into her stance and lifted her fists. One protected her chin, and the other was poised to strike. His heart thumping erratically, he settled into his stance.

"Ding, ding," she said.

His right foot slid backward as he moved out of her reach. Her front foot slid forward as she closed the gap. In and out they moved, as he played defense, doing everything he could to stay away from her jab.

Her footwork was fast, so he huffed and puffed after only a few minutes.

Her gaze intently locked on his, she lunged and jabbed his chest three times before he had the wherewithal to block her punches and back away.

She circled him and attacked again. He did nothing to evade the barrage because every punch set his tingling nerves on fire with a sinful burning so euphoric that he'd sell his soul to remain in the flames.

She stepped back. "Bloody bullocks, Edward. Have you forgotten everything?"

He inhaled, trying to cage the beast within him before it charged and took her to the ground.

Scowling, she reached out and flicked his cheek. "Wake up."

His moan accompanied the sting as pleasure rolled over him.

Her eyes widened, and then, giggling, she pushed on his shoulder.

He growled.

She flicked his nose and then quickly backed away. "Come on." She curled her fingers, calling him forward.

It seemed their game had changed, and he no longer knew the rules. Without rules, he was no better than an animal. "Franny, don't," he said, his words both a plea and a warning.

She stuck out her tongue.

Before he had a chance to prepare, she charged toward him and grabbed him around the waist. Assuming she meant to kiss him, he didn't fight her. Instead, she reached up and ruffled his hair. She dashed to the other side of the ring so quickly that by the time he reached for her, she was already gone.

Her eyes gleaming with mischief, she hopped from one foot to the other. "Come on, Edward. Afraid that a chit will beat you up again?" Tucking her hands in her armpits, she flapped her elbows. "Bock. Bock."

"You are playing with fire, Frances Valentine. You should be tremendously afraid of what I will do to you if I get my hands on your body. I'm giving you fair warning. I am not myself today."

Her chicken wings dropped to her side. "Only if you catch me, Edward Robinson," she said, her voice a sensual invitation.

He cannonballed across the ring and grabbed her. The slippery temptress broke from his grasp and slid between the ropes. Snarling like a bull, he leapt from the ring and tracked her across the gymnasium, his aching cock and balls weighing him down.

Franny dodged exercise equipment to hide behind one of the sandbags. Silly indeed, since he could see her slippered feet and hear her muffled laughs.

"You won't be giggling when I catch you," he called. She'd be screaming his name as he tupped her to death. He pushed the sandbag to the side.

She flicked him on the nose, then dashed to his clothing and picked up his cravat. Taunting him like a matador goading a bull, she circled it overhead.

He plowed toward her but halted to pick up the extra-long rope with the blue dot. She bit her lip as she considered her next move. Seconds later, her eyes lit up and she grinned. Stampeding toward him, she slapped him with his cravat, then whizzed right past.

Whirling, he faced her.

"What do you plan to do with that rope?" she asked. Her chest heaved with her panting, her pebbled nipples poked through her chemise, and her eyes glazed over with ecstasy.

"Tie you up and fuck you senseless," he said.

Closing her eyes, she brought his cravat to her nose and inhaled.

His cock banged on his falls, begging to be set free.

She opened her eyes and fluttered her lashes. "Only if you catch me."

"Oh, make no mistake. I will catch you." Rope in hand, he stalked to her.

They stood nose to nose, their heavy breaths mingling. Her muscles tensed, and he knew she would flee the second he reached for her. He'd also guessed her little secret; she wanted to prolong the chase. Unfortunately, he was ready for the capture. And then, she flicked his nose for a third time. His nose had suffered one too many indignities at the hands of this woman.

He reacted with lightning-fast reflexes, grabbing her around the waist.

Franny squealed as he tossed her over his shoulder. With the rope looped around his wrist and hanging to the ground, he carried her toward her office.

"Put me down." She slapped his arse half-heartedly.

"The hell I will. I'm claiming my prize, darling."

"But I won," she said, in her squeaky, incredulous voice. "Glory," she whispered.

He kicked her office door open.

EDWARD DEPOSITED FRANNY into her office chair, where he loomed over her, giving her his best I-am-man-you-are-woman glare.

"Your nostrils are flaring," she said.

"Your nipples are reaching for me," he retorted.

She peered down at her decolletage and frowned. "Stupid tingly nipples."

"Tingly." He smirked.

She lifted her chin indignantly. "Are you going to tie me up or stare at me all afternoon?"

"I am in charge right now." Even as he made his declaration, he knew how foolish he sounded. A man in charge would not have to announce it. The only reason he hadn't overpowered her was because he didn't want to hurt her. However, if she was going to be incorrigible, he should tie her up and walk away. It would serve her right if she had to rub an aching, damp cunny on the chair.

"Yes, you are in charge," she said.

Damnations. She was humoring him because, even tied up, she would always be in control. Perhaps he was insane, but he didn't want that to change outside this office. He adored the stubborn Franny. It was just right now, for a half hour or so, that he wanted her submissive, but only so she let him gift her with untold pleasure. That, and he needed to rid himself of his damnable fantasies so they could concentrate on her mill.

Walking away with a hard as stone cock would only serve to torment him, so he went to work, securing her to the chair, wrapping the rope around her a few times. She was so passive that he naively let down his guard. Unfortunately, she wrenched her arm free and tickled him under the chin.

He growled.

His precious brat licked his cheek.

He snarled.

She squirmed, trying to pull her other arm free from the binding.

"Hold still, darling," he growled in her ear.

Gods above, the wriggling, giggling Frances Valentine went as still as a statue.

Grasping her hand, he shoved her arm beneath the rope. He circled behind the chair and tied the final knot. Coming around in front of her, he stepped back to take in his erotic artwork.

Franny's locks had come loose from her plait and hung about her shoulders like fire. Her cheeks were deliciously flushed as if she'd already been ravaged. The bindings lifted her breasts so high that the full mounds threatened to spill out over her chemise. Somewhere along the way, she'd lost a slipper, but she still clutched his cravat in her hand.

Grinning like a cocksure fool, he grabbed his cravat.

"What are you doing?" Franny asked, her voice breathy with desire.

He placed it over her eyes.

Her breath hitched.

Taking his time, he secured it behind her head. Bending close, he whispered, "Can you see, darling?"

She let out her breath. "No."

"Do you want me to continue?" he asked.

"Please." And then Frances Valentine, his feral redhead, moaned her submission.

CHAPTER TWENTY-NINE

GOOSEFLESH COVERED FRANNY from the top of her head to the tips of her toes—one wearing a slipper, the other bare. Heat incinerated her body, and every time Edward whispered in her ear, she ached with need.

A second ago, he'd stood on her right side, gently combing his fingers through her hair. Now he was on her left, doing who knew what, because she couldn't see him. However, she suspected he was thinking up ways to torture her for being difficult. Oh, she deserved his wrath, all right. She'd been an unholy imp. But she couldn't help herself. Being chased exhilarated her, and Edward's growl was the sexiest thing she'd ever heard. Lord protect him, because she'd do almost anything to garner that sensual sound. If it weren't so sinful to pray for such things, she would implore God for Edward's torture to include touches, licks, and kisses.

She purred.

"What's wrong, Franny?" Edward asked in that voice that made her inner thighs dewy.

Words failed her, so she shook her head. Lucky for her, he growled at her nonverbal response.

"Do you trust me?" he asked.

With her life. "Yes."

Suddenly, he was so close that his breath tickled her forehead, as though he surrounded her. His finger dipped into the front of her chemise, and he ran the pad of his index finger over her nipple.

She threw her head back and moaned.

Growling, he skimmed his fingertip over her other nipple, and a bolt of awareness shot to her core. His hands, strong and sure, reached into her bodice, cupped her breasts, and freed them from her chemise.

"They are beautiful," Edward said.

If her arms weren't bound against her sides, she would grab the back of his head and pull his face to her "beautiful" breasts.

Her internal pleas worked because his tongue laved one nipple, then the other. He settled in, kissing and sucking. The desire to cradle his head was so strong that she fought to free herself from the ropes.

"Franny, darling, behave," Edward cajoled.

She desperately wanted to please him, so she stopped wriggling and simply felt. Robbed of both her sight and her ability to use her hands, her sensitivity increased exponentially. Every brush of his skin, every guttural sound he made, every time his breath blew across her, her nerves were set on fire.

And then he was gone.

He couldn't leave her! He wouldn't leave her! He must still be there, watching. "Edward?" she called into her dark world.

"Franny." Gentleness replaced his gravelly voice. "I'm here, worshipping at your feet."

It was a good thing that she was seated, because her bones and muscles turned to pudding.

He removed her lone shoe, and his fingers danced over her ankles. Her skirt inched higher as he caressed his way to her inner thighs. She held her breath, willing him higher.

He drew lazy figure eights that morphed into tiny circles. They spiraled inward, until he was so close to her cunny that if she shifted, even a fraction, his fingers would contact her folds.

"I like it when you touch me," she confessed.

Edward chuckled. "Perfect, because I love to touch you." His finger glided inside her cunny.

She slid her hips as far forward as her restraints allowed.

Edward chuckled. Let him. She didn't care what he did as long as he worked his fingers deeper.

He added a second finger, and she moaned her appreciation. First, he pumped in and out of her. Then he curled his fingers in a come-hither movement, driving her into a frenzy. Desperate for more, she ground her pelvis against his hand.

"Franny?" His face must be close to her arousal because his breath blew over her cunny curls. "I'm going to untie you."

He reached around behind her. His chest brushed her cheek. It was too tempting not to, so she licked where she thought his nipple might be. *Hallelujah!* She caught the tiny bud in her mouth and nibbled.

He hissed.

She would have continued to experiment with male nipple sucking, but the tension on the rope gave, and he stepped back to unwind her. A second after the rope hit the ground with a *thump*, he lifted her onto her feet.

Intending to remove her blindfold, she reached for it.

"No, Franny. Leave it on."

She dropped her hands to her side.

"If you want me to stop—"

"Don't stop." Whatever game this was, she desired to play until the end.

Grabbing her wrists, he placed her hands on solid wood and then guided her hips backward, until she was bent forward at the waist. He dragged the hem of her skirt upward until a breeze kissed her backside.

Egad. He must be looking at her bare arse. He cupped her cheeks in his warm palms and squeezed. Who would have guessed that arse-squeezing was almost as pleasurable as breast suckling and cunny licking?

"Brace yourself," he cooed next to her ear.

At some point, he must have removed his trousers because his bare hips pressed up against her buttocks. Was he about to tup her from behind as she bent over her desk? She was hopelessly wanton because the prospect of such debauchery increased the already overwhelming ache consuming her.

He guided his tip to her entrance. *Oh, yes!* Rutting over her desk was exactly what they were about to do.

She was so wet that he easily slid inside her. Her walls welcomed him, squeezing their greeting and pulling him deeper.

"Oh, Edward," she said, between her breathy pants.

"Darling," he whispered. His fingers dug into her waist as he slid halfway out and pushed back in. He settled his lips on her ear and nipped. "Tell me you love my cock inside you."

"I love your cock inside me," she said between her pants. The truth was, she didn't just love his cock, she was falling in love with him.

He rammed into her so hard that her elbows buckled and the desk shuddered from the impact. If they broke her desk, what would she tell Papa and Josie?

He thrust again. Earth-shattering pleasure bolted through her as the desk creaked beneath them. If her furniture became a casualty, so be it. Who needed a desk anyway?

"Harder," she begged as she crashed her buttocks into his hips, over and over again.

His cock grew more rigid with each thrust. Her legs wobbled, threatening to topple her onto her face. The tickling in her core traveled outward and then whirled inward until it formed a tight little ball. Tighter, and tighter, the swirling tornado spiraled until she was certain she would explode.

Edward slammed into her one last time. "Fuck, Franny!" He pulled out of her at the same time she soared from her body.

Pleasure pulsed through Franny as light beams burst behind her eyelids. She collapsed onto the desk. Although the old furniture creaked in protest, it absorbed her weight. Thank goodness, because her muscles had stopped working.

Edward rested his torso on her back and tenderly kissed her shoulder blade. They lay like this for a long while, steadying their breathing.

Eventually, Edward lifted himself off her. She stayed right where she was, still too dazed to move.

"Are you well?" he asked as he helped her to sit up.

She nodded. "Exceedingly."

He sat beside her, his long legs reaching the floor. Her feet dangled. While she'd been senseless with euphoria, he'd reclaimed his trousers.

"Sorry about your dress," he said.

"My dress? Why?"

He wrinkled his nose. "I'm afraid I made a muck on the back of it?"

She giggled. "It is covered in sweat, too, so I shall wash it." She ran her hand over his lean abdomen, humming her appreciation.

"I needed that." He kissed her forehead. "I have been having improper fantasies about you since you bounded back into my life."

"Same."

His brow lifted. "You have been having improper fantasies about me? I thought you hated me."

She shook her head. Perhaps she was still intoxicated from bliss because the words cascaded past her lips. "I don't think I ever hated you. I just get so discombobulated in your presence. Edward, the truth is, I think I'm falling in love with you."

Egad! She needed to cut out her stupid tongue. Cheeks on fire, she stared at her swinging feet.

Edward cradled her chin and gently raised her face until they looked into each other's eyes. His irises were a warm chocolate brown and sparkling. "Thank God, because I fell in love with you the first time I saw you, Frances Valentine."

Happiness bubbling, Franny pressed her smiling lips to his.

CHAPTER THIRTY

AFTER A LONG day of work and a trip to Wagner and Son Jewelers, Edward hailed a carriage, sank into the squabs, and pondered his life.

It had been three weeks since he first made love to Franny, experiencing the most extraordinary moment in his six-and-twenty years. Since then, he'd spent his days making London a safer city. The recovered stolen property was in the hands of its rightful owners, and two weeks ago, he'd closed Lady Milton's case with a quick visit to her townhouse.

Celeste had rested her hand on his forearm. "Are you in love with that red-headed woman?" she'd asked.

"I am," Edward had responded.

"Lucky girl." The dowager had pressed a large sum of blunt into his palm. "I wish you well, Edward. If you change your mind, I will be here."

"Good day, my lady. And thank you for your generosity," he'd said with a gentlemanly brush of his lips over the back of her hand. However, he would never change his mind.

He used the extra earnings to purchase a small emerald that reminded him of Franny's eyes. Part of him wished he could give her a larger stone or the cat brooch with the green eyes, but another part suspected Franny would treasure this unpretentious token of his love. Earlier today, he'd received a message that the ring was ready, so he rushed to the jeweler as soon as he finished an end-of-the-day meeting with the magistrate.

Since solving Lady Milton's mystery, Edward had been assigned a stolen carriage case, an armed robbery that ended in an injured shopkeeper, and a half-dozen petty thefts. He'd found each guilty party and served them writs.

He spent his early evenings at The Silk Knuckles Saloon, skipping rope, lifting the dumbbells, hitting the sandbags, and sparring with the male pugilists. Two nights ago, he'd gone a few rounds with Pete the Trojan. He was not anywhere near The Trojan's skill level, but he enjoyed the challenge and was quite proud that he'd landed some respectable hooks and uppercuts.

Coach was back at the gym doing what he did best, and Franny and Josephine threw themselves into teaching their classes. Once a week, the feisty duo met with the other female rabble-rousers in the upstairs parlor. Although Harry had returned to his duties, he had not fully recovered his strength, so Edward occasionally helped him with chores.

Meanwhile, Franny spent her days training for her fight. In the evenings, once she was done coaching and teaching, she sparred with Josephine while Edward and Wentworth stood ringside and cheered.

Franny's fighting skills never ceased to amaze him. The woman was quick and strong, yet light on her feet. The passion and fire she brought to the ring had earned her an apt moniker. However, that same energy might lead to her downfall if she didn't control it. If an opponent had endurance, Franny might tire before them. Not because she wasn't in excellent shape, but because she was a machine who came out too fast giving everything she had early on.

"Pace yourself," Edward yelled a half dozen times every training session.

Meanwhile, Wentworth bellowed, "Josie, you are too heavy on your feet. You are stuck in a post hole again."

Most evenings, after they locked up the gymnasium, Franny

returned home with Edward. They'd share whatever meal Mrs. Benson prepared and then feed Zigzag. Some nights, they snuck in gentle lovemaking and/or some enthusiastic tupping before he escorted Franny home to her father.

Edward's life was fulfilling; however, a few things gnawed at his peace. First and foremost, he wanted to spend the rest of his life with Frances Valentine. Tonight, he would ask her to be his wife. Without her saying so, Edward knew Franny would want to be alerted to his intentions before seeking her father's permission.

Lately, doubt consumed Edward. Would a woman as free-thinking as Franny want a husband and children? Even if she wanted to be a mother, she would have to wait until she was done fighting to carry a baby. No worries there, he would accommodate whatever she wanted and needed. His greatest desire was to be with her.

Marrying a woman when Edward feared for her safety both in and out of the ring would require a lot of deep breathing. There was no denying that bare-knuckle fighting was dangerous. Deadly even. And then there were his reservations about Lance being responsible for the fire and the beatings. The man had been too flippant. His story lacked details. Lance insisted he was guilty, but it was not unheard of for people to confess to crimes they hadn't committed. With Edward's knowledge of human nature, he would not be surprised if a spoiled aristocrat who wanted to torment his father ruined his own life out of spite.

Edward sighed. Maybe he was needlessly fretting because there had been no attacks on the gymnasium or Franny's inner circle since Lance and his bootlickers had been jailed. Either way, his disquietude did not end here.

Franny's association with men who skirted legality, like Bear, Shark, and Whale, greatly concerned him. But if he meant to spend his life with her, he had to accept that she was a danger magnet.

The carriage halted in front of The Silk Knuckles Saloon. He paid the driver and walked the short distance to the front door, his heart hammering at his chest the entire time. His nerves got the better of him, forcing him to reach into his coat pocket. His quivering fingers brushed over the button from the alley before finding his handkerchief. He pressed on the soft fabric and exhaled in relief because the ring remained safely wrapped inside it.

She will say yes. She loves you, you fool, he assured himself. He pushed on the heavy door and strutted into the building, feigning more confidence than he felt.

The gymnasium hummed with activity. While Coach called directives to The Trojan and an up-and-coming fighter named Thumbs McCartney, Wentworth and Davenport sparred in the other ring. A few men and an athletic-looking woman, whom Edward didn't recognize, hit the heavy bags and hefted weights.

A group of well-dressed ladies stood in the far corner, animatedly chattering with Franny and Josephine.

"Bloody hell," Edward murmured under his breath. He had forgotten that the Ladies' Autonomy League was meeting this evening. As if he wasn't nervous enough, now he would have to wait even longer to ask Franny his important question.

It was as if Franny sensed his presence because she whirled to smile at him. Her face lit up, and she skipped across the gymnasium.

"You are late," she said. "I was starting to worry. How was your day?"

"Quite busy," was all he said. If he told her the true reason for his tardiness, the surprise would be ruined. "How was your day?"

"Rather wonderful. Josie and I went for a fifteen-mile run."

He chuckled. Of course, Franny's idea of fun was something most sane humans found torturous.

"We are about to go upstairs for our meeting," she said. "I ate dinner with Papa. Beef broth and eggs. Not nearly as tasty as Mrs. Benson's broth. I'm sorry I didn't wait, but I was quite famished."

He shoved his disappointment deep. "I'm sorry I'm late. I'll hit the sandbags for a bit." That should settle his nerves. "Then I will see what Harry needs assistance with, and I will walk you home when your meeting ends." The romantic dinner Mrs. Benson had prepared for them might go to waste, but he would not let the change in plans thwart his proposal.

"You won't believe who is here," Franny said.

Edward perused the gymnasium. Thumbs McCartney was present, but he'd been coming in every day for a fortnight. There were other regulars, too, including The Trojan. She must mean the new woman wearing men's breeches.

Edward inclined his chin to the woman, punishing the sandbag. "She looks skilled, but I'm afraid I don't know who she is."

"That is Roseanna Chapman," Franny said. "She has a promising future in prizefighting, but I'm not talking about her. Lady Whitehill is here."

"No," Edward said.

"She told us that her husband will no longer pose a problem because she is joining our cause, and if he doesn't support her, she will make his life miserable."

"No," Edward said again. He regarded the group of women, which included Lady Davenport, Lady Siddons, Lady Hillcaster, Bridget Wentworth, and a few of Bridget's friends. Standing amongst them, wearing a bright yellow frock, was Lord Whitehill's wife.

"Yes," Franny said. "And you won't believe who convinced her to come to our meeting?"

"Surely not that blowhard Lord Whitehill."

"Of course not." Franny threw her head back and laughed. "When we were at The Tea Rose a few weeks ago, Jonathan suggested she align herself with other influential women because she is one of the strongest, most intelligent women of his acquaintance. Apparently, he was making sheep eyes at her for a good cause. All along, the Davenports' and Nicolas's plan was for Jonathan to convince her to support the Ladies' Autonomy League while charming her. Truly brilliant, don't you think? Lord Whitehill will appear heartless if he fights a cause dear to his wife's heart."

"Brilliant, indeed." Edward cut his gaze to the two lords circling each other in the ring. As bloody arrogant as they could sometimes be, they supported Franny's dream and treated him like one of them.

Franny popped onto her toes and pressed a kiss to his cheek. No one seemed to take notice of her inappropriate display of affection except for Josephine, who clasped her hands together and smiled.

"I love you, Edward."

Before he had time to tell her he loved her, the energetic, buzzing Franny skipped across the gymnasium then followed the ladies up the stairs.

HIS SWEAT DRIPPING and his heart hammering, Edward slammed his fist into the sandbag one last time.

"You improve daily," Coach Valentine said.

"I dare say, you will be ready to compete in no time," Lord Davenport declared.

Unaware that he had an audience, Edward turned to face Coach and the two lords. "I don't plan to compete." He paused to catch his breath and swiped a muffler over his soaked brow. "I'm simply enjoying the physicality of pugilism while supporting Franny."

Nicolas Wentworth clapped Edward's shoulder. "Wise, mate. That is the same choice I made, and I have no regrets."

"We are going to grab a pint at The Spotted Octopus," Lord Davenport said. "Would you care to join us?"

"Thank you for the invitation," Edward said. "But I plan to assist Harry tonight."

"Next time," Lord Davenport said.

The three men strolled to the exit, leaving Edward and Harry alone in the now-empty room. Edward removed his mufflers and slid into his shirt and boots. He fumbled with the buttons as he approached Harry.

Although not as angry and red, the burns had scarred Harry's visible skin. Lines creased his forehead, and his hunched posture betrayed his exhaustion.

"Head home, Harry," Edward said. "I'll take over. What still needs to be done?"

"Thank you, sir, but I will finish."

"No," Edward said. "Go home. I insist. I don't mind. I have nervous energy that I need to work off."

"Thank you. I suppose I am quite tired," Harry capitulated. "The floors need to be swept, and the weights should be wiped down."

" 'Tis admirable of you to be working so hard, but you require extra rest to heal properly," Edward said.

Shoulders sagging, Harry left Edward to tackle the remaining chores.

Whistling a cheerful ditty, Edward swept the floor and wiped down the weights with a solution of alcohol and lemon juice. Feeling his long day, he parked himself on one of the wooden training benches and planned the rest of the evening.

Very soon, Franny would descend the stairs, and he would walk her home. The nearby park with the fountain was the perfect place for him to pledge his devotion and ask her to spend the rest of her life with him.

The front door banged, startling Edward. He peered over his shoulder. The lad who worked for the reverend had his arm around the younger Mrs. Brown. Edward swiveled on the bench so that he could watch them approach. Even from a distance, he could see her large bruises and bloody nose.

"Please help her," Charlie called.

Edward rushed to them. Together, he and Harry escorted and then lowered Mrs. Brown onto the bench. Edward retrieved his discarded cravat and gently pressed it against her nose. "Tilt your head back," he softly encouraged.

Edward was no doctor, but he checked her over with the medical knowledge he had gleaned as a lawman. Someone had punched her in the face, broken her nose, and bruised her ribs. He'd wager she'd been crying for hours.

Edward swallowed his fury and aimed for a gentle tone. "Tell me what happened."

Jane Brown dropped her head into her hands and sobbed.

"He attacked her again," Charlie said.

Although Edward suspected he knew the answer, he asked anyway, "Who attacked you?"

"Mr. Brown," the lad answered for her. "They live in my building, and I hear him hurting her sometimes. No one helps her. That's why I want to learn to box. So I can help her, you see."

Edward did see. Clearly. He should have grabbed the damnable minister by his collar and shaken the abused woman's address from him weeks ago.

Mrs. Brown lifted her face, swiped at her tears with her free hand, and met Edward's gaze. "I want to learn to box, too." Her voice was barely a whisper. "I want to be like the boxing ladies. I bet no man hits them."

Not in anger anyway. Sport was a different matter. Edward's mind whirled as he tried to connect the dots. "Does your husband know you want to learn to defend yourself?"

Her unfocused gaze seemed to stare into the past. "A few weeks ago, I told him the ladies here look as though they are having fun. He got angry, called them unseemly names, and told me to stay away."

"And then he hit you?" Edward asked.

She didn't answer his question, but she didn't need to.

"He has been in such a mood. Sometimes I think his brother adds fuel to his anger. Last night, they were at the tavern together. My husband came home very late, and when I asked him where he had been, he did this." She pointed to her cheek.

"Today, I decided to come here to inquire if I could somehow work off the cost of lessons. Unfortunately, he caught me leaving. He insisted I tell him where I was going. I couldn't lie. And then he did this." She removed Edward's blood-soaked cravat from her nose.

Fury and sorrow combined, forming a deadly explosive that sat heavy in Edward's gut.

"I heard him yelling," Charlie said. "I waited until he left before checking on Mrs. Brown." His bottom lip vibrated with his huff. "Why are so many people angry at The Silk Knuckles? I, for one, think ladies fighting and defending themselves is rather amazing."

Rubbing his forehead, Edward searched for the correct words to explain the unpleasant truth about misogynistic, controlling cowards to this young lad.

"Charlie, some men are intimidated by strong women. I suppose many feel that The Silk Knuckles convinces women to stand up for themselves. What they don't understand is that strong women make men better. In turn, society is better."

Even before he finished edifying the lad, the truth hit Edward. He rushed to his greatcoat that lay beneath his mufflers. Bypassing the handkerchief that held Franny's ring, he grabbed the button and presented it to Mrs. Brown. "Do you recognize this?"

She sniffled. "Yes. That is my husband's. He lost it a few weeks ago. Where did you find it?"

The button might not be proof enough for the court, but it indicated Brown had been snooping about the building, which was all Edward needed to know. His fierce growl sent the woman back into her shell, her already diminutive frame seeming to shrink to half its size. Controlling his temper right now was no easy task, but he could not terrify her if he meant to help her.

"What are you doing here, Vicar Williams?" Charlie asked, his unexpected question more of a shocked exclamation.

Edward's loud utterance must have overshadowed the sound

of the front door opening because the pigheaded, seething vicar stomped toward them.

"Charles, Mrs. Brown, leave this den of iniquity right this minute," he said, his tone impervious.

Edward balled his fists by his side.

"I will not," the lad said. "Mrs. Brown needs our help, or her husband is going to kill her."

The vicar's gaze finally landed on the unfortunate woman, and he gasped. "Heavens above, Mrs. Brown. What happened to you?"

"Mr. Brown is what happened to her." Edward stabbed his finger into the vicar's chest. "We tried to tell you, but you refused to listen."

Charlie lifted his chin and squared his shoulders. "Vicar, aren't you supposed to protect your flock?"

"Let me explain something, Vicar," Edward said, his voice an angry snarl. "This lad right here is braver and more of a man than you are."

The vicar's button lip stuck out. "I didn't know," he said, his voice quavering.

What a daft coward, but Edward didn't have time to berate the vicar because he needed to settle a score.

"A doctor needs to attend to her immediately," Edward said.

Charlie jumped to attention. "Yes, sir."

Edward glared at the vicar.

All of his holier-than-thou arrogance left him with a woosh. Williams extended his hand. "Come next door, my dear. The rectory is quite comfortable. I shall fix you a cup of tea. Charlie, run and fetch Doctor Klinger."

"Yes, sir." The lad dashed toward the exit.

"Charlie," Edward called.

The lad faced him.

"Where do you live?"

"My family has rooms at Blackwell Rooms."

"Blackwell Rooms," Edward mumbled under his breath as

the door banged into place. If his memory served him, it was a short walk to the building.

Edward looped his arm around Mrs. Brown, and then, he and the vicar absorbed her weight as they transferred her to a cozy settee in the rectory.

$$\rule{2.5in}{0.4pt}\ \rotatebox{0}{\diamondsuit}\ \rule{2.5in}{0.4pt}$$

CHAPTER THIRTY-ONE

FEMININE POWER CRACKLED as pride swelling, Franny looked out over the ladies gathered in her drawing room. These women were her sisters, and they gave her a greater purpose that she embraced with passion and fortitude. She couldn't imagine another place where women born to privilege and wealth chatted happily with an orphaned pugilist. What a blessing that a daughter of a boxing coach and an ex-governess was also welcomed with open arms into this elite group.

"I have something to add," Lady Whitehill announced.

"Go on, Laura," Lady Siddons said.

Lady Whitehill stood, not an iota of her previous timidity evident. She lifted her chin and pulled her shoulders back as if she were a warrior. "Helena, tell Lord Griffendale to propose your ideas about coverture to Parliament. I will see that my husband does not interfere."

Lady Davenport raised her glass high. "Hear, hear."

Cheers echoed as glasses lifted in solidarity. In recruiting a perfect member to their club, Viscount Jonathan Davenport, the incurable rake who never took anything seriously, solidified Franny's loyalty and respect.

"This is truly going to happen, isn't it?" Josie said to Franny. Meanwhile, joyful side conversations broke out around the room.

Lady Siddons banged her gavel until the chatter quieted.

"Ladies," she said, her tone earnest. "There are still a lot of men to convince. Please do not be disheartened if my nephew fails to make immediate headway." Her jaw set in determination, Lady Siddons scanned the room, making eye contact with her attentive audience. "Even if our proposed ideas do not come to fruition this season, know they will happen. Someday, our daughters, granddaughters, and great-granddaughters will have autonomy. Because we were brave enough to fight, they will own property, vote, and hold seats in Parliament, and every one of you had a hand in creating this equitable future."

Collective emotion swept over the room. Franny swiped tears from her eyes.

Even the skeptical Lady Hillcaster honked into her handkerchief. "I want my granddaughters to have autonomy," she said. "More than I've ever wanted anything."

Surely if they'd won over the stodgy Lucille, they could convince a bunch of single-minded men.

"I suppose that is all for today," Lady Siddons said. "Bridget, is there anything you need repeated for the meeting notes?"

"As usual, I've done a splendid job." The earl's irreverent daughter grinned. "Therefore, I hereby motion for this meeting of the Happy Hoydens from Hell Assembly to conclude. Do I have a second?"

Franny laughed so hard, she snorted.

"Bridget Wentworth." Although Lady Siddon's tone was stern, her eyes sparkled with good humor.

"Oh, botheration," Bridget said. "I hereby motion for this meeting of the Ladies' Autonomy League to conclude. Do I have a second?"

"I second the motion," Franny called. Caught up in this contagious fervor, she felt invincible. She sought Josie's gaze and then sent her a mental message. *Can you believe we are a part of something this important?*

Josie's grin grew until it was all teeth.

As the ladies kissed cheeks and said their good evenings,

Franny and Josie gathered the dirty glasses and deposited them into the wash bucket. Franny's mouth watered as she arranged the remaining pastries in a tin. Once she won this mill, there would be no leftovers because she would eat every last biscuit, cake, and pie.

Josie placed the last dirty plate in the bin, then swiped her hands back and forth. "Let us wash the dishes tomorrow."

Since Franny was anxious to spend time with Edward, she agreed. They descended the stairs side by side.

"Your relationship with Edward seems to grow stronger by the day," Josie said.

Delight rippled through Franny. "Yes, it does."

"Have you made love yet?" Josie asked.

Franny slapped her shoulder. "That is none of your concern."

"With all that manliness, I wager he is an extraordinary lover," Josie said between giggles.

Despite her gasp of indignation, Franny wanted to talk about her physical relationship. However, there was no way she could confess to their rope play, how good it felt when he pushed deep inside her, or the way he devoured her body. "I suspect he has had many lovers in the past. He knows so much." Her cheeks heated. "I hope I suit him. He has had to teach me everything."

Edward lavished her with compliments about her passion, and he seemed to be aroused all the time. Hopefully, he wasn't humoring her.

As they stepped onto the gymnasium floor, Josie's tone turned serious. "I understand that feeling. Nicolas did not have a lot of lovers, but he was engaged before we met. He said the few carnal relations they had were unsatisfactory. However, this comely widow, ten years his senior, schooled him in lovemaking."

Franny snorted. "Lady Milton?"

"How did you know?" Josie asked.

Franny hadn't known, she'd simply been thinking out loud. "She favors Edward, but he told me they were never lovers."

"Don't you believe him?" Josie asked.

Franny clasped Josie's hands and confessed, "I believe him. Josie, he is so very honest. And wonderful. In fact… I have fallen madly in love with him."

"I knew it." Josie wrapped Franny in a hug and squeezed. "Honestly, having a life partner is divine. You have someone to curl up with every night and wake up with every morning. You can talk about anything and everything. Being in love with your husband is rather amazing."

"But he has not proposed," Franny said.

" 'Tis just a matter of time," Josie said. "I see the way he looks at you."

Hopefully this was true, because Franny would leap into his arms, calling out, *yes!* "Since you are being so nosey, it is only fitting that I ask, are you with child yet?" She patted Josie's flat belly.

"No." Josie frowned. "I got my monthly courses last week. Once I am, you will be the second to know. Unfortunately, I won't be able to spar with you then."

How bittersweet.

"In that case," Josie added, "mayhap, Roseanna Chapman will make the perfect sparring partner for you. She is quite good. I am pleased she decided to train with us."

"Mayhap." One of Franny's core beliefs was that life placed individuals in one's path at just the right moment. "The truth is, once I settle my debt to Bear, I don't know if I will continue fighting. Surprisingly, after my original horror, I'm quite excited for this fight. Besides giving up sweets, it feels wonderful to be training. However…"

"What?" Josie asked.

Too many emotions whirled for Franny to understand how she felt about her future competing. She sighed. "I suppose I should stop overthinking and concentrate on my upcoming fight."

"Splendid idea," Josie said.

"By the by, did you truly suggest that I stay with Edward when Papa was recovering?"

Feigning memory lapse, Josie tapped her cheek.

"You little imp." Franny lightly pushed her shoulder. "Seriously? None of you thought a lick about my reputation?"

Josie laughed. "Do not act so put out. We are hardly highborn ladies, and we are already challenging the status quo. We run around in our chemises punching people and telling other women to fight for autonomy. Besides, you were much too stubborn to ever admit you found him attractive. We were simply helping you find happiness."

Franny opened her mouth to dispute Josie. However, every bit of what she had said was true.

"I'm meeting Nicolas at The Spotted Octopus," Josie said. "Would you care to join us? I think your father is with him."

"No. Edward is walking me home. Speaking of Edward…" Franny searched the gymnasium.

"Is something wrong?" Josie asked.

"Edward said he would wait for me, but he isn't here."

"He must be about somewhere. His things are over there." Josie pointed to his pile of clothing and mufflers in the weight area.

"He said he was going to assist Harry. Maybe they are working in one of the offices."

"Probably." Josie kissed her cheek. "See you tomorrow."

Once Josie departed, Franny searched the building to no avail. Disappointed, she plopped onto the bench beside Edward's discarded possessions. Red splotches spattering his cravat caught her eye.

She picked up the sticky fabric. Had Pete the Trojan or Thumbs McCartney given Edward a bloody nose?

She flinched—Edward's poor, wonderful, imperfect nose. As soon as she saw him, she would gently clean his injury, then kiss him until he forgot about the pain.

Tamping down her impatience, she waited.

And waited.

"Where are you, Edward?" she whispered to her empty gymnasium.

CHAPTER THIRTY-TWO

BLACKWELL ROOMS WAS one of at least two dozen lodging houses littering the congested, working-class street. Numerous additions had been connected to the main building, creating an architectural hodgepodge. While staring at the geometrical maze, Edward berated himself. In his haste, he hadn't inquired what floor Brown resided on, and it would not do to barge in on an unsuspecting tenant's evening meal.

"Bloody hell," he said as he kicked at a loose cobblestone.

Thankfully, his little burst of temper temporarily eased his irritation. Now to stay calm, because if he didn't think clearly, he'd make a muck of this. Closing his eyes, he slowly breathed in and out while visualizing a sunny meadow. Colorful flowers bloomed, butterflies fluttered, and birds chirped merrily. His heart rate slowed, and his angry inner voice abated, allowing him to assess his situation.

Coming here was a mistake. He should have waited until he had a writ in his hand and the law behind him. He was not some violent vigilante who ran around London cracking skulls open. He was a logical lawman who thought things through. Ethical men most certainly did not flog arsonists who beat their wives, although they definitely fantasized about it. Edward imagined his whip repeatedly slicing through Brown's skin. And blood as it oozed from the cuts as Brown sniveled like the coward he was.

Edward would not feel guilty for wanting to punish this man because the courts did little to protect women, and cruel bullies needed to be taught a lesson.

His serene meadow morphed into a cyclonic maelstrom of destruction. Growling, he opened his eyes. To hell with his conscience. Justice needed to be served swiftly.

He marched to the closest door and pounded on it. A ruddy-cheeked woman with a halo of gray curls peered out at him.

"Can I help you?" she asked.

"Good day, Madame," he said. "I'm looking for Mr. Brown. Can you tell me where I might find him?"

The woman regarded him through slitted eyes. For a moment, he feared she wouldn't answer.

"Are you his mate?" she asked.

Too angry to control his emotions, Edward snorted.

The woman's skeptical expression softened. She stepped aside and invited Edward into her cozy home. The scent of fresh bread swirled around him, making his stomach growl inopportunely.

"Why are you looking for him?" she asked, her tone more curious than judgmental.

"I work for the magistrate." Damn his honesty. He probably should have lied about who he was since friends and family tended to hide a wanted man's whereabouts from the law.

" 'Tis about time," she said.

Edward tilted his head, waiting for her to continue. His patience was rewarded because after a brief pause, she chirped like a songbird. "That man is as mean as snake snot, he is. Picks fights with everyone he meets. Always out all-night drinking with that no-good brother of his. Goes to church on Sundays, acting like he has God in his soul, but the devil took up residence there long ago. And that's not even the worst of it."

"Oh?" Edward asked.

"I think he hits and kicks that sweet wife of his. Breaks my heart, it does."

Edward's, too.

"The Browns' rooms are on the second floor, but I doubt you will find him there. He's probably at a tavern or a bawdy house, drinking himself into a stupor. The stairs to his rooms are out back. Do not take the side stairs, those lead to the Holme's rooms, and they are a respectable family. Wouldn't want a lawman banging on their door, scaring them."

The respectable people must be Charlie's family. At some other time, Edward would tap on their door and tell them what a remarkable lad they'd raised. But, right this minute, before he changed his mind, he needed to confront Brown. "Thank you for your time," he told his helpful informant.

"Are you going to protect that poor wife of his?" she asked.

He was going to beat the man within inches of his life. Forget about an imagined whip; Edward's knuckles would inflict the damage. Then he would haul him to the local goal without a warrant. He'd simply claim, "I was minding my own business, and this wastrel attacked me in a dark alley."

"Yes. I intend to make sure he never raises a hand to her again," Edward promised.

"Thank you." She rested her hands on her heart, and her eyes filled with affection. "Honorable, brave men like you keep the city safe."

Edward winced. *Honorable* might no longer be a word that described him, because he was about to take justice into his own hands.

As EDWARD APPROACHED the Browns' quarters, his gaze landed on a burlap sack tucked behind the stairs.

He carried the bag to an open space where moonlight eliminated a tinder box, an empty container of whale oil, and a few swatches of charcloth. Hopefully, this would serve as the proof he needed. The fishy stench emanating from the bag stole his breath.

There was no way he could carry it with him for any length of time. He hid the evidence in the branches of a nearby bush so that he could retrieve it in the morning. Thereupon, he climbed the short set of stairs, then cautiously knocked.

The kindly woman was correct; Brown wasn't home. Edward settled into a dark shadow created by the eaves. Brown would have to pass by him to get to the stairs, and when he did, Edward would leap on him, continuing his brutal assault until the ignoramus took his last breath.

Try again, fool.

No matter how much he wanted to, he couldn't kill the blackguard. However, he could approach him and confront him about his misdeeds. Even if he didn't follow through, threatening the blighter would bring him joy. He'd watch Brown squirm, relishing every second of the man's discomfiture. If he somehow got a confession from him, which would be easy to do if he were foxed enough, he could escort him to the goal. No violence needed.

And, once he locked Brown away, his wife would no longer be in danger. Lady Davenport could easily find her a suitable job. Or maybe she could work for Franny and Josie. That was what Jane Brown said she wanted, after all.

Edward smiled. The thought of Franny always filled his heart with joy. Tomorrow, once all of this was over, he would ask her to be Mrs. Robinson. "Mrs. Frances Robinson," he whispered to the darkness.

CHAPTER THIRTY-THREE

F RANNY'S SLIPPERS SLAPPED the floor as she paced the length of the gymnasium. She hadn't realized how annoying the unrelenting *clap* of her short stride was until now. Of course, she'd never spent an evening alone in the massive space fretting about the whereabouts of the man she loved. Halting her frenetic movements, she tried to think clearly but failed miserably.

Frustrated, she again paced.

An epiphany at last. Perhaps Edward and Harry were seeing to something outside. Maybe a shingle had come loose. Or perhaps they were checking on how the repairs were holding up. Although most likely they were enjoying one of the last warm nights before the autumn chill settled over London. Whatever the case, fresh air would do her good.

Laughing at her missishness, she grabbed one of the lanterns, exited the gymnasium, and inhaled. To think, less than a year ago, if she'd taken a deep breath, she'd have choked on the foulness permeating St Giles. Here, on the front stoop of The Silk Knuckles, the breeze tickled her skin, invigorating her.

Holding her lantern high, she searched the arc it illuminated. In the distance, a few carriages moved about, and a gig she didn't recognize was parked in front of the church. No surprise there because masochistic parishioners desiring self-flagellation often visited the nasty vicar.

Even though her surroundings were as they should be, her unsettled fears returned.

"Edward! Harry! Are you out here?" she called.

The chirping crickets answered, their stridulations eerily echoing.

Even though the men were probably around back enjoying the lovely night, prickles of trepidation crawled up her spine.

Her steps tentative, Franny cautiously patrolled the perimeter of the building, her senses on high alert. A loud, hooting startled her. Halting at the back corner of her property, she peered through the darkness, praying her night companion wasn't a vengeful ghost.

Hoot. Hoot. Hoot. Two glowing eyes peered down at her.

The moment called for a self-depreciating chuckle. "Silly goose," she said with her laugh. This wasn't the first time that the owl that normally roosted in the church tower had startled her. She quickly sobered. How could she step back into the ring if even a bird of prey unnerved her?

Something crackled as if a large animal had stepped on a branch. The sound was much too loud to be a night critter. Or a cat. Or a dog. And it certainly wasn't the blinking owl. It sounded like a bear, but since when did bears roam around London? Gooseflesh erupted, and Franny's entire body tingled, but not in the magical way it did when Edward touched her. Someone or something besides the owl was watching her. Her best guess was that her stalker hid behind the greenery that separated the church and The Silk Knuckles.

Her heartbeat sped up and pounded so loudly that the rhythmic *whoosh* of pumping blood echoed in her ears. She needed to get to safety. Once she was inside her building, she would lock the door and wait for sunrise. Since she didn't want to instigate a chase, she moved slowly.

Something behind her crunched. If someone was hiding near the hedgerow beside her, and someone else was behind her, she was surrounded. She needed to charge straight ahead. She picked up her pace and did just that.

The tramp of heavy footsteps followed her. There was no mistaking the danger; Franny was being hunted. She took off, sprinting the length of the building. She was almost to the front corner when someone grabbed her around the waist. Her lantern toppled to the ground. It broke and then fire flared on the path, burning the spilled oil and the hedge.

"I got her," a man yelled.

She elbowed her attacker.

"Ouch, bloody hell." He grunted and let go of her.

She dashed forward but didn't make it far because a second man's arm locked around her neck, cutting off her airway. Franny gripped his forearm and lifted, ducking beneath it. In one smooth move, she came out on the other side of him, twisted his arm, pinned it to his back, and shoved him away from her. He lost his footing and fell face-first, taking his partner to the ground with him.

While the men rolled about trying to get to their feet, she stomped on the fire and then slid out of her blazing slipper. She simply, no matter what, could not allow her building to catch fire again. Picking the shoe up by the heel, she slapped it on the ground until the flames fizzled. Half hobbling, half-sprinting, on her blistered foot, she dropped the charred leather onto the ground.

Her action gave her attackers time to recover. Meaty paws grabbed her arms and yanked, then pinned them behind her. The owner of the rough hands pushed his hips into hers, knocking her backward and off balance. She was powerless with all her weight in her heels, and her shoulder blades pressed against his torso. She attempted to slam the back of her head into his face but was met with air and maniacal laughter.

"Whore," the man spat in her ear. A noxious mixture of cheap gin and stale smoke blew across her neck.

"Who are you? What do you want?" she asked.

"To keep you from spreading your wicked ways to the women of London," he said. "I will see you dead before I let you poison my wife."

Who was his wife? He didn't sound like an aristocrat, and to her knowledge, their newest student, Roseanna Chapman, wasn't married. Franny sorted through all of her companions, coming up blank.

And then a terrifying thought hit her. These men might have harmed Edward and Harry. She had to free herself and find them.

Before she could ask him who his wife was or scream for help, the second man lunged in front of her. Between the dark night and a mask that hid half his face, she couldn't discern his features. He wrapped a gag around her face, shoved the knot into her mouth, and tossed a sack over her head.

She kicked and gave muffled screams as they hoisted her off her feet. One held her hands, the other her ankles. She swung between them like a sagging bridge as they carried her. Assuming they meant to toss her into the gig parked in front of the church, she wriggled and thrashed with everything she had.

"If you know what is good for you, you will stop fighting us," one of the men said.

She would tell him to go to hell if her mouth weren't full of foul-tasting fabric.

"How in the devil are we going to get her into your gig?" the man holding her arms asked. "And once we do, she's gonna have to ride on my bloody lap."

"If she'd stop squirming like a headless chicken, she'd be light," the other said.

She'd be damned if she'd make this easy for them. Besides, she had to escape in case Edward and Harry needed her. She kicked out her arms and legs at the same time. She wobbled in their grip, and her head hit something hard. An excruciating pain, unlike anything she'd ever experienced—and she'd taken her share of facers—seared her brain.

How ironic. It wasn't a blow to her brain in the boxing ring that stole her intellect. Her demise was to come from smashing her head into…something… while being abducted by misogynistic apes. How utterly devastating and disappointing.

"Serves you right, whore," one of the men said, his voice fading to a faraway whisper.

Wait! What served her right? What was happening to her? Edward? Where was Edward? Franny's world whirled into a single point of nothingness.

CHAPTER THIRTY-FOUR

T HE GRAY SKY gave way to the soft light of dawn, and still Brown did not return. It was time for Edward to call this reconnaissance mission a failure, return home, clean himself up, and then report to Bow Street. But first, he had to retrieve his key, which was in his greatcoat pocket—the same greatcoat that also held Franny's ring. Thunderation, his much-anticipated night had turned to utter shite.

He stumbled toward The Silk Knuckles, so exhausted that he couldn't feel his feet hitting the ground.

As Edward neared Tavistock Street, he picked up his pace, only to be met with the reality of his unfortunate situation. His gymnasium key was with his house key, and they were both in his coat, locked inside the building. Instinctively, he reached for his timepiece, which was also in his pocket. He grumbled every unseemly word in his vocabulary. Although Franny and Josie were early risers, he suspected it would be an hour or two before they arrived. Since he had no other choice but to make the most of his misfortune, he would try to sleep while he waited.

Hopefully, Franny wasn't angry that he hadn't walked her home. If the shoe were on the other foot, he'd be bloody furious, but only because he'd be worried about her. Surely, Franny wouldn't worry about him. To date, no one had ever been overly concerned about his whereabouts except for Zigzag, but that was because she eventually got hungry. Well, maybe Mrs. Benson fretted from time to time, but she knew his job kept him away for long periods of time.

At last, Edward reached The Silk Knuckles. He sat on the front stoop, leaned against the door, and stretched his legs out in front of him. Closing his eyes, he tried to relax but instead reevaluated the decisions that led to his unproductive, sleepless night.

His impulsiveness had never served him well, so when he'd devoted himself to being a lawman, he'd traded his besetting ways for careful thought and planning. And now, he had Franny to think about. He would be a worthless husband if he resorted to his youthful ways, especially since she had a wild streak of her own. He didn't need to add fuel to the fire with his obsessive need to fix everything quickly. His overtired brain leaped from topic to topic, leading him to the same conclusion he'd come to hours ago. He should have walked Franny home, proposed, kissed her until they both saw stars, and dealt with Brown once he had secured a writ.

Sighing, he opened his eyes. The rising sun cast a golden ray over something lying near the hedgerow. From this distance, it appeared to be a lantern.

Edward's aching bones creaked as he pushed to his feet. He was almost to the lantern when he stumbled over a hunk of scorched leather. He picked it up and turned it every which way. Why was one of Franny's slippers in the yard, half incinerated, and beside a lantern?

Now that he was wide awake, his heart vigorously thudded.

"Franny! Franny," he called as he searched the area. Unfortunately, he was met with silence.

Dread washing over him, Edward dashed to the front door and knocked. "Franny? Anyone?"

When no one responded, he pounded harder and yelled louder. What if Franny was inside and injured? What if Brown was in there with her? Breathless and with his knuckles bleeding,

Edward continued to pummel.

With every intention of trying to break down an impenetrable door, Edward kicked to the side of the lock, putting all of his body weight behind his heel. To his surprise, the door flew open. Perhaps it had been unlocked this entire time. Odd indeed when the women always locked up before they left. His mournful growl echoed through the empty gymnasium.

"Franny," Edward called as he sprinted from room to room.

Heart hammering and esophagus burning, he returned to his possessions that still sat where he had left them last night. After tossing his mufflers to the side, he slid into his waistcoat and greatcoat, shoved his bloody cravat into his pocket, and collapsed his bone-weary arse onto the bench. Dropping his forehead into his palms, he moaned.

Edward needed to face the truth. He had royally buggered everything. Although guilty of both the theft and threatening them in the alley, Lance was not the arsonist. But this wasn't Edward's biggest blunder because while he'd chosen revenge over common sense, someone had kidnapped Franny.

Every instinct he had screamed it was Brown. Witnesses—or a witness—from his building painted him as a cruel man, and his wife proved him to be so. Then there was the bag of arsonist supplies that he'd found. Though that didn't have to mean Brown was responsible for the fire to the gym, it—along with the way his neighbor had talked about the type of man he was, made him a prime suspect for violence against women.

On the other hand, he'd been mistaken about Lance. But then again, he'd been correct in searching the man's domicile for the jewelry, so he hadn't been completely wrong. He'd just been distracted. By Franny. And now…

Now his best first bet was to follow the instincts that had served him so well in the past. It was Brown. It had to be!

Trying to clear the fog, Edward rubbed his forehead. "Think, you sod." Was Brown fool enough to take Franny to his lodgings? If not, where had he taken her? And what about the lantern? And her shoe? Had she been burned? Injured?

Was she still alive? His heart rose to his throat, making it even harder to think, or even breathe.

No! He needed to cease the pessimistic drama. Of course, she was still alive. He simply had to find her, and to do that, he had to seek out someone who knew where Brown might take her. Luckily, he knew exactly where such a person was.

Edward stormed out of the gymnasium, charged through the bushes, and cut across the front lawn to the rectory. "Williams," he yelled as he pounded on the heavy oak. "Open the bloody door, Williams."

The door cracked open, and a disheveled-looking Charlie peeked out around it. "Sir, what are you doing here so early? Is something wrong?"

Edward pushed past the lad. "Where is Jane Brown?"

"What is going on?" Cinching his robe closed, the vicar hurriedly descended the stairs.

"Mr. Robinson is here," Charlie said, even though Williams had already made eye contact with Edward. "Something is amiss."

Edward met the vicar at the bottom of the stairs. "Where is Jane Brown?"

"Here." A diminutive woman looked down at them from the second-floor landing, her hair askew and her dress rumpled as if she had slept in it. Her eyes were blackened and even from here, he could see they were bloody red from burst vessels.

"If your husband didn't go home last night, where would he go instead?" Edward called.

Her eyes as wide as they could be in spite of the puffiness, she gawked at him. "Well...I..."

"Think, Mrs. Brown," Edward demanded.

"Probably sleeping off the hot coppers in an alley," Charlie murmured.

"Maybe with his parents," Mrs. Brown said, a quiver in her voice.

"Where do they live?" When she didn't respond, Edward's temper snapped. "I believe he has Franny. Tell me the address and be quick about it."

Gasping, she folded in on herself.

Charlie climbed the stairs to her side, murmuring quietly. It seemed to give her courage, because she straightened. "In that case, he is probably with his brother."

"Address," Edward bellowed. "The bloody address."

"Please lower your voice," Williams said. "You are terrifying the poor woman."

"I am not terrified," Mrs. Brown said, her chin lifted and her voice now steady. "His brother lodges on the ground floor of The Bedford, where Bedford Street meets Maiden Lane. To get there you—"

"Thank you," Edward called over his shoulder. He did not need further directions because every lawman in London knew precisely where the rundown tenement was located.

Chapter Thirty-Five

Franny awoke blind and befuddled. She wasn't in her bed, and her tongue was tangled in something putrid tasting. She attempted to rub her aching head, but her arms were tied to the chair. She tried to move her feet, but her ankles were bound together. Since she could wiggle her toes, and the bottom of her left foot itched and burned like the devil, at least she wasn't dead. Slowly, memories filtered in, and she shuddered in horror.

She had been looking for Edward and Harry when two vile men who smelled like a windowless tavern abducted her and carried her to a gig. While fighting them off, she'd hit her head so hard she knocked herself out. And now, here she was, a burlap sack over her head and strapped to a chair, and not in the exciting way Edward had restrained her. These ropes cut into her skin, and the sack and gag were practically suffocating her.

She fought her desire to thrash about. Instead, she cocked an ear toward a faint conversation off to her side and eavesdropped.

"I say we cut the redheaded witch into pieces and dump her in the Thames. Then we leave a note for that ridiculous coach telling him his girl champion is next if he doesn't shut down the boxing saloon. How dare he tempt women with false notions of equality?"

It was a good thing Franny was gagged because it muffled her outrage and kept her from calling attention to herself.

"No, Jackson. We stick with the original plan. We send a note to the coach telling him that if he ever wants to see his daughter again, he needs to close The Silk Knuckles Saloon immediately and permanently. Then we hold her captive until the sign is taken down and the building is empty."

The man she assumed was Jackson harrumphed. "I'm worried about that big officer who follows her everywhere. He doesn't seem like the type of man to take kindly to threats. He might come looking for us."

"Mother says Williams isn't happy about being next door to the house of she-devils. If the lawman gives us trouble, we'll convince the vicar to lodge a harassment complaint with the magistrate. Besides, no man in their right mind is going to want that place to reopen."

Franny knew it. The vicar had something to do with this. Still, she did not know these men or their mother.

Shuffling through her memories, Franny landed on the Mrs. Browns. The older Mrs. Brown had mentioned having two sons. *"...both good men who have welcomed God into their hearts."* The younger Mrs. Brown's eyes had been filled with desperation. Now it all made sense. The timid woman wanted to learn to protect herself from her husband but had been afraid to approach Franny in front of her mother-in-law. Perhaps her husband had found out and had tried to stop her. If true, then his young wife's interest in The Silk Knuckles might have intensified her beatings.

Good men, Franny's arse. They were deplorable knaves, and when Franny freed herself, they would rue tangling with her. Testing out the tension in the rope, she twisted her wrists. As she suspected, the binds were tight. She attempted to circle her ankles, and the rope cut into her skin. Interestingly, the men hadn't secured her calves to the chair. Maybe they had run out of rope. Or perhaps they were dimwitted and didn't realize how strong her legs were. The clod-pates were so single-minded they probably didn't understand that women could kick. A grave miscalculation on their part because this "red-headed witch" could crack a man's skull between her thighs. Especially if she was angry.

Or furious.

"It seems the whore is awake," one of the men said.

Franny winced. Unfortunately, she had called attention to herself with her subtle movement. She held her breath as their footsteps moved closer. One of the men rested his lips against her ear. Thank heaven for the burlap that kept their skin from touching.

"Do you understand that you are being punished for peddling nonsense to the fairer sex? What do you think will happen to these ladies after you turn them into heathens and no man wants them?"

If only Franny could talk so that she could tell them that these remarkably strong women were better off on their own than with abusive husbands.

One of the men ripped the sack from her head, yanking her hair in the process. She blinked until her eyes adjusted to the light. The men who stood before her could have been twins, except that an ugly thunderbolt scar started at one of the brothers' brows. It cut an angry path that split his eyelid, then traveled down his cheek. The other brother was missing the top button on his rumpled tailcoat.

Hadn't Edward mentioned finding a button?

"Do not try to yell for help," Jackson said. "No one in this neighborhood will come to your rescue."

Scowling, Franny perused the barely furnished, filthy space searching for an escape. A large window on the opposite side of the room. A couple of wooden chairs. Litter piled on the table. A mattress on the floor.

Franny concluded two things: Number one, she had no idea how to free herself. Number two, whichever brother lived here had fallen on hard times. How they managed a horse and a gig was anyone's guess. Although arses like this were not above thieving.

"I'm going to take off the gag," Jackson's brother said. "Keep your voice down, or we will punish you. Do you understand?"

Wanting to be rid of both the gag and the knot that was choking her, Franny nodded in agreement. Truthfully, they could sod off. She had no intention of following their arbitrary rules.

Once he unwound the gag, Franny swallowed. What she wouldn't give for a large cup of water.

"Where am I?" she croaked.

"Good try, wench," Jackson said. "You will get no information from us."

The name-calling was getting old.

"You won't get away with this," she said with all of the defiance she could muster. "Edward will find me."

Jackson chuckled. "Eventually. But he won't like what he sees." He turned his back to her to retrieve a knife from the overfull table. When he faced her, half his mouth grinned. The scarred side of his face twisted, and it was as if she was looking into the face of a monster. Brandishing the knife like a child proud of a new toy, he bent over her. "Lucky chit, my brother wants you alive for the time being. I agreed to the compromise as long as I get to carve up that pretty face of yours."

How apropos. Then she could be as hideous as he. Sighing, she rolled her eyes. She would not be baited. He was a cowardly buffoon trying to intimidate her and she refused to take him seriously.

"Jackson," his brother reprimanded. "We need her alive and unharmed if we are to make the deal."

"Richard, I told you that wife of yours is making you sentimental," Jackson hissed.

Richard must be Jane Brown's husband, the poor thing. No woman should ever, for any reason, be saddled with such a burden.

"Mayhap," Richard said with a snarl. "But at least I don't have scars from a bloody whore."

"Bugger off," Jackson said.

The brothers engaged in an epic battle of glares. Perhaps if they exchanged their scowls for fisticuffs, and beat the shite out of each other, Franny could escape.

"Which of you is your mother's favorite?" she asked.

They turned their angry gazes on her.

"What the bloody hell?" Jackson asked.

"She is trying to turn us against each other," Richard said.

Franny itched to ask him why he had been cut. She wagered he hadn't paid for services rendered. Or maybe he had gotten too rough. Probably both. Inquiring into his business would not garner the results she needed; however, a bit of manipulation would.

Feigning indifference, she shrugged. "Richard, when your wife and mother visited my gymnasium a few weeks ago, your mother mentioned she had two sons. She said one was an angel going to heaven and the other a devil going to hell. Jackson," she rambled on, "I wager that after the prostitute sliced you up, you decided to punish all women. I suspect you also convinced your brother that the best way to handle his wife was to beat her. 'Tis rather pathetic when you think about it. One brother gets a lovely wife and the other has to go to a brothel for cunny."

Jackson lunged, pressing the tip of his knife into her neck. He lowered his face until their noses were inches apart. Every time he growled, his saliva spattered her cheeks. "Go tack that note on the door, brother. Before I make this witch as ugly as me."

Well, that had not gone as planned. Instead of making the brothers turn against each other, she'd incurred the devil's wrath all to herself.

Jackson pulled the blade back, and relief coursed through her. But a second later, he settled the tip against her cheek.

Blast, he wasn't bluffing. He truly was going to mark her face. As terrified as she was, she could not let these men know. Beneath their bluster, they were cowards who were petrified of women. She must use that fear.

She met Jackson's gaze and stared into his putrefied soul. "I am not afraid of you."

Growling, he stepped back. The knife caught a ray of sunlight shining through the window. If only someone would peek in, see Franny, and come to her rescue. Unfortunately, she suspected that no one would take notice, or care, if they were in one of the rookeries.

Jackson stabbed her cheek. A trickle of sticky blood dripped. As much as she wanted to cry out and beg him to stop, she couldn't. If she meant to save herself, she must remain brave, think clearly, and fight back.

Maybe she could kick him in the bollocks. She'd have to lift both legs simultaneously since they were tied together, but she could manage that. She had one chance to inflict pain because after that, they would anchor her calves to the chair's legs. Ultimately, her sally wouldn't save her because she would still be their prisoner, but it might buy her time and halt the incision Jackson was slowly and gleefully carving into her face.

You can do this, Franny assured herself repeatedly as she steadied her nerves. Ignoring the burning in her cheek, she squeezed her ankles together and engaged her quad muscles at the same time that a face appeared in the window. She blinked and looked again.

Edward brought his index finger to his lips.

The brilliant man had found her. Edward Robinson would forever be her hero.

CHAPTER THIRTY-SIX

THE CUR HAD a knife pressed to Franny's cheek, leaving Edward with no other choice. He needed to break into The Bedford right this second. If only Bear hadn't confiscated his bloody pistol.

Edward rubbed his temple, trying to rid himself of the nightmarish image he had just witnessed. He hadn't detected an iota of fear from Franny. Her chin was lifted, and her jaw was firmly set as she stoically stared her assailant down. Knowing Franny, she had given the Brown brothers one deuce of a fight before they tethered her to the chair.

Since a good stiff wind might blow the poorly built tenement to France, Edward should be able to kick the door down with little effort. Without weapons, his only option was to barge in and talk sense into these wretches. If that didn't work, he had two capable fists.

This time, he should double-check to see if the door was locked before using his leg as a battering ram. He gently pushed, and the door opened. He cautiously peeked into an empty entranceway. With utmost caution, he slipped inside and gently pulled the handle until the door clicked into place.

On silent feet, he glided across the floor to peer around a corner which afforded him a clear view of Franny and the brothers. The rat with the knife still leaned over her, and blood dripped down her cheek. God help Edward, he wanted to strangle this man and watch as the life drained from his body.

Franny met Edward's gaze, and her lips quirked upward. The confounding woman who had stolen his heart grinned as if she were at a sunny picnic. Meanwhile, a lunatic was mutilating her.

The knife wielder followed Franny's gaze to stare into Edward's eyes. His face turned red, and his nostrils flared. "Where the bloody hell did you come from?"

Holding up his hands to show he was unarmed, Edward stepped into the room.

The other brother faced Edward, and his eyes widened. "Jackson, why don't you ever listen to me? I told you the lawman would be trouble."

As if in slow motion, both of Franny's legs shot upward, smashing Jackson in the bollocks. He screamed, and the knife tumbled from his grip. It barely missed stabbing his boot before clattering on the floor. He bent double, clutching himself.

Time sped up. Franny stood and with the chair still attached to her arse and back, she whirled like a dervish. Never had Edward seen such a sight. Apparently, neither had the brothers because their mouths hung open in shocked awe. Still holding his crotch, Jackson stepped back, barely avoiding a collision with the spinning chair.

On her third turn, Franny smashed the chair into Jackson. This must have been her intent all along because she called out, "Huzzah!" as they tumbled to the ground. Franny landed on top of Jackson, the chair between them.

"Get off me, witch," he screamed at the back of her head. "Would you fuckin' help me, Richard?"

Frances Valentine, the human rocking horse, seesawed while trying to roll off Jackson. He cried out in pain as the chair mashed his face and torso a half dozen times.

Undeterred by the weight on top of him, Jackson stretched his arm until his fingers brushed the knife. Luckily, he struggled to grasp the handle with Franny and her chair precariously teetering on top of him.

Edward lunged for the knife at the same time as Richard. There was no way in hell Edward would lose this battle; the protective violence raging within him would see to that. Before Richard could grab the knife, Edward threw him against the wall. Richard's legs buckled, and he collapsed to the floor.

Looming over the dazed fool, Edward clenched his fists and exhaled loud, angry breaths.

These men had kidnapped and cut Franny. They'd injured Coach. They'd tried to burn down The Silk Knuckles and had left Harry scarred for life. They had stalked Josephine. Hell, they had even attacked Edward the night he came to Coach's rescue. And one of these good-for-nothing rats had beaten his wife numerous times. All to keep women subservient so they felt powerful and superior. These were not honorable men. They were virulent piles of dung.

Richard unsteadily climbed to his feet. "If you can't control your chit, we will," he said.

Edward's temper snapped. "You bloody arse. I don't need to control anyone but you." He grabbed Richard by the neck and smashed the back of his head into the wall.

Richard howled as unshed tears glistened in his eyes. Edward could not allow himself to feel pity. The brothers might win this battle if he showed an iota of mercy, and that might leave Franny a casualty.

Edward launched three successive jabs. Richard's head flew back, and blood flew from his nose. Steadying himself, he called Edward outrageous, filthy names, some quite poetic in their originality. Edward let him finish his diatribe and then delivered the *coup de grâce*, a precise uppercut to the jaw. Richard wobbled before crashing onto his back.

With one adversary down, Edward turned his attention to the second. At some point during the melee, Jackson had managed to gain his feet despite his injured bollocks, retrieved the knife and was poised to stab Franny in the back of her head. Edward dropped down, grabbed the man's wrist, and bent it backward until the bone snapped with a satisfying crunch.

Jackson screamed.

Removing the weapon from Jackson's fingers, Edward pressed it against his jugular. "Give me one good reason not to butcher you like the pig you are."

"But you are a lawman," Jackson said, his voice tremulous.

Although it was an excellent reason, Edward remained unconvinced.

"Edward, don't kill him," Franny said from atop the pile. "I don't want you to live with the guilt. Just let me slice off his bollocks."

It took Edward a moment to realize Franny wasn't serious. She must be taking as much pleasure in Jackson's mewls as he was, because her giggles vibrated the back of the chair, crushing Jackson's nose.

"Bloody hell, what happened here?" someone who sounded like Baker asked.

Edward raised his gaze to find Baker and Jenkins holding their tip staffs high. Baker wore a shite-eating smirk. He'd probably look the other way if Edward sliced through Jackson's pulsing neck. Either that or he would blackmail Edward for the rest of his life.

Sighing, Edward let the knife hang by his side. "How did you know I was here?"

"A young boy," Jenkins said. "He works at the church next to The Silk Knuckles Saloon."

"Charlie. A damn fine lad," Edward said.

Franny cleared her throat. "Could you gentlemen cease with the gossip and untie me?"

Edward couldn't help himself. He bent forward and slammed his lips over hers, the best part being that she couldn't punch him since her arms were shackled to the chair. Even more wonderful than that, Franny Valentine kissed him back with all of the passion of a woman totally and completely head over heels in love.

MRS. BENSON HAD outdone herself. She'd prepared another romantic meal for Edward and Franny, and she wasn't the least bit angry that her efforts the previous evening had been wasted.

"I'm so happy you are both safe," she said after hearing about their harrowing misadventure. "You must be starving. Please eat while everything is warm. Have a wonderful evening." She winked at Edward.

Upon entering the kitchen, Franny clapped and popped onto her toes. " 'Tis so lovely and romantic, don't you think?"

"Indeed," Edward said.

A vase of fresh flowers sat in the center of the table. Beneath it lay a new linen embellished with embroidered strands of ivy. Well-placed candles cast a warm glow over the room and brought out the golden highlights in Franny's fire-colored hair.

Edward and Franny never ran out of things to discuss as they enjoyed roast lamb and potatoes. Throughout their meal, Franny's eyes sparkled. Afterward, she sipped wine and belly laughed about using the chair she had been tied to, to defeat her kidnapper.

"Ironic, don't you think?" she asked.

"Indeed." Edward chuckled. Now that she was safe, he could temporarily appreciate the humor of their Shakespearian farce in spite of the sticking plaster covering the cut on her cheek. Fortunately, the doctor had told them it wouldn't require stitches, would soon heal and most importantly, with luck, it would not leave much of a scar.

Demanding attention, Zigzag meowed as she rubbed against Edward's calf. He bent down to scratch her between the ears. When he sat up and met Franny's affectionate gaze, warmth washed over him. This was how he wanted to spend every evening for the rest of his life, and now was the perfect time to tell Franny.

"I know you have been worried about climbing back into the ring and feeling cowardly, but you were heroic and brave today." Before she could argue with him, he confidently took her hand in his. "Frances Valentine, I love you with all of my heart. Will you do me the honor of becoming my wife?" He retrieved the ring from his pocket and slipped it onto her finger.

Franny stared at the emerald and then gawked at Edward. It seemed he had shocked the loquacious woman into silence.

Then, as if his question finally dawned on her, she gasped and brought her hand to her mouth. "Are you sure? I am quite difficult."

"Exceedingly difficult. And I have never been more sure of anything."

She squealed with delight. "Yes!" Cradling his face in her palms, she rubbed her nose against his. "It would be my honor, Edward Robinson."

Edward's heart soared.

"Could we move this celebration to your bed?" she asked, rolling her shoulder coquettishly.

He leaped from the table and pulled Franny onto her feet. Maybe it was his overwhelming love, or perhaps it was the romantic dinner. Although most likely he was just his usual randy self, because he tossed his fiancée over his shoulder, carried her to his bedchamber, dropped her on his mattress, and tupped her until they were boneless piles of sated flesh.

CHAPTER THIRTY-SEVEN

AFTER SENDING EVERYONE away, Franny sat in the corner of Bear's office, centering herself. It had been delusional to think she could do this because there was no way she could step into the ring. *But you gave your word, Frances Valentine, you milksop.* And even if she hadn't made a deal with Bear, it was too late to back out. At least a hundred and fifty members of the Fancy were there to see her, leaving her with no other choice. Closing her eyes, she inhaled and exhaled to slow counts of eight. Then, she visualized Ruth the Jewel, the notorious panderer, lying at her feet as the ringmaster held her hand high, declaring, *"The winner of tonight's contest is Fiery Franny."*

A knock interrupted her woolgathering. She opened her eyes and glared at the door.

Bear peeked in at her. "You have a visitor."

Franny groaned. She didn't want to be ill-mannered or un-grateful, but she had repeatedly told her loved ones she needed time alone to prepare mentally.

"Miss Franny, you will want to see this person." Bear stepped aside and ushered in Laughing Lucy, who looked lovely in a purple dress and matching bonnet.

"Frances, how delightful to see you." Lucy approached and kissed Franny on the cheek.

"What are you doing here?" Franny hadn't intended for her

question to sound rude, but she was surprised to see her old opponent. Not only that, but she was also relieved that the woman appeared quite alert. There was no evidence that Franny had once delivered devastatingly brutal blows to her head.

"I heard you were fighting again, so I came to cheer for you. I find Ruth's behavior rather appalling."

Unsure of what to say, Franny simply swallowed.

"May I be honest with you?" Lucy asked.

If Lucy was here to remind Franny of the unfortunate day that plagued her nightmares and talk her out of fighting, she was a bit late. Franny hesitantly nodded.

"I heard rumors that you were afraid to get back in the ring after our mill. Since you haven't competed since that day, I assume they are true. I wanted you to see that I am well. I wanted to tell you that if you wish to return to the ring, you shouldn't be fearful. Although I hope you weren't pressured into it by those overly aggressive promoters named after animals."

Franny snorted. "Overly aggressive, blackmailing promoters who don't take no for an answer." Although her words rang true, Franny had developed a soft spot for Bear and Whale. She'd even come to appreciate Shark and his ridiculous teeth.

"I assumed as much," Lucy said. "They knocked on my door as well, but my days of fighting are behind me."

"I'm sorry about that," Franny said.

" 'Tis not your fault." Lucy waved her hand as if shooing a fly. "Furthermore, you do not owe me an apology. I am quite content in my current situation. Think of it this way, as violent as this sport is, it is doing much to elevate women. Remember the remarkable accomplishments of Elizabeth Wilkinson Stokes, one of the greatest fighters ever. Because of her, the world knows women are as fearless as men. We can be athletes or anything else that we desire. We can choose our own path. We are not property to be owned."

Franny dropped her gaze to her wrapped fists. This was true, and *overly aggressive promoters* aside, she wanted to climb back into the ring to prove that she could. Tomorrow was another day in which she might choose a different path. She wasn't sure she wanted to compete forever, but whatever she did, it was her choice, and hers alone. Edward and The Silk Knuckles were now her passions, but for today, right this second, she wanted to fight.

Bear stepped back into the room. "It's time, Miss Franny."

Franny leaped to her feet. "I'm ready."

"Remember, give Ruth hell," Lucy called over her shoulder as she exited.

"How is that burn on your foot feeling?" Bear asked as he wrapped his arm around Franny's shoulders and escorted her down the hall.

She had been much too nervous to give the injury a second thought. "Fine," she said.

"Good." Bear gave her an affectionate squeeze. "I know I'm not supposed to choose one of my fighters over the other, but I hope you knock Ruth to the moon."

SPECTATORS PACKED THE basement of The Purple Rabbit. Men even lined the stairs and hung over the handrail, waving fists full of blunt. Franny climbed through the ropes. As she warmed up, she searched the room.

The crowd was so dense that Franny struggled to locate Edward. She feared he had left, not because he wasn't supporting her, but because he might not have the stomach to watch her get hit. He still became agitated when discussing the Buffoon Brothers slicing her face. She often reminded him that she was safe because the men were currently locked in Newgate awaiting their trials.

Or perhaps Edward had to leave to deal with a crime.

Or, maybe, the crowd had discovered a lawman in their midst and forced him to leave. They might assume he was here to prevent the fight from happening, when his sole purpose was to support her. The mere thought of this unruly crowd harassing Edward forced a ball of acid up her esophagus.

But at last, she spied him standing with Nicolas, Viscount Davenport, and the Duke of Griffendale. Edward blew her a kiss. She flung one back, and the crowd roared enthusiastically. She smiled. Tonight, these individuals tossing around money and calling for blood accepted Edward as one of them.

Acting as the ringmaster, Bear waved his hand until the crowd quieted to a dull hum. "Welcome, ladies and gentlemen. Are you ready for the fight of all fights?" he called into his speaking trumpet.

Not that she would tell Bear, but this was hardly the fight of all fights. Josie had already won that championship. This was an illegal underground match between a woman who had not fought in a year, and a thespian with questionable morals who pandered to the lowest dregs of the Fancy. However, this crowd did not seem to care about Bear's exaggeration because they cheered and stomped until the basement walls shook.

Bear again raised his hand to quiet the uproarious spectators. "In this corner—" palm up, he presented Franny "—returning to the ring for the first time in almost a year, we have one of the beloved owners of The Silk Knuckles Saloon and an up-and-coming coach in her own right. Please show the aptly named 'Fiery Franny' some love."

"Fiery Franny," the crowd chanted.

Despite despising theatrics, Franny played along. She peeled down the top of her loose round dress and tied the sleeves around her waist to anchor the skirt in place. With the top of her chemise displayed and her breasts tightly bound beneath the fabric, Franny curled her bicep and contracted her muscle. As the crowd roared their appreciation, she strutted the perimeter of the ring.

"You've grown soft," Ruth yelled.

Ruth had always been soft, but Franny held her tongue because she did not favor the rubbish-talk that was currently in fashion.

"Soft as a kitten," Ruth yelled.

At least Franny hadn't painted her face as if she were a jester.

Ruth pretended to hold a small animal in her arms. She even feigned petting it.

Franny rolled her eyes.

Ruth snarled as she pantomimed wrapping her fingers around the kitten's neck and squeezing. At least that was what Franny thought she was miming.

"And in this corner—" Bear swung his upturned palm to Ruth—"we have a crowd favorite, the always colorful Ruth the Jewel. Please show the lovely Ruth some appreciation."

"Ruth the Jewel," people cheered.

Like she did every single fight, Ruth peeled to her chemise and flashed her tit to the lecherous crowd. Bringing her hand to her mouth, and widening her eyes, she feigned embarrassment. After she had titillated the crowd into a frenzy, she tucked her breast into her chemise. Not a single person in that audience was fooled. Every member of the Fancy knew that Ruth and innocence did not go together. However, many still enjoyed her show, and Ruth took advantage of their prurient natures. The woman was shameless.

One of the umpires motioned for Franny and Ruth to join him in the center of the ring. "Remember the rules agreed upon," he said. "Irish fighting style. No kicking. No biting. No weapons. No hair pulling. And absolutely no direct hits to the mouth. Once someone goes down, they have ten seconds to get onto their feet. If they are unable to stand, the round is over. There are thirty seconds between rounds. The mill will be called if I think either of your lives is in danger. Do you agree to these terms?"

Franny nodded more enthusiastically than she would have predicted.

"We will begin the mill in a few moments. Are you ready?"

"Yes," they both said.

Franny strutted to her corner and settled onto Papa's knee.

He took her hands in his and double-checked her wraps. "I'm

proud of you. I know this wasn't easy for you." He wiped a tear from his eye.

Josie, her bottle woman, held a cup of protein beer under Franny's nose. "Remember, pace yourself. Don't come out too hard and fast," Josie said.

Although she wasn't thirsty, Franny sipped, knowing she required nourishment in case the mill lasted half the night.

Again, the umpire motioned for them to come forward.

It was time! Franny's heartbeat thudded in her ears, and her legs trembled uncontrollably. *Deep breath in. Deep breath out. I can do this.* Franny was the superior fighter, after all. *Yes. Indeed. Undoubtedly.* Franny's shaking ceased.

Her shoulders thrown back confidently, Franny strutted to the scratch line and tapped Ruth's knuckles. Ruth snarled at her. Embracing the moment, Franny growled back.

Placing her toe on the line, Franny settled into her stance, raised her fists, and waited for the bell.

CHAPTER THIRTY-EIGHT

E DWARD HELD HIS breath, his focus fully on the woman in front of him.

Wearing a simple gray dress, Franny stood in the center of the ring, looking like a fierce goddess preparing for battle. Her toned shoulders led to well-formed arms that were capable of both hefting heavy items and actively participating in strenuous bed sport. Only the most lionhearted or insane would think of approaching a combatant with such intensity etched across her visage. Even with the top of her chemise exposed, her sleeves tied around her waist, and a cut on her face that hadn't yet healed, Franny was the embodiment of a powerful female warrior. Her crowning glory was the red braid that hung down her back.

The second the bell rang, Franny's left fist shot out, gauging her distance. Quick jabs followed, the first hitting and the second brushing Ruth's shoulder. As Ruth retreated, Franny stuck to her like glue. Ruth grounded herself and prepared to jab, but Franny's hip twisted twice and powered two right hooks into Ruth's oblique. The crowd called out boisterous directives as Ruth backed away.

Viscount Davenport leaned close to Edward and shouted over the din, "I dare say, Franny is on fire. She isn't wasting any time."

Edward's sleepless night had been for naught, and his fretting had been pointless. Of course, Franny would win this fight. She was a force of nature. Determined. Skilled. Strong. Resilient. And soon this amazing woman would be his wife. He was the luckiest man in this overcrowded establishment.

So far, Franny's shorter stature and bulkier muscles had not been a disadvantage against her taller, lighter opponent. Moving with the agility of a panther, she circled Ruth, her right fist protecting her chin as her left fist shot out, throwing one jab after another. If Ruth didn't find her rhythm, this fight would be over in the next few minutes, leaving a very unsatisfied audience. Edward, on the other hand, would be relieved to have this night behind him.

Franny ducked beneath Ruth's extended arm, jammed her opponent's reach, and hammered on her midsection.

"You've got this, Franny," Edward yelled.

Eventually, Ruth shook herself from her stupor and broke away. Franny slid forward, stalking her. Ruth halted her retreat, settled low, and flung out her fist, walloping Franny's shoulder.

Experiencing a sympathy pang, Edward rubbed out the imaginary sting in his shoulder. Meanwhile, Franny was undaunted. She slid back, lunged forward, and snapped out a series of impressive combinations that continued until both her footwork and her hand speed slowed. Her fire had run out of fuel. Edward's stomach soured.

Their expressions resolute, the women caught their breath as they circled each other. Edward took the opportunity to breathe with them. If he didn't calm himself, his heart would give out from overexertion.

The break in action was too short for Edward's liking. Fists again flew, and he was certain he could hear the *thwack* of knuckle against skin. Although this had to be his imagination because the loudly cheering spectators would drown out any low sounds emanating from the ring.

Franny's flurry of jabs followed by her cross knocked Ruth backward. Ruth quickly regained her balance and followed

Franny, throwing speedy combinations that put Franny on the defensive. Ruth unleashed a wicked cross, but Franny ducked and came out on the other side of it, only to have the taller woman whirl and punch her breadbasket so hard that Franny doubled over. Her opponent used Franny's moment of weakness to her advantage, gaining the upper hand and dominating the ring for the next few minutes.

Although Edward continued to cheer enthusiastically, his heart ached. As he feared she might, Franny had come out too strong, tired herself out, and now Ruth had the edge.

Ruth delivered a right, left uppercut. Franny stumbled, ricocheting off the rope, proving Edward's unfortunate theory was indeed correct. Luckily, she found her balance and did not crash to the ground.

"Ruth has improved since I last saw her fight," Griffendale said.

"Mayhap she learned a few things when she was in prison," the viscount said.

Edward was much too overwrought and concentrating entirely too hard to listen to these aristocrats and their pointless drivel. He glared at Davenport.

"What?" Palms up, the viscount shrugged. "I'm sure lady prisoners have to learn to protect themselves if they mean to survive."

Although this was true, Edward couldn't think about anything but the woman he loved struggling to maintain her stamina. Hoping to send her a long-distance infusion of energy, he pushed through the crowd. "Come on, Franny," he hollered as he edged as close to the ring as the throng allowed.

No matter how much he willed her to regain her vigor, Franny continued to fade. Eventually, blood dripped from her perfect nose, and he had to look away. A sense of hopelessness washed over him. There was nothing he could do to help her, and she would be devastated if she lost this fight, especially to a woman anyone in the know considered an inferior pugilist.

By the time Edward found the resolve to return his attention to the ring, Ruth had cornered Franny and was unleashing a steady barrage of punches. If Franny didn't get out of the corner, this fight would soon be over.

The only thing Edward could do was to love her with all his heart. Right now. After she lost. And every day until forever. "Franny, I love you," he yelled.

Leaving her chin unprotected, Franny met his gaze. The defeat written across her face broke his heart. He couldn't let her give up.

"I love you, Frances Valentine," he called. "My brave warrior, I bloody love you. Now, cover your chin and get out of that corner."

Even from this distance, he saw the spark ignite behind her eyes. He watched in awe as she came back to life with an audible roar. Instead of protecting herself, she drove her fist up and under Ruth's chin. As Ruth's head flew back, Franny ducked and came out on the other side of her.

Ruth pivoted to face Franny, then seemed to shrink to half her size. Perhaps she sensed Franny's raw tenacity. Franny threw jabs and hooks until Ruth was the one in the corner. Settling into her stance, Franny hammered on Ruth's midsection.

"You've got her, Franny," Edward screamed.

Franny dispatched a right-left-right uppercut combination. Ruth wobbled, then toppled, arse backwards. Luckily, her head hit the rope, softening her landing.

Breathing hard, her fists clenched at her side, Franny stood over her supine opponent.

"One. Two. Three…" one of the umpires counted.

Edward held his breath.

Franny bent forward and gasped for air as thunderous cheers echoed off the purple walls.

"…Eight. Nine. Ten." The umpire grabbed Franny's hand and held it high.

"Fiery Franny! Fiery Franny!" the jubilant horde chorused.

Either most of these people had wagered on Franny, or they simply appreciated watching her come back from the brink of what looked like defeat. Meanwhile, Coach and Josie held Franny in their arms as Ruth's knee man and bottle man tried to shake her to consciousness.

Suddenly, Griffendale, Wentworth, and Davenport surrounded Edward, clapping him on the back.

"Damn good fight," Davenport said.

"I might have my new champion for the next Duke's and Dame's Mill," Griffendale added.

Even over the raucous noise, Edward heard Franny calling him. He was shoved about as he fought through the frenetic throng. By the time he reached the ropes, his body had taken quite a bit of abuse. Although, to be fair, he had not experienced a fraction of what these lady pugilists had been through.

Franny stood above him, tears pouring from her eyes. "Edward, I couldn't find you." She grabbed his arm and tugged on it until they stood face-to-face in the ring.

"I've been here the entire time." He wrapped her in his arms. "You were amazing, darling. Why are you crying?"

"I don't know. Mayhap I'm happy because I won and you are here with me." She sniffled. "But I made a grave error in underestimating my opponent." Her words were almost drowned out by the pandemonium. "And then I panicked and couldn't catch my breath. I didn't pace myself."

"But you didn't give up," he said, drying her tears. He untied his cravat and used it to gently clean the blood from her nose. At the rate this was going, he would need to work his old Drury Lane shifts to earn enough blunt to purchase new cravats.

Franny's gaze slid to Ruth, and she bit her lip. "Will she recover?"

Edward held Franny against his chest and rubbed the back of her neck, whispering soothing words until Ruth's eyes opened and she was helped onto her feet.

"Oh, thank heavens." Joy radiating from Franny, she turned

back to him and smiled the most radiant smile he'd ever seen. "Even though I couldn't see you, I heard you say, 'My brave warrior, I bloody love you' and I felt as if you were sending me your strength. You thinking I am brave gave me my second wind."

"Franny, my darling, you are the most courageous woman I've ever met."

"And together we are invincible." She stroked his cheek. "Did Bear return your pistol?"

"Yes. Right after we got here."

"Now that I have kept my end of the bargain and you have your weapon, let us collect my winnings, leave this over-loud place, and go tell Zigzag how we conquered the world."

"Perfect." Edward chuckled. "My cat will be happy to receive the good news."

"Our cat." Franny's grin grew so wide that her adorable nose wrinkled. "Papa will be so tired he won't notice I'm missing, so you should give me a nice warm bath." She fluttered her golden lashes. "And since I won, I would like you to be naked while you massage the soap into my skin."

"Hell, yes, please, and thank you," Edward bellowed, as he victoriously thumped his fists on his chest. Thereupon, he escorted his fiancée, Fiery Franny, tonight's female champion, through her adoring fans.

EPILOGUE

One month later…

NOW THAT HER bookkeeping was complete, Franny exited her office and regarded her kingdom, pride washing over her. All of her dreams had come true. Well, almost all of them since she had recently discovered she had a new, secret desire.

Her gaze landed on her shirtless husband, and her mouth watered. Oh, the things she would do to his scrumptious body later tonight.

Sweat coated his shoulders and pectorals, and his muscles flexed as he sparred with Nicolas in the farthest ring. And to think she and Josie had once made a pact to never marry or let a man consume their thoughts. Young girls and their silly notions. Franny sniggered. But how were they to know that in the future they would fall in love with these loving, heroic men? Men so supportive that they thumbed coverture laws, going so far as to sign documents that even after marriage, their wives remained the owners of The Silk Knuckles. Adding to this, Nicolas tempered Josie's wild streak, and Edward matched Franny's passion.

Smiling, she slid her gaze to Papa. The man was in his element as he stood outside the closest ring, calling directives to The Trojan and Thumbs McCartney.

Off to the side of Papa, the Duke of Griffendale was showing Roseanna Chapman how to properly punch the sandbag, a lesson that Roseanna did not need. The woman could murder a sandbag with one hand tied behind her back. However, she seemed to be listening intently. Or maybe she was feigning interest so she could inhale the alluring duke's scent. Franny chuckled.

In a strange twist of fate, the duke had asked Franny to be his champion at the next Duke's and Dame's Mill. Franny had declined. She had conquered her fears, climbed back into the ring, and proven to herself that she wasn't a coward. But now that her goals lay elsewhere—The Silk Knuckles Saloon, The Ladies' Autonomy League, and her husband—it was time to put her competitive days behind her for good.

After Franny turned him down, Griffendale swore and kicked at something invisible. He had quickly gotten over his temper and, days later, turned his attention to Roseanna. In Franny's humble opinion, Roseanna, who wore men's breeches and hid her hair beneath a large black handkerchief, was the perfect choice to fight the Amazonian Lady Paulsgrove in the next prestigious championship.

Franny's gaze traveled to the calisthenics area where Sky and Charlie were hefting about weights, trying to mold their adolescent bodies into Roman statues. Both lads had extraordinary work ethics, so with solid nutrition and a year or two of maturity, they would undoubtedly meet their goals.

Meanwhile, Josie led the ladies' exercise and self-defense session. The class had grown too large for the ring and now spread over the back half of the large room. Lady Davenport meandered from the lesson to stand beside Papa. Her silk gown was more suited to courting than to exercise. She tapped Papa on the shoulder and smiled at him.

He awkwardly smiled back before returning his focus to his fighters. He pointed and yelled at Thumbs, more than likely telling him to keep his wrist firm when throwing hooks—that was Franny's advice on the days she coached Thumbs.

If only Franny could convince Papa to forgo his bachelor ways and promenade with the delightful dowager. Oh, how happy the two lonely souls might find themselves. But Papa was impossible.

"What would a fine lady want with an old codger like me?" Papa often asked.

"Your companionship," Franny told him. "And I think you are the most handsome man in the world. What woman wouldn't want you?" *My mother, who was brilliant and beautiful, wanted you.* But these were bittersweet words Franny couldn't bring herself to say out loud.

Harry exited Papa's office, approached, and doffed his cap.

"What are you still doing here?" Franny asked. "Aren't you supposed to be meeting Grace's parents tonight?"

"I am, Miss Franny. I just wanted to see if there was anything you wanted me to do before I left for the evening?"

"No. You've worked hard. Go enjoy yourself."

"Could I ask your opinion on an important matter?" he asked.

"Of course. As you know, I do so love expressing my opinions."

Harry chuckled, then quickly sobered. "Lady Davenport insists that Miss Grace and I have the wedding breakfast at Greenpark House, but I haven't asked for her hand yet." He exhaled a breath rife with concern. "Should I decline the viscountess' offer, me being a working bloke and all? Then again, doesn't Miss Grace deserve the very best? She is a splendid girl."

"Oh, Harry, that's wonderful. Lady Davenport hosted my breakfast as well." Franny's cake had been three layers high and covered in delicate iced roses. Fresh hot-house roses had filled the vases, and the sideboard had been piled high with delectables. Franny's floral headpiece had been a gift from Mrs. Benson, who had also embroidered tiny roses onto the neckline of a pink satin gown. Their families and friends had filled the dining parlor, visiting well into the evening. Franny sighed at the happy memory. "Keep in mind that Grace has been a beloved servant in the Davenport household for years, and you have been quite loyal to The Silk Knuckles Saloon, which is dear to Lady

Davenport's heart."

Harry nodded. "I hadn't thought of it like that. I see your point, Miss Franny. I'll ask her father's permission tonight. Then I'll ask Miss Grace, and if she says yes, we shall allow Lady Davenport to host the breakfast."

"I'm sure Grace will say yes. I've seen the way she looks at you."

Harry grinned. "I hope you are correct."

"I'm always correct." Franny chuckled.

Harry nodded. "Well, you were right about your saloon and gymnasium."

"Oh?" Franny asked, her curiosity piqued.

" 'Twas your idea, Miss, and then the three of you brought all of these people together." He pointed at the two boys curling the dumbbells, then in Edward and Nicolas's direction. "From young working-class lads to influential aristocratic men." His gaze traveled to the other ring. "There you have two male champions." He inclined his chin to Roseanna. "And an up-and-coming lady fighter." Palm up, he swung his hand toward the class. "Look at all those aristocratic ladies who come here despite what society says. You even made a place for Mrs. Brown."

The young Jane Brown was now the hostess and barmaid of the upstairs saloon, so ladies could visit even when Franny and Josie weren't available. Harry had turned one of the upstairs offices into a bedchamber, so Jane had a safe place to live. And twice a week, she attended the ladies-only classes.

Franny swallowed the lump in her throat and wiped a rogue tear of happiness from her cheek. "Go." She playfully flicked her fingers, shooing Harry toward the exit.

His step buoyant, Harry made his way to the door.

A commotion drew Franny's focus to Bridget Wentworth. She stood in front of the ladies in a low lunge. Fingers wide, the side of her hand chopped the air. Her limbs windmilled willy-nilly as she hopped her opposite leg forward and repeated the movement.

Josie stood hands on hips, shaking her head.

Bridget scampered through the ladies as they imitated her.

Josie threw her hands in the air and marched away.

Something must be wrong because Josie never let her sister-in-law commandeer her class, although Lord knows, Bridget tried.

"Are you angry?" Franny asked as Josie approached.

"No." Josie's eyes sparkled. "I just don't have it in me to make Bridget behave right now. I have other things on my mind."

Franny inclined her chin to the ladies who lumbered about chopping and kicking the air like convulsing spiders taking their last breath of air. "At least they are moving, which I suppose is exercise, therefore beneficial."

"Bridget thinks she is an ancient Oriental warrior." Josie peered over her shoulder to watch the ladies, then burst into hysterical laughter.

Franny joined her, and soon they guffawed until tears ran down their cheeks.

Josie dried her eyes and straightened. Her voice serious, she declared, "I have something to tell you."

This must be the night of confessions. Not that Franny minded. She loved helping her people. "Go on," she encouraged.

"I have not had my monthly courses, and do you see this?" She pointed at the tiny pink bumps covering her face. "Either I am a girl of ten and four again or I am…"

Franny grabbed and hugged her. "With child."

"*Shh*. They didn't hear you in St Giles," Josie whispered.

"I'm sorry." Franny lowered her voice. "Nicolas must be thrilled."

"He is keeping it a secret until I tell you and your father. I shall tell Coach tonight before I leave. Tomorrow, Nicolas will tell Bridget, which means by tomorrow night, all of London will know."

"True," Franny said. Probably all of England as well.

Jonathan Davenport, who had been noticeably absent the

past few days, sauntered into the gymnasium. A man wearing a hooded cape, who was slightly shorter and much slighter than the viscount, walked beside him. The viscount's palm cradled the man's lower back.

"How very odd," Josie said.

"Indeed," Franny agreed. Although the viscount was exceedingly amicable, he didn't escort men about the city with a protective hand on their person.

The viscount inclined his chin toward Franny's office. "May I speak with you both privately?"

Once the four of them stood in Franny's office, the viscount extended his palm. "May I present Her Ladyship, Jabbing Josie Wentworth, the future Viscountess of Shiredale, and Missus Fiery Franny Robinson."

The cloaked figure proffered a delicate hand with slender fingers. Seeming unsure of himself, he withdrew his offer and removed his hood.

Franny didn't mean to gape, but she did, quite indelicately. She also gasped like a horse's arse because he was a she, and she was lovely. Skin as pale as a ghost, eyes as blue as sapphires, and so willowy thin, Franny would wager she hadn't eaten a solid meal in ages.

"And, this is Gen," the viscount said. "Will you please help her?"

EDWARD FAVORED HIS home the day Mrs. Benson first presented it to him, and now, with Franny here with him, his attachment to his cozy abode had grown. He wouldn't mind filling it with tiny Robinsons, if and when Franny was ready, that was. He rested his head on his pillow and closed his eyes.

The memory played in his mind…

"Are you staring at my breasts?" Franny hissed in his ear.

Of course, he was staring at her breasts. They were glorious.

Franny stepped back and glared at him. "You bloody arrogant arse!" She pommeled his nose. Blinding pain shot to his brain as blood spattered. He shielded his face with his forearms.

Her breath heaving from both anger and exertion, Franny turned her back to him and stomped to the opposite side of the ring, taking his heart with her…

Five years later, his burning questions from their first encounter had been answered.

Her breasts were large but firm and bounced joyfully when she rode him. Her nipples were pink like her lips and reminded him of rose petals opening to the sun. The curls protecting her quim were the same scarlet shade as her long, wavy locks.

Keeping his eyes closed, Edward listened to their chamber door open. Franny's bare feet padded across the floor. As she drew closer, the scent of her rose soap tickled his nostrils. The mattress sank as she climbed into bed. To his delight, she straddled him.

"Mmm," he murmured as she leaned over him, the soft fabric of her chemise brushing his face. *Hallelujah!* She was going to ride him like a prize thoroughbred.

She gripped his elbow and extended his arm above his head. Fabric wrapped around his wrist as his little nymph tied him to the headboard.

He opened his eyes to find her bosom hovering over his face. He tilted his chin so he could watch her work. Her expression serious, she knotted his cravat, then guided his other arm into place, using a second cravat to tether him to the headboard.

Beneath the counterpane, his cock twitched. "Franny," he moaned as he ground his hips against her.

Franny lowered her torso until they were face-to-face. "Behave." She flicked his nose.

"Fuck," he murmured.

Franny pulled back the counterpane and raked her gaze over his bare chest. Her eyelids drooped, and she licked her lips.

"Use me, darling," he said in the husky voice he knew drove

her wild.

His command worked. She gasped and shivered. However, a moment later, she countered with a bold demand.

"Do not tell me what to do. I am in charge right now," she declared.

Oh, he liked this game, as did his cock that had grown so hard it stood upright, stabbing Franny.

She rearranged her hips and pulled the counterpane to his ankles. The cool air danced over his heated flesh.

"Husband, you are beautiful," she said as her soft palms slid over his chest.

In all of his sensual explorations, he'd never been rendered so helpless. He did not have a submissive bone in his body; in fact, his fingers itched to touch her. Yet passively accepting Franny's caresses thrilled him as much as taking control and restraining her.

Franny's hair tickled his shoulder as she leaned forward and suckled one nipple, then the other.

"God Almighty, you are good at that," he said.

She peered up at him, her green eyes shining with mischief. Her gaze glued to his, she licked and kissed her way down his abdomen. The closer she got to his arousal, the louder his blood seemed to pump.

And then she was there, laving his twitching cock with long, luxurious licks.

"Bloody hell," he repeated a few times as she boldly flicked her tongue along his length.

Taking the head of his cock into her mouth, she sucked as Edward growled guttural sounds. His once-innocent wife had become quite skilled at satisfying his wanton needs. Lucky for him, she was also an eager pupil who aimed to please.

"Use your hand," he demanded.

She seemed to have forgotten that she was the one in control because nodding enthusiastically, her tongue swirled his cock as she fisted his girth and gently twisted.

"That's it, Franny. That's perfect," he rasped.

Seeming to enjoy his praise, she subtly grinned. What a beautiful sight. His wife smiling as he fucked her mouth. Without warning, she sucked him so deep that his cock brushed the back of her throat.

This might just be one of the best nights of his life. "I'm going to come," he said in a throaty rumble.

"Not yet." In one swift move, she straddled him, her strong thighs squeezing his hips as she guided his cock into her tight, warm cunny.

"My God, Franny."

She lifted her hips ever so slightly, then gently lowered herself until he was so deep, they were one.

As heavenly as this felt, he had to stop her. "Franny, I don't have my sheath on."

"But it feels so good without it," she said.

"Indeed." Unfortunately, he would have to be the voice of reason. "Darling, since you have me at a disadvantage, you will have to slide it on me."

"I want you to orgasm inside me. Please."

As much as he didn't want this to stop, he needed to make sure she was thinking clearly. "Are you ready for the consequences?" he asked.

"Yes!"

Oh, thank God. His excitement added to his building euphoria.

She eased her hips down, throwing her head back in ecstasy. Her tight cunny perfectly gloved, then warmed his bare cock, heightening the pleasure barreling to his limbs. No longer able to fight his desire to touch her, he ripped his hands from his restraints, gripped her hips, and slammed her down hard.

"Edward," she cried.

He crashed her cunny onto his cock until his balls ached, and his muscles tensed. He was so damn close. However, tonight, he needed them to fly together.

"Come with me, darling," he whispered.

A shiver wracked her body. "I love you, Edward." She leaned

forward and kissed his lips.

Her sweet words of love. Her tongue now tangling with his. Her cunny pulsing around him. His body tensed until he exploded, his seed shooting deep inside his wife.

Franny's walls shuddered, then quaked. "Oh, Edward," she called as her insides milked every last drop from him.

Their gasping breaths mingled until they slowed, morphing into contented sighs. Franny toppled forward, resting her bosom on his chest.

"That was lovely," she said.

"*Mmm.*" He settled his lips on her ear. "I think I need new cravats. Again."

Giggling, she rolled off him. She curled up beside him, resting her head on his chest. "I dare say…"

"What, darling?" He peered down at her and kissed her forehead.

"Every once in a while, I would like to tie you up and have my way with you."

"Hell, yes," he said.

"And the rest of the time, you can tie me up."

Fine by him.

"But we don't always have to tie each other up. Sometimes we can just have a good ol' romping tup."

Edward chuckled. "Whatever you want, my darling."

She sighed, then stilled. Soon, a gentle hum rippled from her lips.

"I love you, Frances Robinson," he whispered into her hair. "And I shall love our children. And, most importantly, I shall cherish every day of my life with you by my side."

Smiling, Edward closed his eyes, clutched Franny to his chest, and snuggled his arse into the mattress.

The End

Up Next: Viscount Jonathan Davenport and
Lady Genevive Bailey's love story.

Acknowledgements

Thank you, Pennsylvania Golden Gloves Champions Jessy Ringquist and Heather Joerg Eberly, for the many years you both spent patiently coaching me to move and think like a pugilist.

Thank you, Edie Cay, for generously sharing your research on the history of Women's Bareknuckle Fighting.

Thank you, Alexandra Gall and Maggie Sims, for being my first readers and loving on Franny and Edward.

Thank you, Cynthia Blackburn, for appreciating my silly humor and the time you dedicated to editing my scandalous ladies and the men who love them.

And finally, thank you, Kathryn LeVeque of Dragonblade Publishing for believing in my female pugilists.

About the Author

Nicki Pascarella writes Historical and Contemporary Romances. She loves to make her readers laugh and swoon. Using her twenty-nine years of experience as a high school teacher and her background in creative writing and journalism, she is passionate about helping artists break through creative blocks. When she isn't writing, she reads, runs, and hangs with her husband, daughter, and Shetland sheepdogs. Nicki also performs with the multi-award-winning belly dance troupe, Troupe Hayati.

Website: www.nickipascarella.com
Facebook: nickipascarella
Instagram: nickipascarella_author
TikTok: Nicki @nickipascarella
Amazon: amazon.com/author/nickipascarella_author
BookBub: bookbub.com/authors/nicki-pascarella
GoodReads:
goodreads.com/author/show/21532142.Nicki_Pascarella